ANTHONY PATHFINDER

Fair GAME

BOOK ONE OF THE STREET CHRONICLES

The cataloging-in-publication data is on file with the Library of Congress.

ISBN 9780615633183 (paperback)
ISBN 9798405329260 (hardcover)

For more information, or to contact the author:

authoranthonypathfinder@gmail.com
www.anthonypathfinder.com

This book was printed in the United States of America.

Love Life and Live Life!

Believe not because some old manuscripts are produced, believe not because it is your national belief, believe not because you have been made to believe from your childhood, but reason truth out, and after you have analyzed it, then if you find it will do good to one and all, believe it, live up to it and help others to live up to it.
~BUDDAH

Before I begin, I would like to thank the Life Source for life. Without its guidance, none of this would have been possible. Secondly, I want to thank you, the readers. Life is not a smooth road, and it's unpaved with myriads of signs and obstacles. Along this road called life, I decided to pave some of the avenues, streets, lanes, and boulevards and remove some of the obstacles, and only then, did my dream of accomplishing this goal become a reality. I'm so humbled to be in this position.

I would like to thank several people who I felt were instrumental in seeing me through this project, whether it was a word of encouragement or an honest critique. Joy and Lil Jermaine, I appreciate the feedback. Thanks for the honest criticism and support. Olga, I want to thank you for your constant support and for being there for me. I also want to recognize my brother Roy and Andrea aka Indian. I think about you guys every day. RIP.

To my immediate family, I thank you and love you for your support. Much love to the wonderful assembly of people who worked their magic and brought to life the final product. Big up to all the people who worked behind the scenes, thanks. Finally, I want to thank all the doubters who said it wasn't possible. Every single one of you was my motivation, and I thank you.

Episode 1

"Come here, Sugar."

"What's up, baby?"

"I want you to keep an eye on Dana tonight. She's gonna be on her own and I want you to break her in and give her the lowdown," Kenny Maverick said.

"Why? Is she that important to you? It's that young pussy, huh, Kenny?" Sugar never got to say another word as she ate a right hand straight to her mouth.

"Bitch, shut the fuck up, and stop asking so many questions!" Kenny snapped.

"I was just saying…"

"Don't say shit, a'ight! Just do as you're told before I put my foot up your ass."

2 | ANTHONY PATHFINDER

"Okay, baby!" she replied, telling the other girls to get ready.

Sugar was one of Kenny's oldest working girls, and although she was no longer his favorite, he continued to use her to keep the other girls in check. Her days as his number one were winding down, and although she was only thirty years old, in the pimping game that was considered over the hill. Kenny used to sleep with her back in the day. However, he had begun sleeping with Star, a twenty-seven-year-old who didn't look as worn out as Sugar.

When I came on the scene everything changed. I became his main squeeze. In the beginning, he was very reluctant about putting me out on the street, but I knew it would only be a matter of time before he would convince me to do so. Chocolate brown in complexion with brown eyes, and weighing one hundred and twenty-five pounds, I was a natural beauty. Standing five-seven, I had a gorgeous figure any man would die for.

Sugar was genuinely nice to me on my first night out. She told me not to leave the block and to make sure the tricks turn their car engines off, and if they started arguing with me to holler for one of the girls.

"Dana, it's fifty dollars for a blow job and a hundred for a fuck, that's how Kenny calls it, and that's how it is, he won't take any shorts. Make sure you use a condom all the time, every time. And watch out for the po-po at all times," Sugar stated.

"Okay."

My first trick was an older man who looked to be in his early fifties. He was tall and had brown skin with handsome features. He went crazy when he saw me. He kept telling me how pretty I was, and how I would make a nice wife someday. At first, he wanted a blow job but then changed his mind. He wanted us to spend the night together at a hotel. He was willing to give me six hundred dollars. The whole thing sounded great, but I remembered what Sugar said.

Seeing that he was eager and hyped, I told him we could do it in his car, but that the price would remain at six hundred dollars. He eagerly agreed. He then put on a condom and climbed on top of me. He was breathing rather heavily, and as he humped and grunted for what seemed like three minutes, he finally came. As I stared at his old ass, I began thinking of my father whom he reminded me of, and all the bad things he had done to me.

***

I remember the first time my father sexually abused me. It happened three months before my mother died. I was nine years old. I was an only child, but my Aunt Mary, who would often visit told me my mother had two miscarriages because of the beatings from my father.

My father was a casual drinker until it became a problem. The drinking and his constant arguing led to a lot of fighting. Aunt Mary told me my mother loved me dearly. I knew she did and that she was genuinely concerned about me. She would lavish me with love and spoil me at the same time. She loved playing her old-school CDs. We listened to the radio a lot, and whenever the deejay played her favorite song, *Ooh Child* by the Five Stairsteps, she would jump to her feet and begin singing and dancing. She had a lot of energy and was constantly smiling, except for when my father drank. Her expression would immediately change from her normal outgoing self to one of sadness. Although I was young, I knew they were having problems. There were times when I would see her crying.

"Why are you crying?" I would ask.

"I just hope the good Lord will keep you healthy until you can take care of yourself," she would say.

My mother, Alice Baines had a chocolate brown complexion, stood about five-six, and was exceptionally beautiful. According to my grandmother, all the men vied for her attention as a young lady. Her family was very prominent in the upper-middle-class neighborhood of Spectrum, South Carolina. A lot was expected from her as a young lady and she did exceptionally well. She graduated at the top of her class from Spelman College.

Upon graduation, she met and married my father, Richard Marcus Estick, who had graduated from Morehouse College a year earlier. She taught high school and later became the principal at one of South Carolina's all-black boarding high schools.

My father was also from a very prominent black family in Spectrum. His family traced their roots back to the early 1700s. His family operated the first black-owned newspaper as free men in South Carolina. He was a tall man of medium build and light in complexion with dark green eyes.

My mother and father were financially secure by the time I was born. Father was the owner of several tractor-trailer companies. He was also a senior partner in one of the state's most prestigious accounting firms. Both my parents were reared to succeed. Anything else would have been a disappointment and a disgrace to their families. Maybe it was the added pressure to succeed, that led to my father's drinking. The drinking was driving him insane. At times I would see him talking to himself and strangely looking at me. I never paid any attention to it, because I thought it was the alcohol getting the better of him.

I was watching television late one night when he entered my room. I knew something was wrong. His behavior was unsettling, and fear overcame me unlike anything else that I had ever experienced, and as he tucked me in bed his hands began to shake uncontrollably.

"Daddy, what's wrong?" I asked, looking him in the eyes.

"Hush, baby!" he said, placing his finger on my lips.

I felt his hands touching me in places where Mommy had said to never let anyone touch me. His hands were all over my body. But this was Daddy, this wasn't just anybody. I felt as if I had stopped breathing. I could feel him touching my growing breasts. I tried to move his hands, but he told me everything was fine. I was crying as he began fondling my vagina. I cannot recall how long this went on because I fell asleep. What I do remember is that I couldn't look into his eyes the next morning. I knew what he had done to me the previous night wasn't right, but what could I do? So, I pretended as if nothing had happened.

My mother was sick during this time and I recall her spending a lot of time in the hospital. She had a massive heart attack and her health was rapidly declining. There came a time when I was not allowed to visit her at the hospital. Both my parents had agreed upon a housekeeper to look after me. I knew my mother had died after seeing the look on our housekeeper's face. My father had informed her of my mother's death, and she broke the news to me.

My father's relatives and other family members visited after my mother's death. They were crying and telling my father to be strong. The house was filled with a bunch of snooty, rich black folks, who were only there to admire what car Uncle Jeffery and Aunt Simone drove, instead of mourning my mother. I watched the men with trepidation, sadness, and anger as they placed my mother's coffin into the ground. I was crying. I wanted my mother. She had been my only protector and now that she was gone, what would I do?

***

By my thirteenth birthday, we moved to the town of Crisppen, South Carolina. The memories in our former home were too much to bear, so my father decided to relocate. He spoke about a new beginning and I believed him. He bought a beautiful house by the ocean. The thing I liked about the house was that I could look out my bedroom window and see the rolling waves crashing against the huge rocks that lined the shallowest part of the water.

He built a ladder-like bridge in the backyard and oftentimes I would just hang out there with my friends or we would go and hang out on the beach. It was fun hanging out on the beach. It was the only time in my life when I could escape from the turmoil taking place in my young life. None of my friends knew what was going on between me and my father. However, there were moments when I would withdraw into a shell. They would notice this and ask if I was okay. I would respond by telling them I was fine.

To keep my sanity and to keep from falling behind in my studies, my father and I reached an agreement. The only time he could fondle me was on the weekends. During the week, I had school and had to study. Six months after my thirteenth birthday, he broke his promise. I was shocked and disappointed.

On this particular night, I realized that he no longer wanted to just fondle me. This was the first of many occasions that my father would have sex with me. I was very mature physically and he would always remind me of it.

I felt lonely and lost. I had no one to turn to. I became a recluse and my classwork suffered, but I never said a word to anyone, not even my paternal or maternal relatives. I resisted the temptation of telling them or anyone else about my father because it was our secret. By my eighteenth birthday, I had already had one abortion. And it was then that I decided to talk openly about it to someone who I considered a friend. Brian Washington was a friend of my father and he was at least six or seven years his junior. Handsome, confident, and trustworthy, Brian was a strapping six-two. I felt he was the logical choice as far as having someone who could understand some of the motives behind my father's actions. I always had a gut feeling that Brian knew my father was sleeping with me. However, he said he had no idea until I mentioned it. He would listen attentively whenever I spoke about my father's behavior. I felt at ease and quite comfortable with him. He was well aware of his control over me, but that didn't stop us from becoming romantically involved.

Within a short time, I was sleeping with someone other than my father. I wished it had been with someone my age and not my father's friend. Maybe that's the reason why I have always dated older men.

Brian would get angry and agitated whenever we spoke about my father. On several occasions, he asked me why I was still living at home.

"You're eighteen years old. If you decide to move out there's nothing he can do," he stated, one day.

"I know, but where would I go? I have no money and I won't have access to my trust fund until I'm twenty-one."

"Listen, why don't you come and stay with me?" he suggested.

"I can't," I said, sobbing. "I wish I could, but he would kill us both. I can't do that."

"Think about it."

***

During our relationship, my father came home early one night and decided to take his usual walk on the beach. To my surprise, he caught me and Brian having sex. Terrified and unsure of what he would do next, the only thing I could think of was him getting his shotgun and shooting us. Instead, in a somber and angry voice, he told Brian to get off his premises. I was in shock as he told me to take my ass back to the house. I felt in my heart that I would never see Brian again. *Maybe he did have a gun under his shirt*, I thought.

My heart was pounding as I walked toward the house. I was listening for the sound of gunshots. I was relieved when I heard his footsteps behind me; at least I knew he had not hurt Brian. He told me to go take a shower. He was waiting for me when I came out of the bathroom. He grabbed me by my hair and dragged me to his bedroom, where he began beating me. He called me a bitch and a whore as he ripped off my bathrobe. I tried to fight my father for the first time in my life. He was surprised, but he was too big and strong and quickly overpowered me.

He tore off my nightgown and proceeded to rip my panties. I was crying as he began to rape me. It was at this moment that I decided it was time for me to get the hell out of his house and get as far away from him as possible.

After raping me, he fell asleep. I cleaned myself up and took the keys to my car, one of his credit cards, and four thousand dollars from the safe he kept by his bed. I was so scared that he might wake up, that I didn't even bother taking any of my clothes. I realized that I would never see him again, but it didn't matter to me.

I called my best friend, Jenny. She and I first met at a Jack and Jill career day event for the rich and influential in Greenbridge, South Carolina. I told her about my situation and what I was about to do. She had run away from home on several occasions and knew her way around. I guess you could say she had enough experience for both of us. Jenny and I decided to head to Los Angeles.

As we drove, all we talked about were the movie stars, the nightlife, and hanging out at the latest hot spots partying. This was all new to me, but for her, that wasn't the case.

After reaching Los Angeles and settling down, we both found jobs. I was working in a very upscale boutique and Jenny worked in a French restaurant. Whenever we were off from work, we would head down to Venice Beach and relax with surfers, musicians, basketball players, and muscle-bound weightlifters who looked like they were on steroids.

One night after partying, I saw a shadowy figure staring at me and Jenny as we walked to her car. I couldn't see the person's face, but I could tell it was a man. The figure slowly began to approach us. When I realized it was my father, I screamed as loud as I could at the top of my lungs, but he kept on coming. As fast as we ran, he was still behind us. Thank God a patrol car was cruising by. Jenny ran into the middle of the intersection, where she got the officer's attention. She told the officer that a strange man was following us. The officer immediately called for backup and my father was accosted, thrown against the officer's patrol car, and handcuffed after becoming boisterous and physical.

"Is this the man who was following you?" the officer asked.

"Yeah, that's him," I said.

I looked at Jenny, then at my father who never flinched. He coldly stared into my eyes and bit his bottom lip as they led him away. I knew he would be out in an hour or two or maybe even minutes. I had to get my ass out of Los Angeles and fast. I had to get to another state, even another country, if necessary. Seeing him only brought back all my pain. It was like a damn nightmare all over again. I realized all the shit he did to me would not go away. It would take a long time before I could ever become the person I wanted.

***

As Jenny and I sat on the bus heading for New York City, I thought about my mother and what she would have said to me. I thought about her smile and how she used to hold me in her arms. I thought about the whole episode with my father and concluded it was partly my fault. I thought about my family members in whom I refused to confide in. I thought about Brian and although he was older than me, I loved him. He was a great lover and treated me well. I certainly missed him. I turned and held Jenny's hand and began to cry, unlike any other crying I had ever done before. As she held me, she too began to cry. We thought about what kind of life we would encounter in New York City.

Finally, the bus pulled to a stop inside the Port Authority Bus Terminal. I was anxious, relieved, and scared. I didn't know what to expect. No sooner than we got off the bus, we were approached by several young men who wanted to know how we were doing and if we were visiting or planning on living in the city. We were about to respond when two young men who were on the bus with us, told the group to take their bullshit elsewhere. Jenny and I looked at each other as the men explained to us that they were pimps, drug dealers, or thieves and for us to be careful. We thanked them and headed toward Eighth Avenue. Jenny immediately contacted Trina, a girlfriend of hers who lived in the Park Slope section of Brooklyn. She allowed us to stay with her until we found a place of our own.

Episode 2

O ur stay with Trina didn't last long and Jenny saw to it that we wouldn't be homeless. She rented a two-bedroom house in the same Park Slope neighborhood.

I was doing fine until I met Kenny. I was nineteen and he was thirty. We met in 2004, one year after I arrived in New York City. I didn't know anything about him or what he did for a living, but I fell madly in love with him. I was surprised when I found out he was a pimp, a so-called player. I don't believe any words in Webster's Dictionary could have described or summed up how I felt.

In the beginning, our relationship was great. But in a matter of months, I found myself working as one of his street girls and getting high. Despite the other girls that worked for him, I was the apple of his eye. I was his number one girl and to be that I had to do whatever it took to please him. And I did that by getting his money on time and pleasing him sexually.

Not only had he turned me out sexually, but my mannerisms and speech had changed. I became more familiar with all the latest street slang. I was turned on by the thug in him that was always on display. Yet, he had a sensitive side, which he liked to keep hidden. I cared for him and it was no secret. The other girls knew I was his and he knew it. It didn't take long for things to unravel and take a turn for the worst.

It was a cold and gray afternoon when I stumbled onto the front porch of the house that Jenny and I shared. I was cold, freezing, and trembling without a winter jacket. When Jenny opened the front door, looking bewildered and scared, I stumbled into the house and fell to the floor. With my lips chapped and mouth dry, I was barely able to murmur for her to give me some water. As I drank the water, I began thinking about the ass-whipping I had gotten earlier from Kenny.

"That so-called man of yours did this, huh?" Jenny asked, in an angry tone. "Are you gonna continue to see that no good bitch ass mutha-fucka?"

"No, I'm not!" I said though I didn't believe it. "This is it; I'm leaving his ass. Ooh, ooh, oh shit! Every time I move my right leg hurts."

"You know what? You always say the dumbest shit and then turn around and go right back to him. When are you gonna get some sense? Honestly, I think you should leave the ass-kicking and drug shit alone. It's fucking you up; you've stolen from all your friends including me. How could you?" she asked, with a disappointed look on her face.

She was right. I was on a mission and I didn't care. I had an urge for drugs and whenever I needed them, I had to have money, so I stole.

"Come on, let me help you to your room," she said.

Despite the pain I was in, I drifted off to sleep. I had not slept in almost twenty-four hours. It was sometime around six o'clock the next day when Kenny aroused me from my sleep.

"Where the fuck was you last night?" he barked at me. Before I could answer, he slapped me across my face and started beating me.

"What the fuck! Don't you see the bruises you're putting all over my body?" I pleaded.

"I don't give a fuck about no bruises! What you need to do is to go out there and get my money. Bitch, go wash your ass and pussy and get my fucking money!"

I tried telling him that I was tired and needed the rest. He sneered at me, balled up his fist, and began yelling and ranting.

"What the fuck is wrong with you, huh? First of all, you're a crackhead. No, you're a former rich girl who was fucked by her daddy, who then moved to New York to become a dick-sucking crackhead ho. You're a dope head, a cocaine user, a thief, and you sell your pussy. I'm your new mutha-fucking daddy. No one wants you, loves you, or gives a fuck about you. What the fuck you think, Dana? Time is money, now get up off your stink ass and go make my money."

I didn't know what to think or do. I was crying inside. I was hurt and felt useless. I began blaming my mother for dying and leaving me alone in an unkind and cold world. As I thought about my father the tears continued, because if he hadn't done those things to me, maybe I would not have experienced some of the things I did.

Kenny was about to leave when Jenny walked in on us. She had a look of disdain on her face as she grilled him. He didn't say a word to her. Instead, he turned, looked at me, and told me to be ready in two hours, slamming the door behind him. Jenny was really upset, and she began arguing with me, which I didn't mind because I thought I needed it.

"Dana, I'm tired of this bullshit. You need to get yourself together. All you do is let that fool disrespect and use you. Why did you let him in?" she asked, as I stood there dumbfounded.

"I didn't let him in, he has a key," I said, turning away from her gaze.

"What? Did you give that bitch a key? Oh no, what the fuck is wrong with you?"

"I don't know," I sobbed.

"For starters, I'm going to change the lock on the door," she said.

***

Kenny hadn't always been a bad person. He graduated high school and had thoughts of attending college. His mother worked unbelievable hours to provide for him and his older sister, a prostitute. He tried his best to shield her from the streets, the sexual violence, and the pimps and johns she encountered daily. But it wasn't long before she became a victim of violence at the hands of her pimp, who slit her throat.

His mother was never the same after his sister's death. Kenny was devastated and along with several of his buddies, they decided to dish out their form of street justice. They confronted his sister's pimp late one night and shot him to death. After that incident, Kenny got involved with just about any and everything illegal.

"You name it, I did it," he would say to me. "A nigga's dream of going to college was just that, a fucking dream."

After failing to protect his sister he was never the same. He blamed himself. He felt he had let his mother down, and this disturbed him deeply. He was very protective when it came to his mother. She was all he had, and he was going to provide for her by any means necessary.

And if it meant dying while seeking his fame and fortune that's a chance, he was willing to take.

"You know I had second thoughts about getting into this game because of what happened to my sister. I wanted to kill every pimp I came in contact with. I was a conflicted soul. My whole life has been a paradox. On one hand, I knew the shit wasn't right because I saw what it did to my sister. But on the other hand, I wasn't gonna starve," he said, one day while we were talking.

"You could have gotten a job. Why didn't you?"

"No doubt, you're right but it was the money, the respect, and all the other shit that comes with the game. I need to shine that's the shit that keeps me going. I don't know Dana, but I think I'm caught between a rock and a hard place."

That was the only time I ever saw him so vulnerable. It seemed as if he was crying out for help but at the same time, he wasn't willing to take it. He was trapped and alone. The big dreams that he had before his sister's death were a thing of the past and his hopes of leaving the streets behind never came to fruition because the life, he led wouldn't allow it.

***

Jenny came over and held me. She whispered in my ear that she would help me through my ordeal. The warmth I felt as we hugged triggered a series of emotions and urges throughout my body. The urges that I felt would only happen whenever I was about to fuck. It was strange, but I was getting aroused as she softly kissed me on the neck. The softness of her body made my pussy jump. Sure, she and I had hugged on numerous occasions. Yet something was inviting and curious about this hug. I loved what I felt and wanted more. She never pulled away or attempted to let me go. She held me even tighter.

My heart rate increased as my swollen nipples drove me wild. I then felt her hard nipples protruding as if they were trying to rip apart the wife-beater she was wearing. I felt her warm, but arousing breath on my neck. Her hands slowly worked their way down to my ass. We kissed passionately as I pulled her pants down in one motion. I then stuck two fingers inside her wet love canal. She shrieked in ecstasy as her juices began to flow.

She moaned as I worked my fingers in and out of her.

She was kissing my nipples while playing with my pussy. Her fingers were dripping wet with my cum. She put them to her lips and ran her tongue over them before slipping them into her mouth. I was turned on. I wanted to taste her. I pulled my fingers from her honey nest and put them in my mouth. I had never tasted anything like that before. She tasted great.

She told me to lie on my back and to keep my legs open. My mind was reeling back and forth anticipating what she was going to do next. My throat felt dry. I closed my eyes as her face got closer to my honey nest. I felt her warm breath and lips touching my swollen pussy.

I moaned, as her tongue slithered over the lips of my pussy, before entering me. "Yeah, right there! Don't stop, Jenny! It feels good!"

I held her by the head and gyrated my pussy over her face. I lifted my ass off the bed and rocked back and forth in a slow-moving motion as she gripped my ass without missing a beat. Suddenly, she eased her body on top of mine. Her pussy was on my face. I was startled for a second, but my instincts quickly took over. I couldn't help myself; I stared at her wet, clean-shaven coochie. I kept my eyes on it as I licked, kissed, and fingered it. I spread her ass cheeks and stuck my tongue deep inside her. Jenny parted my pussy lips and began sucking my clitoris, as she slowly ran her finger over my ass hole. I was going out of my mind. Although this was my first time getting it on with a female, I instinctively returned the favor. She was making love to me and it felt good. It was different, but she knew all my weak spots.

After an hour of making out, we headed for the shower. "Wow, that was exhausting," she said.

I couldn't look her in the eyes. I felt like when my father had sex with me, embarrassed and scared. I guess I will always have a problem with that. Yet there was a part of me that was comfortable with our lovemaking. I was a willing participant and I enjoyed it. I didn't know what to say to her. I was nervous as hell, but somehow, I managed to respond.

"Do you know what we just did?"

"Yeah, I know. We just fucked!" she said. "I have always wanted to sleep with you."

No, she didn't just say that I thought to myself.

"Wow? I can't believe what you just said. So, you've been on my shit for a while, huh?" We both laughed.

I was about to lather my body when she placed her arms around me and said, "I've always wanted to do you from the first time we met at that Jack and Jill event."

"You don't say! So that means you've been stalking me the whole time without me knowing about it, huh?" I laughed, as she smiled and gave me a deep wet kiss.

After our shower, we continued our conversation about Kenny. Jenny was right; I had to decide. I knew it wasn't going to be easy getting away from him, but I was going to do whatever it took.

***

The next day, I confronted Kenny on the front porch and told him that I no longer wanted to work or be with him. He bit his bottom lip.

He was furious. He immediately snatched me up, barged his way inside the house, and began beating me.

"Bitch, you ain't gonna play me like that. Are you out of your fucking mind? What the fuck you think I am? You one of my high-paid hoes, bitch. You ain't going nowhere until I say so."

He was being very disrespectful and adamant, but I didn't give a damn. I wasn't going to take it any longer.

"Fuck you, Kenny!" I screamed at him, as blood poured from the punch to my mouth.

"Fuck me, huh? That's what you think? I'm gonna make sure another nigga never looks at you and says you're pretty," he snapped, snatching me by the throat. He was about to cut my face when I heard a door slam and the voice of Jenny.

"Nigga, if you make another fucking move, I'ma blow your black ass away! Put the blade down and get the fuck up off her!" she screamed at the top of her lungs.

He slowly loosened his grasp from my neck. The look on his face was one of disgust and contempt as he turned and stared in the direction of where the voice was coming from. My eyes were blurred. It was only after I regained my sight that I noticed the nine-millimeter Glock in Jenny's hand, which was aimed at Kenny's head. I was shocked.

"Yeah, mutha-fucka! What now?" I screamed. "You ain't so bad now, huh? You a punk-ass bitch! Get this through your head; it's over and done with. Did you get that? It's finished mutha-fucka!"

"Okay, Dana, that's how you and your lesbian girl rollin'? You gonna play a nigga like me like that? A'ight bitch, I'ma get up out your crib," he snarled, nodding his head.

"Shut the fuck up and get out already!" Jenny screamed.

We were relieved when he finally walked out the door. We both were apprehensive about him coming back to get even. Nevertheless, we were praying that he would just move on and leave us alone, especially me and he did. With Kenny out of the way things would be different, or so I thought.

Episode 3

$\mathcal{I}$ had to make some changes in my life, and Jenny was going to make sure I did. She introduced me to a friend of hers named Bradley. An accountant and a graduate of Baruch College in Manhattan, he seemed like a nice guy and he liked me. He was handsome and had it going on. He was the athletic type and stood six-two with a dark Wesley Snipes complexion. He also had a weird sense of humor. He always made fun of the way I spoke.

One minute he wanted me to speak "Ghetto Ebonics", as he put it, and in the next breath, he wanted me to talk "Proper", whatever that was. It was quite hilarious, stereotypical, and stupid. But what the heck, I figured I could look past all that.

He and I started seeing more of each other and it wasn't long before we became intimate. Still, it didn't stop me from seeing other men.

Bradley was about to start graduate school, and he was busy with his accounting job and other extracurricular activities. I had heard through the grapevine that he was close with several of his female co-workers.

I was working as an assistant manager at Macy's on Thirty-Fourth Street in Manhattan and had saved up enough money to purchase a used 2001 Ford Explorer. I had seriously thought about attending college, so I applied to New York University where I was accepted. Although I was only granted part-time financial aid, I was more than happy to get started with this chapter of my life. The light at the end of the tunnel was finally coming into view. My living situation remained the same. But because of the problems we had with Kenny, Jenny and I relocated to Brooklyn Heights. We knew that son of a bitch was crazy, and we didn't want to be anywhere close to him.

There was an emptiness inside of me that needed to be filled. Instead of finding something other than weed and alcohol to fill that void, I began doing both a lot more. What harm could some marijuana and alcohol do to derail the optimism that I had? I didn't foresee any problems at all.

After a couple of months, things began to sour between me and Bradley. He was so freaking hyped it was ridiculous. As intelligent as he was, he was a prick. At times he was nagging and just plain stupid. One night as I lay in bed reading The Write Lover by Brooklen Borne, my doorbell rang. It was him, and in his hands were a bouquet and a leather bag. I let him in and went back to reading.

"Hey, baby! How are you?" he asked, giving me the flowers and kissing me on the cheek.

"I'm fine. Can you make me a cup of coffee?" I asked, in my sexiest cat woman voice.

"Sure, no problem!" he said, walking into the kitchen. "Oh, I see you're still reading that romantic novel, huh?"

"Yeah, it's a great story; Brooklen Borne is a hell of a writer."

"I can tell because every time I visit, he takes up most of your time."

"No, he doesn't, but I promise tonight you will have my full attention."

"Okay," he smiled, handing me the coffee.

I put the book down after finishing my coffee. It wasn't long before he was all over me. While we were bumping and grinding and doing our thing, this fool out of the blue told me he had a surprise for me. He reached for the black leather bag, and in it were all sorts of sex accessories. Some of the sex toys were cool like the vibrator, the oils, and the blindfold. I wasn't into the handcuffs and some of the other stuff. Well, let me see, damn, I'm lying. I think the handcuffs were something I may try in the future. But I couldn't believe my eyes when he pulled out a strap-on dildo.

I was like, "Nigga please, I know you're not thinking about using that on me?"

"No, I'm not. I want you to talk dirty to me and do me."

"What! Mutha-fucka you gay or something?" I asked, in one of my southern drawls. I was beside myself and I stared curiously at him.

"Hold on Dana, let me explain," he said, getting serious. "I should have told you I was bisexual. I just didn't know how to convey it to you. When Jenny…"

I quickly interrupted him at the mention of her name. "Does Jenny know that you sleep with guys?" I shot back at him.

"No! We never spoke about it."

Isn't this some shit? I asked myself. I could sense that he wanted me to use the dildo on him. The more we talked, the more excited he became. "So, Bradley, let me get this straight, you want me to fuck you with the strap-on dildo?"

"Yes!" he said, eagerly.

I was going to fulfill his desire but on my terms. I made sure the strap-on was well-oiled before shoving it in his ass.

"What the fuck! What are you doing? Be gentle," he said, in a voice, I had never heard before.

"My bad! You mean gentle like this?" I asked, not being as rough.

"Yes."

I was smiling on the inside as I suddenly let loose on his ass. *Take that, and that,* I said to myself.

"Stop! Stop! What the fuck are you doing?"

"This mutha-fucka!" I snapped at him, as I took the strap-on off. "Get the hell outta my apartment!"

"What?"

"I said get the fuck up outta my bed. You wanna hear ghetto ebonics? Take your shit and your 'I'm better than thou attitude' and get the fuck up outta my crib. Bounce bitch and don't call my digits. Matter of fact, you're fired, step the fuck off."

I knew his ass was hurting from the way he was walking. I kicked his butt out of my apartment and my life. I couldn't believe what I had witnessed. Here was this strapping handsome man who had allowed me to punk him. I mean, who does that? Although I ate some coochie every once in a while, why would I want to be with a man like Bradley? I want my man straight. Just because I like girls doesn't mean I have to be with a man who likes other men. I guess when Bradley was getting familiar with the girls on his job; he was also getting familiar with the guys. I shrug the whole thing off and went back to reading Brooklen Borne's, The Write Lover.

***

I was now focused on my job and school. I was determined to make something of myself and my life. After taking care of my financial aid, I felt relieved knowing that I was now a full-time student and I would only have to come up with a quarter of my tuition instead of half. I headed to the bursars and the academic department to make sure they had everything in order and to see my academic counselor. The beginning of the semester was always a hassle, so a sister had to take care of her business.

I registered for five classes. In the previous semesters, I was a part-time student. However, for my third semester, I told myself that it was time to get my act together. I attended private school my whole life and I was always one of the top students in my class. And I damn sure didn't want to spend five or six years completing my bachelor's degree.

One of the classes I registered for was Sociology 204, Human Sexuality. Forty students were in the class. I was one of the lucky ones that were registered. There were at least ten or twelve students, including my girls, Tanisha, Monique, and India, who were trying to get permission from the sociology department to get into the class. Six students were allowed in and my girls made it.

"Girl," Tanisha said, with her chocolate brown complexion and pretty face, "this professor is hot and he's a brotha."

"For real?" I asked. "I wanna see what he looks like."

"Shit, that's the reason why we were trying to get into his class," Tanisha replied.

"Where is he?" I asked as I stared toward the front of the class.

"Right there, the brotha in the black Guess shirt and Sean John jeans!" an excited Monique yelled.

"Whaaaaat!" I said. "That's the Professor? Dayum, he's fine!"

They laughed and said, "Bitch, you crazy!" I didn't mind though because he was fine. They too appreciated a fine-looking brother. Not only had they earned the right to speak on such matters, but they were also smart, charming, gorgeous, and beautiful.

Tanisha was five-four with shoulder-length hair and hazel eyes. She weighed one hundred and twenty-four pounds. I knew her weight because she constantly talked about it, unlike the others. Monique had dark brown eyes was light in complexion and stood five-ten. She kept her hair in a Toni Braxton-style cut. She had a model physique; tall, slim, and pretty. India was of Jamaican Indo-Afro ancestry. She had flowing jet-black hair with dreamy brown eyes. Not only was she beautiful, but she and I were the same height. Most men were afraid to approach us. Our pretty looks intimidated them. You could see it in their eyes. I appreciated the intimidation factor because it prevented the ones who weren't up to any good from approaching us.

Tanisha and India grew up in the middle-class neighborhood of Rosedale in Queens, New York, where they attended several of the best public schools. Monique grew up in the same borough. However, she lived in the hard-knock section of South Jamaica, where she was constantly surrounded by the sound of gunshots, drugs, thugs, and poverty.

Tanisha and India met a pregnant Monique on a crowded Q 34 bus early one morning as they headed to school. After giving her seat to a fatigued-looking Monique, Tanisha introduced herself. Tanisha and India attended Townsend Harris High and Monique was enrolled at Bowen High. Located directly behind Townsend Harris, the girls saw each other a lot and soon became fast friends.

Life was difficult for Monique and her son, Lil Jamel. She worked tirelessly at her job at Foot Locker. But her dedication to her schoolwork paid off and allowed her to attend New York University. She was the last of the girls to get in because of her financial aid situation. She was given the full financial aid package instead of the part-time status.

The professor's name was Charles Anderson. He was anywhere from five-eleven to six-one. He was the athletic type. He was about one hundred and eighty-five pounds and his body was ripped. He wasn't built like those iron-pumping steroids-looking, brothers. He was dark brown in complexion with brown almond-shaped eyes. His lips were full, soft, and succulent. He kept a nicely trimmed goatee, a bald head, and an earring in his left ear. I was amazed to see such a fine young professor because a lot of the professors that I saw were middle age or older. He could have been a classmate of mine.

Human Sexuality was an incredible class. In almost every class session, Professor Anderson showed a few still and moving pictures of naked women, men, and children in some remote Third World countries. These people's cultures varied sexually and were quite different from ours here in the Western part of the world. The guys in the class stayed awake during the moving pictures. Naked Third World women meant a lot to them.

I saw so much dick and pussy being flashed across the screen that after a while I became a dickologist and a pussyologist expert. The names penis and vagina were no longer a part of my vocabulary. I was breaking things down for the professor in class. The girls and I were at the head of the class. I pretty much was getting good grades. The first three exams the professor gave to the class, I passed with flying colors. The girls did well also.

Like most of the girls in the class, I tried to get familiar with Professor Anderson. But he wasn't paying me any attention and I wasn't going to sweat him like the others were. I wasn't about to play myself. I laid back and chilled. I wanted to prove to him that I could pass his class with an A average without being the teacher's pet.

Soon thereafter, he began to lavish a lot of attention and praise on my participation, focus, and work. I was elated and skeptical all at the same time. He wanted to know my major.

"It's Political Science," I said.

"Have you ever thought about a major in Sociology?" he asked, his eyes widening.

"No, I haven't," I smiled at him.

"Well, you're one of my top students so maybe you should think about it."

I couldn't help myself as I stared first at his crotch and then his ass, as he turned to walk away. The girls were staring at me as I tried not to laugh. They playfully hated me.

"You should let him hit it," Tanisha said.

"Hit what?" I asked. "You mean my pleasure zone with the vice grip muscles?" We were laughing so hard, it was ridiculous.

After regaining our senses, we talked about the size of his dick. We wanted to know if he had a big one. Our eyes were like radars as they settled on the front of his crotch every time he stood up and faced the class.

"Damn, that nigga got a nice size dick," Monique said.

"How the fuck you know that?" India asked, laughing.

"That bitch has x-ray vision and she's been looking at the bulge in the front of his pants the whole time," I said.

"Like y'all ain't doing the same thing! That shit looks like something I could work with. Y'all don't see the imprint?" Monique asked with a sigh, as we all admitted that we were dick-watching the professor.

The next day my fascination with Human Sexuality and Professor Anderson hit a huge hurdle. Before returning my paper, I felt his eyes piercing my body like a sharp knife. When he handed me the paper, I was astonished to see a big fat C- in red ink.

"What the fuck? How could he do this to me?" I said to the girls.

I was furious. Never in my wildest dreams did I expect anything like this. Monique and India both received A's and Tanisha a B+. My mind was reeling back and forth. I grew angrier by the second, as he avoided my eyes. He seemed as if he was awaiting my usual upbeat self and participation, but I was too pissed. I can't recall what he lectured on that particular day.

I was about to storm out at the end of the class when I was abruptly summoned by Mr. Fine Ass Anderson who wanted to have a word with me.

"I sensed something is bothering you," he said, as he took a sip from the bottle of Dasani water on his desk.

"Oh!" I muttered under my breath. *Can you believe this son of a bitch? He thought that something was bothering me after he gave me a C-*, I thought to myself.

"Ms. Estick is there a problem?"

I kept quiet as I stared at him with a glare that would have stopped traffic on Fifth Avenue. Finally, I pointed to my paper and said, "This!"

"Well, I know you're upset. But on several questions on cultural imagery of women amongst the Bantu people of South Africa, your explanations were not quite what we focused on in class. You seemed to have strayed somewhat from what was pertinent to the subject matter. I know you certainly could have done much better. The grade I gave you is the grade you earned.

You're a highly intelligent young woman and I know that you're quite capable of far superior work than this. I noticed Tanisha Peters, Monique Johnson, India Reid, and most of all you, the first time you guys entered my class. At the start of the semester, you guys were always clowning. Nevertheless, I was glad to see that your behavior has changed for the better. You guys have done quite well, and you all have received A's in my class so far, which you have deservedly earned. As for today's result, it would have been unfair for me to give you a grade that you didn't earn. You were not focused and that's the only reason why you did not get a higher grade. I'm quite confident in your capabilities, and I do believe that you will do quite well on your midterm."

This mutha-fucka! I thought to myself. *And to think I thought he had it going on.* But as upset as I was standing there listening to him, he was looking hot. I barely heard him as he continued talking and writing his office hours on a piece of paper.

"If you need any help, please let me know." He smiled and handed me the piece of paper.

"Sure," I replied, trying to downplay my anger. I noticed him taking my clothes off with his eyes.

He stretched his hand towards me — grasped my shaking, sweaty palm, and shook it. At first, I was like, *damn, I'm about to cum.* My coochie was jumping. But I immediately composed myself and mumbled under my panting breath, "Thanks, Char...I mean Professor Anderson."

He smiled at me and replied, "Take care and see you in class next Monday."

"Bye," I said in return, giggling. I left the classroom on wobbly legs and headed toward the Student Union.

***

After weeks of trying to convince me to meet her in her favorite online chat room, I finally showed up. Tanisha was already there when

I logged in. We immediately pretended to be lovers. It was hilarious as we played around with the men. They didn't seem to care if we were lesbians. Quite a few straight women were also in our conversation. The thing is I never took it seriously. I always thought that people who frequented chat rooms were nothing more than losers.

Nevertheless, one night I was bored and decided to check out the Hot and Frisky chat room. I logged in as Sugar and Spice. It was feminine, sexy, and attractive, which was me. No sooner than I entered the room, I was bombarded by a group of men and women with several sexually explicit names. My private box lit up with the colors yellow and red as the messages kept coming. I tried to respond as fast as I could but ended up ignoring several of them. I tried to be nice about the whole thing. I told the chat room applicants who wanted to talk in private to come and do so on the main screen.

Eventually, I became bored and was about to log out, when I received a private message from someone named Energy. The conversation we had was the opposite of the one I had earlier. He wanted to know if this was my first time in the chat room.

"In this particular chat room?" I typed.

"Yeah."

I said yes. I then asked him if he was a regular. He lol, (laugh out loud), and said yes. He said that he lived in Manhattan and that he was in his late thirties.

"Are you cute?" he asked.

"Well, I've been told that all my life."

"Okay, can I see for myself?"

"How would that be possible?"

"Easy, just send me a picture. If you've been told all your life that you're beautiful then I would assume that you must have a picture or two laying around."

I laughed and typed, "Yeah, I do have pictures but not online. Do you have one?"

"Sure, I do, but I would like to trade pictures with you if you don't mind."

"But I told you I don't have any online," I reminded him once again.

"Get one online and then we can trade. I can wait."

We spoke for at least an hour. Still, neither one of us wanted to say too much about our personal lives. I damn sure wasn't. No way was I going to meet a guy in an online chat room and tell him my business. Nonetheless, we shared a few things such as basketball, football, chess, and listening to Rhythm and Blues, Hip Hop, and Reggae music. But I wasn't about to get carried away. As we chatted, several girls were typing his name across the main screen as if he was some sort of celebrity.

"Wow, you must be the man in here. Do these girls have pictures of you?" I typed it in bold letters.

"Only one and she's not in here at the moment," he typed, and lol.

"Okay," I typed, grinning as I read the bullshit he was typing.

I could tell he was somewhat decent. He said he wanted to get to know me and I was somewhat curious about him myself. However, I wasn't about to go out of my way to do so.

"I have some business that I need to take…"

Before he could complete his sentence, I asked, "Do you have a wife or a girlfriend?"

"A wife, no, I have a friend, but it's not serious. Why do you ask?"

"Nothin', I hear you," I typed thinking, *what a lying bastard*.

"Keep in touch," he typed. I promised that I would. We then exchanged email addresses and said we would stay in touch.

***

I was two years younger than Jenny and although we left South Carolina together; she stayed in touch with her parents. Although they did not appreciate how she got up and took her ass to California and then to New York, they got over it. They never held it against her and despite the many stories her mother heard about New York, she allowed her to withdraw money from her trust fund. Things were going great for her. She had taken a few real estate courses, studied her butt off, and got her license. Along with a mutual friend she did some research and started her own real estate business with some of the money from her trust fund. Matter of fact, the trust fund money helped in more ways than one because she lent me some cash.

Jenny shared some of the things that happened to me with her mother. She told her mother that I had to leave home because my father tried to rape me and that when I resisted, he got physical with me. Her mother was speechless and wished me the best. I was glad she didn't get into all the details with her.

When I first met Jenny at the Jack and Jill function, she was singing my mother's favorite song. My first impression was, *wow, she's pretty, sexy, and cool and she's singing our song*. I knew right there and then that we would become friends. Jenny was the spitting image of Beyoncé. With her smooth ebony complexion, she stood out in any crowd. She was five-eight and very outspoken. She was one of three sisters who attended some of the best elite Black schools in South Carolina. Her father, James Thornton was a respectable banker and her mother, Ingrid, a pediatric doctor had a practice of her own. Her mother was known throughout South Carolina by many rich and influential black families. Her family's reputation was respectable and highly regarded.

Jenny had a lot more freedom growing up than I did. I guess her father wasn't sleeping with her like mine was. She would hang out for days with many of the privileged kids, who were rebelling against their parents. She had a badass chicken-head cousin from the hood named Kim. She would always take Jenny with her to the hood and introduce her to the thugs, rude boys, hood rats, chicken heads, wild sex parties, and the beer-drinking brothers who were up to no good. She was hitting the purple haze and drinking beer before I knew what the hell purple haze was. The only thing that I was doing before her was having sex.

Jenny lost her virginity at the age of fourteen, along with her cousin Kim, in the Red Square houses in the south end section of Oceanville. This was a place where kids dreamed of becoming dope slingers, gangsters, whores, and pimps, instead of doctors, lawyers, and teachers. It happened with a guy named Craig, who I once met. He was twenty-five years old and had three kids by two different women in the same housing project and his trifling ass wasn't supporting any of them. Yet he wanted to get Jenny pregnant. Despite him wanting to be her "baby daddy", she stayed with him right up until she left South Carolina with me. I never judged or hated her. She was my friend and I loved her.

Like me, she was into older guys. I have always believed that older men are better lovers and they know how to satisfy and treat their women. In the same breath, Jenny would let you know that making out with another girl was the icing on the cake as far as she was concerned. She was the one who showed me the ropes. That's why it never bothered me that we slept together because I knew she was a loving and caring person.

Jenny was doing great as far as her love life was concerned. She was seeing a guy named Greg, and an attractive young girl named Ebony. I don't know how she managed to pull that off, but I always told her that I wanted to be like her when I got older, to which she would laugh and say, "I ain't mad at you."

***

I told Jenny what happened between me and Bradley. She immediately began laughing at the mention of his name and said she wasn't surprised at all.

"What the fuck you mean you're not surprised?" I asked as we both laughed.

"Didn't you know?"

"Know what?"

"He gave up on the sisters and this I just recently found out," she remarked with a faint chuckle, taking a sip from the Snapple bottle in her hand.

"Damn! He could have given me a disease. Suppose the condoms had burst?" I tried to be calm and not let my emotions take over.

"If it's AIDS, you're talking about I don't think he has it."

"Hmm, all I know is that he asked me to do him in his ass, uh, uh, no," I said, as we fell out laughing once again.

"You're not right. This is serious stuff we're talking about and you're making me laugh."

"Seriously," I asked, trying to control my laughter, "did he tell you that he isn't HIV positive?"

"Yeah."

"Okay, but that shit is scary."

"I know, but you did use condoms every time he hit it, right?"

"Oh hell, yeah! I'm not that stupid. But I'm still leery because I've been with several brothas with some big dicks and the condoms burst. I don't know if it was done deliberately or not, but I know I was scared. Then you've got those brothas who put the condoms on and let them slide off without letting you know. The worst ones are those who put the shit on knowing they put a hole in the tip. Then they wanna fuck you and cum all in your shit, fuck that."

"True, girl! That's some real grimy shit."

"So, all this time you didn't know he was sleeping with men?"

"Girl, I didn't know that when I hooked you guys up. If I had known that I wouldn't have introduced him to you, anyway, enough about Bradley, what's going on with you these days?"

"Do you remember that professor I was telling you about?"

"Yeah, what about him, you fucked him?"

"No, bitch, not yet, but I wanna hit it though. Did I say that?"

"I thought you said you weren't gonna sweat him anymore? Look at you."

"Girl, what I said and what I see, hmm." I smiled, as I bit my bottom lip.

"You're a damn freak."

"I know, but I just wanna hit it one time that's all. Other than that, I'm doing great. And, oh yeah, I'm still feeling out some of the brothas in the chat room. Remember that other fool I told you about? The one I kick it with on a regular in the room?"

"Oh, that guy Energy?"

"Yeah."

"What about him?"

"He seems kinda cool, so I'm gonna see what's up with that."

"Be careful, you know how some of these negroes are in the chat rooms."

"I know," I said, as she got her car keys.

"I'll be back in a minute. It's food time. Do you want Chinese, Jamaican, Spanish or Italian? My treat."

"I'll have the Spanish, but no pork. A six-pack of Corona and a bag of weed would be nice," I said.

"Okay, bitch!" I closed the door behind her.

Episode 4

I passed Professor Anderson's class with an A average. He was right about me not being prepared for the exam that I had failed. Moreover, I had straight A's in all my classes. I was on a roll. The girls also passed his class with straight A's and we all had a lifetime of sexual fantasies. I still had my eyes on the professor and now and then I would stop by his office to see how he was doing. Okay, I'm lying; I went to see him so I could check out his fine ass.

I was now a lower junior and feeling good about myself. The computer and chat room became my second life and Energy and I would chat for hours. We were still reluctant about exchanging our pictures. I would have traded pictures with him in a heartbeat if he had sent me his. But I guess he was playing hardball so I went along with the back and forth to see how long it would continue.

I met Dax around the same time I crossed paths with Energy. Dax, whose real name was Robert Jackson, respectably approached me, and he was saying all the right things I needed to hear. Instead of taking my time and approaching the situation with caution, I gave in. Unlike Energy, Dax wasn't feeding me any of the bullshit that he was saying to me. You can always tell when someone is trying to play games with you, and that's the impression I got from Energy.

I didn't have a picture of myself on my computer, so I downloaded several, and Dax and I exchanged pictures and cell phone numbers. The feedback and karma between us were wonderful. Besides, he was a cutie which made things a lot easier. He was a stockbroker on Wall Street the financial capital of the world. Thirty-four -years old, single, and the father of a five-year-old girl named Chrissie.

Dax and I spoke often on the phone and a month after our initial meeting on the internet; we met one Friday evening at Junior's Restaurant famous for its cheesecakes on Flatbush Avenue in Brooklyn. He was even finer in person. I don't know why I thought he would be wearing a suit. I guess because he worked on Wall Street, I assumed he would be wearing one. I mean, isn't that how a stockbroker dresses? Nevertheless, he was dressed in a pair of black Sean John slacks, a light gray Girbaud sweater, and black and gray Timberland boots. He looked and sounded like a typical brother from the hood instead of the smooth-talking educated person I spoke with on the phone. His Morris Chestnut complexion was even more awesome in person. He stood six-three with full lips and sleepy laid-back brown eyes. His body was nice and firm. He looked so scrumptious that I wanted to take a bite out of him.

I was looking gorgeous dressed in black Prada shoes and a black Versace pantsuit that hugged my sexy body in all the right places. My hair was cut in a close-cropped Jada Pinkett style. I was like eye candy the minute he laid eyes on me. His face lit up like a Christmas tree. I knew he wasn't disappointed. I had wanted to make an impression and I did.

We ordered our cheesecake to go and decided to catch a movie. We spoke about the things we wanted to achieve in the future. We talked about the things we had in common, our likes and dislikes. We even joked about how two individuals as expressive, ambitious, and progressive as we were, had no reason to be in a chat room. We laughed and talked about all the gossip and nonsense that goes on in chat rooms.

I was somewhat shocked when he said, "I don't think it's a good idea for you to go back to the chat room. You don't have anything in common with those guys."

"Excuse you?" I asked, staring into his eyes.

He laughed and uttered under his breath with a shy look, "You don't need to because I'm here for you already."

"Oh? How do you figure that?" I asked, studying his face.

"Well, I won't be talking to any of the women in the room anymore."

"Is that so?"

"I mean, I will say hi and talk for a minute, but that's about it. It's gonna be all about you from now on. I like what I see, and I like what I've heard from our conversations over the past weeks," he exclaimed with a devilish but cute smile on his face.

The only thing I could say was, "Hmm, we'll see what you think in a few more weeks."

***

Robert and I had been hanging out a lot and in no time, Jenny came with the questions.

"Girl, you look happy. You must be getting some good dick? What's his name? What's the 411?" she asked, laughing.

"Well, I'm seeing a man, mother!" I giggled, as I continued making my grill cheese sandwich.

"You hooked up with that negro Energy from the chat room, didn't you?"

"No, it's this other guy and his name is Robert. He's thirty-four years old. We met about a month and a half ago in the same chat room and we've gone out a few times. The brotha is fine! He looks good, no shit! He's dying to hit this shit." I laughed, as I patted the front of my coochie.

"Did he get a sniff?"

"Hell, no!" I stated as we laughed even louder.

"So, when am I going to meet him?"

"Hush, you will. I'm supposed to meet him in two hours. So, let me go and wash my ass."

"A'ight, have fun and have him wear a condom," she insisted.

As I sat in my jeep waiting for Robert, a black BMW X5 with tinted windows pulled up next to me. The windows slowly began rolling down.

Shit, I thought to myself, *Kenny has caught up with me finally.*

Instead, I heard a voice say, "Excuse me beautiful are you waiting for anyone in particular?" It was Robert and boy was I glad to see him.

"What the fuck you doing rolling up on me like that and whose shit is this you're driving?" I yelled at him.

"Don't worry it's paid for. Park your shit and get in." He said that he had picked up the BMW over the weekend. The ride was hot.

"What happened to your Mercedes SL 500?" I asked.

"Nothing, it's home!" He then drove off with the tires screeching.

"So, what's on the agenda for today?"

"First, I have to make a quick stop at my apartment. Do you mind?"

"No, it's okay."

He lived at Eighty-Fourth Street and Tenth Avenue on the Westside of Manhattan. Upon arriving, he pulled into an underground garage of a luxury condo apartment complex. As I contemplated whether I should get out of the car or not, I realized that my legs were shaking uncontrollably.

"Come on up, I won't bite," he insisted, reaching for my hand.

He was staring into my eyes throughout the elevator ride. My heart rate rapidly increased as we entered his apartment.

"I'll be right with you make yourself at home," he said, assuring me that I had nothing to be afraid of. "I need to take a shower. Work with me, okay?"

"It's cool, go ahead."

His apartment was quite impressive. He had two elegant bedrooms with sizable attached bathrooms. The smaller of which was probably his daughter's. The wooden floors which adorned the apartment throughout were clear and sparkling and I could see my reflection. He had a gourmet kitchen with state-of-the-art appliances. Drop-dead ten-inch ceilings and a spacious living room with a panoramic view of the New Jersey skyline.

He was in the main bathroom with the door closed when he hollered, "Are you okay?"

"Yeah," I replied.

I was looking at several photos of him and his daughter when he came out of the shower with water dripping all over his upper body. He had a towel around his waist. My legs immediately became wobbly. I quickly sat down hoping he wouldn't notice my shaking legs.

"Care for a drink?" he asked, mischievously.

"Yeah," I said, hoping the drink would relax me. He poured me a glass of Krug.

What the fuck is happening to me? I've been through shit like this before. Girl, hold it down, relax, relate, release, be calm, I screamed to myself. Halfway through my drink he reached for my hands and held them for what seemed like an eternity. He kissed my lips ever so lithely. Damn, I was getting turned on. My panties were wet and within minutes my blouse and pants were off.

He was about to take off my bra and panties when he whispered, "don't move," and used his teeth to remove my bra. He planted a kiss on my hot pussy and began removing my panties with his teeth. He somehow managed to use his tongue and play with my clit as he pulled them off.

"Right there," I moaned, reaching for his clean-shaven head.

He got up and walked to the refrigerator butt naked. Wow, he was packing. I was like *damn, all that for me*? He returned with a can of whip cream which he meticulously sprayed over my tits, navel, and pussy. My legs were wide open as he ate the whipped cream off my body. He licked and sucked his way down to my pussy. My body was on fire. He ate me out for half an hour. I came over and over on his tongue and face. I shoved him back on the couch and took his dick in my mouth.

"Yeaaah! Baby, ooh baby! Just like that! Don't stop!" he panted. I felt his manhood grow inside my mouth. "I don't wanna cum, not yet. Baby, slow down! Please don't make me cum," he pleaded.

His manhood jerked in my mouth as if it had a mind of its own. I slowly released it from my grip because I was ready to fuck him. He slid on a condom and began to kiss me once again. His tongue darted in and around my mouth, and as he slid his manhood deep inside of me, I moaned as his balls slapped against my ass.

He was banging my pussy like there was no tomorrow. No doubt about it. I got on top of him and lowered myself onto his hard rock.

I was gyrating my hips when he told me in a calm and sexy voice, "Keep the pussy still."

He began talking nasty to me and I had to stay still. The whole thing was driving me crazy. My pussy was jumping, and his dick was doing the same inside of me.

"Oh, God! Yes, right there!" I moaned as we quickened our pace.

He was working overtime. He was putting it on me. I couldn't speak.

"Here it is, take it!" he yelled.

"Yeah, baby! Fuck this pussy! Fuck me, Robert. Fuck it!" I screamed.

We couldn't hold it in any longer; we exploded in unison soaked in each other's sweat. He held me close and whispered in my ear that he was falling for me. I kissed him and told him that I felt the same way. He asked me to move in with him. I told him I wasn't ready for such a move. Instead, I got an apartment of my own on the Lower Eastside of Manhattan. I felt it was time for me to be on my own. Jenny didn't like the idea at first, but she understood and gave me her blessings.

***

Robert had introduced me to one of his close friends, a young man by the name of Jason Parcell. I was meeting all these fine black men who were financially established and educated. Jason was quite the looker and rather easy on the eyes. He stood six feet with a light brown caramel complexion and an Adonis body. He was confident about himself and he believed that his lifestyle and world were above and beyond others. The same age as Robert, he was intelligent and condescending at times. He had graduated in the top five of his graduating class at Princeton University where he earned degrees in Political Science, Sociology, and a minor in Philosophy. He later enrolled at Colombia University law school where he graduated in the top three of his graduating class.

I first met him at Robert's apartment, where he was in an in-depth conversation with several people. He had an air of superiority about him and behaved as if he was solely responsible for redefining the lazy stereotypical and derogatory labels which were oftentimes placed on many young brothers. He was quoting Socrates, Kant, and Nietzsche. He was quite the intellect as he spoke about the Old, Middle, and New Kingdoms of Ancient Egypt.

Damn, I'm out of my league, I thought to myself. I kept my mouth shut as they continued talking.

"It's time I drop some science and knowledge on you youngsters," Jason said, pouring himself another drink.

Certainly, I was familiar with some of the things he was saying. But I wasn't on his or the level of the others. I was still an undergraduate trying to get my academics together. He dominated the conversation. He kept staring at me and it wasn't that 'Hi, how are you doing?' stare either. It was more like, 'Hi, can I get a fuck?' There was a certain aura about him, and it emanated assertively, and it sparked my curiosity. He mentioned how he hated those brothers who sold nickel-and-dime drugs. He said it wasn't right for young brothers to poison their communities.

Then I thought to myself, *isn't this brother a criminal lawyer? And didn't Robert say that many of his clients are drug dealers?* He was saying all those things, yet he was defending them in court. He was the biggest hypocrite.

I was listening to hear what else "Preacher" Parcell had to say and he did not disappoint me either.

He went on to say, "Laziness, procrastination, and low self-esteem are some of the crutches that niggas like to use. Anyone can make it if he or she wants to. A lot of these fucked up thinking niggas who are afraid of challenges ain't shit! There is no challenge too great where a nigga cannot overcome, you feel me?"

I almost fell off my chair when he said, "You feel me?" And how he kept using the "N" word, and he was a lawyer. Unbelievable, he was something else.

***

Several days later, I was with Robert in his apartment. The place was filled with toys and nursery rhyme books. I suggested to him that he might need a larger apartment to store all those books and toys.

"Don't you think you need a bit more space?" I said to him, instead he shrugged it off and said his daughter loved to read. According to him, she was with her mother or grandparents. Besides, I rarely saw her so who was I to question him about that? What's more, I was having fun hanging out with him and his friends. We would drive to New Jersey, Long Island, Connecticut, and upstate New York, where many of his friends were professional and rich. I loved the power affairs and ritzy engagements; they reminded me of my childhood. My parents were either inviting or being invited to some posh affair with their rich and powerful friends.

It was at one of these affairs that Jason decided to make his move. We were at the home of Derek and Hally Robinson both corporate lawyers when I had to use the bathroom. Robert and the others were jamming by the pool except for Jason. I had been to the house on a few occasions but as always it took me a while to find the bathroom. As I walked past the kitchen and headed down the hallway, there he was. The closer I got the finer he looked. I tried avoiding his eyes but that didn't go too well.

He began walking towards me and suddenly my knees felt weak. The tension was unbearable. Without saying a word, he pushed himself on me and started kissing me. I resisted at first, but I couldn't help myself as I felt his hard body pressed against mine. His hands began caressing my ass and pussy. My knees buckled and my body was in heat. I reached for his dick as we kissed passionately. He was pulling at my bathing suit, but I told him this wasn't the right time or place, and for him to stop.

"Why not, don't you want to fuck me?"

"Yeah," I said, his dick almost bursting out of the Speedo he was wearing.

"So, let's do it right here," he said, as he continued playing with my pussy.

"I have to get back outside," I pleaded, pulling away from him. "Robert knows I went to use the bathroom."

He pulled my bathing suit to the side again and planted a wet kiss on my pussy, his tongue quickly darting in and out of my love tunnel. He finally loosened his hold on me which I didn't want. However, I didn't want to look suspicious, so I greeted Robert and the others as if nothing had happened. But I couldn't get Jason out of my head. I knew from the moment our paths crossed that he wanted to sleep with me. Shit, none of the other girls at the pool party had anything over me. Jason kept staring at me the whole time. I was scared that someone may have noticed the chemistry between him and me, so I kept my eyes off him. Now and then he would stare at me and smile, especially when

Robert would pull me close or kiss me. I couldn't wait for the party to be over. I couldn't take it.

Episode 5

"Hello, what's up?" I asked Jenny, holding the phone close to my ear.

"Listen. I have some information concerning your father."

My father was the last person I wanted to talk about. I hadn't thought about him for quite some time.

"What is it?"

"He was arrested last month for beating on his girlfriend and he was in the hospital."

"The hospital?"

"Yeah, and guess what?"

"What?"

"His girlfriend is only twenty years old."

"Hmm."

"That's right and they got into a fight because he thought she was cheating on him. When she came home, he beat the shit out of her, and she clocked him upside the head. They both had to get stitches and she pressed charges against him. He's spending a lot of his money on her and her family. Your uncles and aunts are worried about him losing his business. They believe that his girlfriend and her family are taking advantage of him. Girl, he's always talking about how you ran away from him and that you're the only thing that matters to him. And he wants to know where you are so that he can make your trust fund available to you."

"Your mom told you all this?"

"Yeah, she did. You know they still go to those bourgeoisie-ass parties and talk shit. Your father is a snap. He's got a young girl." She laughed.

"Don't tell your mom where I live because you know that fool would be here in a New York minute."

"Girl, you don't have to worry about shit like that. I would never play you like that."

"I would love to get access to my trust fund. But I refuse to get in contact with him right about now. Maybe I will sometime in the future. But as of now, I don't think so."

"I don't blame you. You do what you have to. Just remember I've got your back," she assured me before hanging up the phone.

***

I was about to get dressed after taking a shower when my telephone rang.

It was Robert, "Hi baby," he said in his usual sexy voice.

"What's up?"

"Meet me at Eighty-Sixth and Broadway in an hour."

"Okay, I'll be there."

He was waiting on the corner like he said when I pulled up. I was surprised to see him without his car.

"Where's your ride?" I asked as he sat next to me in my car.

"Oh, it's in Long Island. I have to go and get it."

"Why is it in Long Island?"

"One of my business associates borrowed it. You know how it is sometimes," he said nonchalantly.

"I guess." I never questioned him when it came to his business. He and his friends always drove each other's cars. "How do I get to Long Island from here?" I asked, heading South on Broadway.

"The Navigation system and I got your back." He then leaned over and kissed me on the cheek. He wanted to know how my day was.

"It was shit. I've had a rough week."

"What you need is some good loving from your man." He placed his hand between my legs.

"I do *need* some loving, but I don't think I need it good. I want some *bad* loving." I giggled.

I pulled into the driveway of a huge house in the Hamptons. Several luxury cars were parked in front of the house and the driveway. *This must be the home of a celebrity*, I said to myself. Robert and I approached the entrance to the house. A butler, looking and sounding like Mr. Belvedere led us into the living room. Growing up in South Carolina, we had a huge house and a Nanny and most of my classmates and neighbors had beautiful homes. But damn, this house was something else. The street was filled with million-dollar homes. Even the freaking air I was breathing smelled of money. I was hanging around folks with million-dollar homes and yachts.

An older-looking gentleman no taller than five feet and with a baldhead and a booming baritone voice walked over to Robert and hugged him as if he hadn't seen him in a while. I was like, *damn, that's a little ass man.* Even I was taller than him. Both men were laughing as Robert introduced me.

"Jimmy, this is my baby, Dana."

"Hi, nice meeting you," Jimmy said, as he lit a cigar. "Is my smoking bothering you?"

"No not at all, it's okay."

"Now I see why you call her your baby, Rob." Jimmy laughed in his booming baritone voice.

"Isn't she beautiful?" Robert asked smiling and blowing me a kiss.

I was overwhelmed by all the attention. Yet I loved every minute of it. Mr. Belvedere brought me an apple martini and Robert and Jimmy excused themselves. Laughter and voices were coming from a room down the hall. I couldn't hear what was being said so I decided to be nosey.

As I got closer to the room, I saw several sharply dressed men and women snorting what looked to be cocaine from a large platinum dish. I wasn't in any way, shape, or form startled or suspicious, because I had seen Robert's friends snorting cocaine before in small amounts, but never from a large dish. I figured those folks were just having fun like they always seemed to have whenever there's any kind of affair or party. I was if anything in awe of the house after I was given a personal tour by Mr. Belvedere.

After about two hours, we were on our way back to the city. Knowing I had a thing for BMWs because I wouldn't stop talking about them, Robert suggested that I drove his. I was cruising behind him as he drove my ride. I parked his car in front of my apartment and hopped into my ride with him. He said that he was hungry and wanted to know if I would fix him a meal. I said yes. We stopped at the fish market where I picked up some snow crab legs. We then headed to the supermarket where we purchased lettuce, red peppers, tomatoes, cucumbers, and four cans of Colt 45 beer, and drove to his apartment.

Once there, he got in the shower. I seasoned the crab legs and placed them in a pot with the beer. This was a favorite of my family. To complete the dish, I made a salad. After eating, he and I sat down to watch some television. As we cuddled together, we sipped on a bottle of imported French wine. I loved my man and I wanted to please him. Our lovemaking that night was intense and torrid.

"I love you baby and I want you to be my wife," he said to me, in a halting voice. I was startled beyond belief. I didn't know what to say. "Say something, come on now. I'm ready to take this to the next level."

"I do wanna marry you," I shrieked, as he kissed me.

Although we had only been seeing each other for a few months, I loved him, and he treated me wonderfully. I had hoped the answer I had given him wouldn't be taken as a green light for us to run out and get married the next day, because I still wanted to sow my oats so to speak, as the guys would say, and go on a few dates. Yet I was more than willing to be with him for the time being.

Episode 6

$\mathcal{I}$ was now a floor manager at Macy's and although things were not quite where I would have liked them to be. I was confident that my situation would get better on my terms. Then again, Robert saw to it that my finances were taken care of and although I objected and would give him a difficult time whenever he would offer me large sums of money. He never wavered on the stance that he took. He would get pissed at me whenever I would go on a job interview. It was no secret that I needed another job because I wasn't making enough money at Macy's. I just wanted to be my own woman.

I still had moments where I would get down on myself. Whenever I would get depressed or upset, I would hum the lyrics to my mother and my favorite song, and it would lift my spirit. The song was a source of strength for my mother and I guess it was for me as well. Come to think of it, she would always play it after a night of arguing and fighting with my father. I would hear her sniffling through her tears as she hummed along with the song. There were many nights when I would lay in bed feeling sorry for myself. I would cry and sing for hours thinking about her until I fall asleep. I missed her. I wonder how she would have reacted to me being on my own.

I was still busting my ass in school. I had no qualms about the twenty-one-credit load I was carrying. I was on a mission that was possible and inaction or failing was not an option.

Charles and I were having lunch quite frequently. The chemistry between us was taking on a different feel. I knew he was falling in love with me. He was single and didn't have a girlfriend or children. He was absorbed in his work and didn't want to get involved in a relationship where he couldn't give one hundred percent. He made it clear to me that he was not looking for a good time, but that he was looking for something serious.

"Going through the motions and games in a relationship isn't something that I look forward to," he politely said. "I want a down-to-earth relationship and I want to settle down with someone willing to love and start a family."

Wow, I said to myself, *he's serious*. Did I feel the same way? Regardless of the drama that I was going through with Robert and Jason, I fully understood where he was coming from.

Charles and I continued having lunch at several restaurants off-campus. We were very discreet about when and where we would eat. We limited our interaction on campus as much as possible.

"Shit, you know what people would say if they caught us together?" I would say.

"I know where you're going with this."

"I'm glad you understand because that's grounds for dismissal."

"It's funny that you're the one saying all of this to me." He laughed.

I was always on my best behavior even though I wanted to suck up the professor like a hot biscuit with gravy. I felt extremely comfortable knowing that he and I were about to embark on something special.

***

A month after Robert's proposal of marriage, Energy and I finally agreed on a date. Robert and I never made any plans as to when the marriage would take place and so I felt I was still available. But overall, I still loved him. It was November and the weather was not as cold as it normally could be. This was my kind of weather. I have always believed that fall was the perfect time to show off your wardrobe. I told Energy I would be wearing a black Versace leather suit and black Prada shoes. My hair was stylishly done. I was looking fierce. I gave myself a round of applause. My shit was tight.

I guess this was my moment of truth as I waited on the corner of Broadway and Forty-Third Street. I was finally going to meet another brother from the chat room. One whose picture I had not seen. I was nervous because I was hoping and praying that he looked good. He said that he would be wearing a brown leather jacket, brown mock neck shirt, brown Tommy Hilfiger slacks, and brown snakeskin shoes. I was waiting on the corner when I noticed Professor Anderson walking toward me.

As he made his way through the crowd I yelled out, "Hi, Charles."

He seemed surprised to see me and greeted me with weary eyes. *What the hell is the professor doing here,* I asked myself. Then it dawned on me as he got closer and I noticed his attire.

"Oh, shit!" we both gasped.

"Energy?" I asked, shocked.

"Yeah. Spice? Isn't this some shit?" I nodded in agreement. He was smiling.

I was glad to see him although I never expected anything quite like this. I was somewhat embarrassed because we'd had cybersex, ouch, and we shared some of our sexual fantasies. From the glow on his face, I could tell that it did not bother him.

"So, what are we going to do now, Mr. Energy?" I asked mockingly, as he hugged me. We had made plans to catch a movie, grab a bite and then head to the Shadows nightclub and get our dance on.

"Let's stick to the plan. Let's go and check out a movie first." He smiled.

"Are you sure?"

"Sure, I'm sure, do you have other plans?"

"No. Wow, you sounded so different on the phone."

"I know. I sounded more down to earth as Energy, didn't I?"

"For real." I giggled.

"I guess Energy is a bit freaky, huh? You were so straightforward about the things you shared. But let's not forget the things I said I was capable of doing with my tongue."

"Oh, boy!" I winced.

"Remember I told you that my tongue was long?"

"Yeah, let me see?" I asked smiling. "Stick it out! Wow, it's long, hmm."

He then put his arm around me and pulled me close to him as we headed to the movie theater. After the movie, we ate at Vito's an upscale Italian restaurant on Fifty-Seventh and Madison Avenue. I felt wonderful as he held my hands throughout our meal. This was nothing like when we ate off-campus. This was different. We weren't looking over our shoulders or worrying about anyone walking upon us. The atmosphere was equally romantic; everything was perfect. Charles stared into my eyes and gently stroked my fingers. The food was great, and we left holding hands.

We hopped in a cab and headed to the Shadow's Night Club. Kanye West's *All Falls Down* was playing as we entered. The place was filled with excitement. I quickly noticed a group of groupies staring at my man…oops, I meant Charles.

"What do you want from the bar?" he asked.

"Some Cristal would be fine," I answered over the loud music.

We were sitting and talking when the deejay dropped some old-school music. The Cristal was already in my system when the deejay played Lauryn Hill's *Doo Wop (That Thing)*. Charles and I got on the dance floor and started doing our thing. I could feel his rippling muscles as he held my hips and gyrated on my coochie. The more he swayed his hips, the hotter I got.

I turned around and started backing my ass into his crotch. I felt his manhood trying to bust loose out of his slacks. He grabbed me around the waist and pulled me even closer. We danced nonstop for quite a while before taking a seat.

As I headed to the lady's room to pee, I ran into the club groupies who earlier had tried to give Charles the eyes making another attempt. I made sure they saw the look on my face as I gave them the evil eye. It was my way of telling them that he was off-limits. I was tipsy and so was Charles after partying all night long.

"Why don't you come and spend the rest of the night at my place?" he suggested.

"Okay!" I barely whispered knowing what he had in mind.

My mind ran across Robert, but I felt as if Charles and I belonged together. Maybe it was the crush I had on him. But whatever it was I didn't want it to go away so soon or to end abruptly.

We took a cab to his apartment in the Chelsea section of Manhattan. His place was genuinely nice. He kept it quite clean. Somewhat like Felix Unger from the television series *The Odd Couple*. It didn't take long for him to make his move. He slowly began kissing me, sticking his tongue deep inside my mouth. I could feel it moving around as if he wanted to polish my gums. I was sucking his tongue while he played with my breasts. Oh God, it felt good. I had to stop for a minute. I excused myself and headed to the bathroom. I returned in my bra and panty. He had that look in his eyes; one of lust as he stared at me.

He walked over to me and told me to lie on the couch. He began eating my pussy with my panties on. It drove me wild, but I wanted to feel his whole tongue inside me. I took my panties off and he stuck his tongue deep inside me. He was right; his tongue was long. He worked his magic. It felt as if his dick was inside me. Within minutes, I came all over his face. I held his head as he kissed all over my coochie. He pulled his head from my honey nest and began removing his clothes. My eyes were glued to his boxers as he removed them. And that's when I saw the dick that my girls were going crazy over. It was fat and long and I was going to make sure I felt it. I wanted to taste it. So, I began sucking it.

His eyes were almost closed as he moaned, "Ohhh, Dana! Dana! Yeah, just like that!"

"Look at me," I said, as I deep-throated his dick.

"Oh, God!" he wailed.

"Look me in the mutha-fucking eyes, Charles!" I repeated taking more and more of his magic stick in my mouth. He couldn't look into my eyes.

"Please don't say another word," he begged.

Charles was caught and bagged. He was whipped. We were out of control and in a frantic state. He turned me around facing the wall and entered my wet love tunnel.

"Oh, shit!" I moaned.

I felt his dick opening my love canal. His manhood was inching further and further inside me. It felt as if there was no end to it. He began to pump in and out nice and slow. I stuck my ass out and gyrated my hips. We caught our rhythm and began working our hips as one. It felt so good! He had me lie on my back. He put my feet on his shoulders and began banging me. I could see his magic stick going in and out. He fucked me like that for forty-five minutes nonstop. He was the man and there was no shame in his game. We were sweating profusely. He told me to get on my stomach. I couldn't take it anymore. I was getting intoxicated on his dick. I felt it growing, expanding, and touching places that had me delirious.

I tried to pull away, but he pulled me back on it and continued hitting it. I felt my body shake and my inside building up. My muscles tightened. I was about to cum. I stayed on his dick and began working my pussy. He lost control of his body. He kept jerking and twitching. I picked up the pace. My thrusts were meeting his at a frantic pace. Our bodies contorted and jerked as we screamed and exploded together. We lay there tired and out of breath.

After a night of sweet lovemaking, he began talking about his childhood. "I grew up in a single-parent household and growing up I used to see and hear a lot of people who believed that children reared in a single-parent household can't make it."

I was listening intently to the things he was saying, and it made a lot of sense. It seemed he went through a lot growing up. Not having his father in his life bothered him.

"My mother had to raise me and my younger sister."

"Are you from a large family?"

"No, it's just me and my sister."

"What's her name?"

"Paula," he said as he continued talking.

My father divorced her when I was eight years old. He continued visiting us for the next two years until, one day, he just stopped visiting. I can recall my mom arguing with my father about our financial needs. However, being the rational and concerned father that he was, he vanished from our lives," he said sarcastically. "I never laid eyes on the bastard again until I was much older and in graduate school. My father was not a rich man, but he was comfortable. He owned his own business. My sister and I were born and raised in the suburbs of Riverdale, New York. When my father decided to leave my mother, we had to move to the projects. My dad always had an excuse. I guess he had to support his other family because he never spent any of his money on us. He never gave us shit! My mother worked her ass off." He said this as if he wanted me to agree with him. "She could have accepted the city's handout, but she chose not to. She had a lot of pride."

"What was her reason for not getting on the city welfare payroll?"

"According to her, our situation was not great, but it wasn't that terrible either. Not being on public assistance allowed someone else who truly needed it to receive the help they needed. Those were her words and she stood by them."

"Wow!" I said as he handed me a cup of coffee.

"I know that I'm boring you with my life story."

"No, not at all! I wanna hear more."

"Anyway, that's the type of woman my mother is, reasonable, caring and a realist and I'm quite sure I've acquired some of those traits. Sure, life had its ups and downs when I was growing up. A lot of my friends were poor, and I mean poor, you know what I'm saying?"

"Yeah," was all I could say.

"As my sister and I got older, our mom instilled in us certain qualities which consisted of hard work, education, respect, love, honesty, dedication, desire, and determination. My mom's favorite quote was and still is 'if you're not doing it, someone else is, which is somewhat self-explanatory. That quote became a part of me and was the premise for my outlook and journey in life. That is why I work so hard at what I do. I can remember when I first told my mother that I wanted to become a college professor; she was thrilled like any mother would be. Yet, whenever our family members visited, she would tell them, 'Here's the next CEO of some major company and if that doesn't work out, you're looking at the next Johnny Cochran.' It was a toss-up between Business, Law, and Graduate School. My mom wanted me to attend Law School. But I always knew that teaching was in my blood. I was sure that I wanted to teach on the college level."

"Thank, God!" I said under my breath.

"What did you say?" he asked with a puzzled look on his face.

"Oh, I said I needed a bite."

I was glad that he didn't hear me. I didn't know how he would have reacted, and I didn't want him to think I was obsessed with him. He was being low-key as we entered his kitchen. I wanted to know everything about him, so I urged him on.

"Oh, please continue." I smiled.

"I mean business is good and so is the law. But that wasn't me, and I didn't see myself lying for some punk who may have committed a vicious crime."

It's funny how Charles felt about criminal lawyers and the job they do compare to Jason, who makes thousands defending the bad guys, I thought to myself.

"As funny as this may sound, I don't want to become some old whiner in my later years, babbling about how I should have listened to my mother and become a CEO or an Attorney-at-Law."

We both fell out laughing.

I was really in tune with everything he said. The chemistry between us that night made me realize that he was my soul mate, or pretty close to it. I knew I had some serious soul-searching to do, and I wanted to see where our friendship would take us.

Episode 7

Robert invited me to one of his partner's high-powered parties in the Cambria Heights section of Queens, New York. I was sitting on one of the leather couches that filled the spacious living room, chitchatting with several of the girls whom I was familiar with, including Tara James. Tara and I first met at the Robinsons. We immediately liked each other and became good friends. Tara was dating Marques, a fine-looking redbone brother, who thought he was God's gift to women.

We were all chilling, listening to R. Kelly's *I Decided* when we heard a crashing boom coming from the front door.

The door flew off its hinges as a sea of men in light blue jackets stormed into the living room, yelling, "Police, don't fucking move! Get on the floor! Keep your hands where we can see them!"

Several guns were shoved in my face as they ran toward the back of the house. I was crying hysterically. Tara looked upset but she wasn't crying. I was surprised, confused, angry, and scared. I didn't know what the hell was going on. Just the thought of going to jail frightened me. I thought about Jenny. She always had an answer for everything.

Robert is my man. He's a stockbroker making mad money on Wall Street with lots of connections. So why the fuck is the po-po rolling up in a private residence where everyone is supposedly law-abiding and professional except for a few, who were getting their sniffs on? I asked myself.

I was handcuffed and taken to the precinct with the others. Nothing like this had ever happened to me when I worked the streets for Kenny. I was lucky enough never to get arrested. I was placed in a holding cell along with Tara, Gwen, Tiffany, Babs, and some other girls we didn't know. We were then put on a bus with a group of prostitutes which freaked me out because of my past. The others were drug-addicted, alcoholic-looking women. The silence was unbelievable.

The bus came to a stop in the underground tunnel at Central Booking. We were fingerprinted and had our pictures taken. Despite our situation, we were all dressed in the latest designer clothing. We were high class compared to the other women. But we all had one thing in common our asses were locked up.

Several thuggish-looking hard-core women were staring at us. They looked angry, but I wasn't about to act like a punk. If a fight was going to break out, or for that matter anything else, it was going to be on my terms, fuck that! I was ready to defend myself. We spent the night waiting to see a judge. When we finally saw him, he had a stoic look on his face as he warily observed us.

"This judge doesn't bullshit around," Gwen whispered.

What the fuck did I do to deserve this shit? I was so afraid, that I thought I shitted on myself.

"None of us did anything to deserve this shit," she replied, with a worried look on her face.

The district attorney was young and black. He had a reserve disposition about him. However, looks can be quite deceiving as I soon learned. He began ranting and raving about the house being a known drug location, which over the years had harbored numerous drug dealers.

"Oh, my God!" I murmured, almost fainting.

"Your Honor, the men, and women standing here are all members of the Playaz Club, a violent drug organization," the district attorney stated.

"The Playaz what?" I blurted out, as our court-appointed lawyer calmed me down.

It just so happened that the Playaz Club lawyers who were to represent us were out of town.

The judge agreed with the district attorney. He set our bail at ten thousand dollars apiece. I was pissed! We were taken to a holding cell to await the bus for the ride to the Women's House on Rikers Island.

But as faith would have it, minutes before the bus arrived a correction officer yelled out, "Estick, James, Johnson, Smith, and Davis form a lineup front! You have all made bail." I was overjoyed. Tara and I smiled and hugged each other.

Relieved, I couldn't hide my excitement as I stood in front of the courthouse and took a deep breath. Tara and I were crossing the street when we noticed Jason sitting in his black 350 Mercedes Benz.

"Get in!" he said, sounding agitated.

We got in the Benz, and I immediately lost my mind. "What the fuck is going on? And where the fuck is Robert?" I asked, yelling.

"Ladies, Robert, Marques, and the others are chilling out right now. You will see them later tonight or tomorrow," he said, as Tara with a frown on her face just shook her head.

"Fuck that, I wanna see Robert now! I wanna know what the fuck is up with all this drug shit! Do you know I almost ended up in jail for shit I knew nothing about? Jason ain't you the one who said you didn't like drug dealers because they were killing the community?"

"I said nickel and dime drug dealers. If you're gonna quote me, quote me right."

"Whatever. I thought Robert was a stockbroker and you a lawyer?"

"We are, but it's a long story. You'll know everything in a few minutes. Tara, did you say anything to her?"

"No," she replied.

"About what?" I asked, but Jason repeated he would explain everything.

As we rode to Tara's apartment, she and I exchanged numbers. After dropping her off, I told Jason to take me home. I was about to give him directions when he started driving as if he knew exactly where he was going.

I never told him where I lived, so how in the world would he know where to go? I asked myself.

As he drove, he coolly stared at me and said, "From now on I'm your official bodyguard." He claimed that it came straight from Robert's mouth. But it was nothing but a bunch of bullshit.

"Oh, please! You must be out of your mind," I said in a condescending voice. "Nigga, I thought you said I would see Robert later? How long is later?"

"What's up with the nigga bullshit? There's no need for that."

"Okay, I'm sorry. I shouldn't have said that but why did you lie?"

"I'll explain everything to you once you get yourself together. Don't worry about it. You'll know exactly what's going on."

I was somewhat apprehensive about having Jason in my apartment. But I figured he was the only one who could tell me what the hell was going on, and what I had gotten myself into. I checked my messages and there were several calls from Jenny, my co-workers, and Charles. I should have returned Charles's call, but decided I would do so once Jason leaves. Jason sat down and turned the television on. I couldn't believe my eyes. The Cambria Heights raid was on the early morning news. I was hoping and praying they wouldn't show me in handcuffs, and I was relieved when they didn't. However, the news crew shed some light on what had taken place. The bust had been an ongoing sting operation. The house had been wired with surveillance cameras and pieces of audio equipment for several months. The drug operation had made millions over the past three years.

The alleged bosses of the operation are said to be several professional people. Unconfirmed reports state the operation is being financed by several high-ranking contacts in South America, said Sandy Lang of Channel Seven eyewitness news.

"Say something!" I snapped at Jason.

"Damn it! Give me a second here, go get yourself together. I'll tell you what's going on."

"Okay!" I yelled, heading to the bathroom. I had to get rid of the jail stench and my clothes.

"Will you please get rid of these clothes for me?" I asked, getting in the shower.

"How am I supposed to do that?" he shot back, entering the bathroom.

"I don't care. Put them in the fucking incinerator in the hallway!"

I could see his horny ass trying to size me up through the shower curtain. Eventually, he picked up my discarded clothes and walked out of the bathroom.

I was feeling fresh and renewed after the shower. I smeared lotion on my body and put my robe on. As I entered the living room the smell of bacon and eggs filled my nostrils. He had gotten comfortable. He had removed his jacket, shirt, and shoes. I was furious and was about to read him his rights and remind him that he was in my apartment. But I changed my mind. I was hungry and the food smelled great.

This nigga is a trip, I laughed to myself.

"Here, this is for you," he said, handing me a plate.

"Now what's the 411?" I demanded as I began tearing up the bacon and eggs.

"Hmm, Robert is not who you think he is."

"Okay."

"He's married and…"

"Married?" I almost choked on the bacon. "What, he's married? Oh, hell no! What about his daughter? Is she his only child?"

"He's married and he has three kids, a boy, and two girls. They live with him and his wife in Westchester County."

"So, what about the apartment and the pictures of the little girl? That's his daughter, right?"

"You're not listening to me. I said that he has two little girls. Chriss is the younger of the two. The apartment you're talking about that's his ho apartment. That's where he keeps his mistresses." I was speechless.

He knew the things he was saying were hurtful. Yet it seemed he wanted to hurt me even more.

"You're not the first. He has met numerous girls like you on the internet over the years. You're one of the lucky ones because most of the girls become his drug mules. You do know what a drug mule is, don't you?"

"You fucking right I know what a drug mule is. Fuck! I can't believe this shit!" I muttered.

"As I said, you're one of the lucky ones."

"Whoa, slow down. What do you mean by lucky?"

"Let me see how I can put this. He never used you as a willing and upfront drug mule. He kept you in the dark about all the shit that was going on. Nevertheless, you did accompany him on several runs and you also did a few yourself, didn't you?" he asked, with a sly look on his face. I almost fell out of the chair.

"Shit! For real? When was this?" I asked, eager for his response.

"I'll start with the most recent. Remember the house you visited on Long Island where you met Jimmy? Didn't Robert tell you he had to go and pick his car up?" I couldn't say a damn thing. "Then there was the house in Pelham Park, and I believe you drove that car? Let me put it this way, whenever you two were together and you switched cars or drove his, you were transporting a lot of drugs, Cartel style. Let me digress for a second. Didn't you ask me if Robert was a stockbroker earlier? Oh well, he is. All the people you've met are professionals. The thing is they are also involved in the drug trade."

"What about you?" I stuttered.

"Who me? I'm a Playa and I'm also Robert's lawyer. Didn't he tell you? I thought he was your man?"

I didn't answer him. I was so confused and scared. I didn't know what to say or do. But I wanted to know why he was telling me so much.

"Why are you telling me all these things?"

"We will pretty much know where your loyalties lie in a few weeks, don't worry about it."

"The Playa's Club does exist?"

"What the fuck is wrong with you? Didn't I just tell you I'm a member? Yeah, it does, and you're a part of it."

My legs were shaking, and my palms were sweaty. My breathing intake was short and quick. I wanted to run but I couldn't.

"Although you're not a major player in the organization as of yet," he went on, "we'll continue to work on you. By the way, I prefer to use the term organization instead of crew, gang, or posse. Those terms are used too loosely. To me, they signify 'Dah hood' wannabe low-budget niggas who are unorganized and don't know what the fuck they're doing. We're a highly organized and very profitable organization. We have connections within every realm of society that you can imagine. You are a member; you do know that? Oh, I almost forgot, Robert never told you? Hmm, let me fill you in. It's like you gave your consent but you didn't. So, he did it for you, and that makes you a member," he stated empathically.

I was shocked. I had to pee, and I couldn't hold it any longer. To my dismay, he followed me to the bathroom and stood there as if he wanted to watch me. I closed the door and he stared at me with an unpleasant look on his face. After taking care of my business, I walked to the living room and sat down on the couch. He began talking.

"You and the others were bailed out by the organization on the orders of your lover. By the way, some of the other girls know about the organization. For those who don't know they're not being updated as you are. So, you should be glad to know that we consider you very special. Hey, how is your friend, Jenny? I guess she must be living it up with her trust fund, huh?"

I was dumbfounded. How did he know about her? "She's fine," I stuttered.

"Well, let's keep it that way. Don't forget you're a long way from South Carolina." I was scared as shit. I was sitting there biting my fingernails. "I cannot emphasize it enough, because normally a person in your situation wouldn't be sitting here right now. Chances are you would be lying somewhere in Greenpoint or Woodlawn cemetery taking a nap, you feel me? Game is money and money is game. This is bigger than you always remember that."

"Yes."

"So, are we clear now?" he asked with a scowl on his face.

"Yes."

"Do you know that in this organization we share and can have whatever is appealing to the eyes?"

"Yes."

"Is there anything around here that might be appealing to me?"

"Yes."

"What is that?"

"Me," I said, catching a flashback to my father.

"You know what I want, don't you?"

I nodded my head and said, "Yes."

"Take off your robe!" he commanded. He quickly got naked and told me to give him oral sex. I did this for several minutes before he stopped me and said, "Do you remember that night in the hallway at the pool party?"

"What about it?"

"Robert told me that I could have you. Didn't you notice he wasn't concerned about you?" I was sitting there stunned. "He knew about us. Welcome to the Playaz Club, where the motto is share and share alike."

"Please," I begged, "can you wear a condom? I don't want to get pregnant."

He put the condom on and straddled my almost lifeless body. He was ranting and raving about how sweet my goodies were and how he had wanted to sleep with me from the first time he laid eyes on me.

"Dana, it doesn't have to be this way," he moaned.

I was emotionless. It felt as if I was dead. I felt like taking my own life. He wanted me to respond to him physically, but I couldn't. It felt as if I was being raped and tortured all over again. The whole episode reminded me of what my father did to me. He was sweating profusely, and I realized that he intended to make it a long process. Knowing this, I began gyrating my hips and no sooner than I started he came. I was so glad.

He then got up and took a shower. I thought about calling the police but quickly changed my mind. I knew I would have to deal with Robert and the others. After taking his shower, he deliberately took his time getting dressed. He then reminded me that the organization was family and that it was first and foremost.

"Nothing else matters," he snarled. "Oh, say hi to Jenny for me." He tried to kiss me, but I resisted. I thought he would get angry, instead, he smiled and closed the door behind him.

I wanted to wash away the filth and that's exactly what I did. I was a total wreck and as I lay in bed curled up under my covers, I unplugged my home phone and turned off my cell. I felt as if my desire and drive to live were at their lowest. I turned on my CD player and listened to my favorite song. I fought back the tears for as long as I could before falling asleep.

Episode 8

I felt better the next day and although I was still upset, I knew I had to get on with my life despite the arrest, Jason raping me, and all the lies that Robert told me. I was in no mood to go to work. I called Jenny and told her I was taking the day off.

"What are you doing later?"

"Nothing at the moment," she said.

"Wanna hang out?"

"Sure, I'll meet you at Junior's in an hour."

"Cool."

I was about to leave my apartment when my cell phone rang. I instinctively thought it was Robert, but as I took a closer look, I realized it was Charles. I wasn't in the mood to talk. Whatever he had to say was directed to my voicemail. I felt bad but there were issues I had to resolve before I could even think about being with him.

***

"Girl, you look fucked up! What happened to you?" Jenny asked, before entering Junior's Restaurant.

"It's a long story."

"Having trouble with Robert, huh?"

"Yeah, something like that."

"Well, Jenny is here for you. Tell me what's going on. I'm listening," she said, glancing at the menu. I had to say something, but what? Jenny wasn't the type to be easily fooled. However, I wasn't about to disclose everything.

"Do you know that Robert is married with kids and lives in Westchester?"

"Goddamn girl, when did you find that out? Did he tell you?" she said, with a surprised look on her face.

"No, it was Jason. You remember his lawyer friend I told you about?"

"Yeah, but ain't that his boy? I bet that negro was looking some ass."

"He was, but I wasn't having it," I remarked, lying my ass off.

I wanted to tell her a lot more, but I just couldn't do it at that particular time. I knew if I did, she would be looking over her shoulders constantly. And knowing the type of person she was I didn't want her to get her Glock and go after Jason or Robert. I didn't want her to get hurt.

For what it was worth she remained cool before asking, "Have you seen or heard from Robert?"

"No, I haven't. I tried calling his cell and his apartment but this mutha-fucka won't answer."

"Damn, I told you how some of these grimy-ass brothas are. Here's a typical example of a brotha living foul. I told you to leave those bullshit-ass negroes alone. But no, you wanna see what's up with them. Girl, the only thing that's up with them is their dicks. Trust me; all they want is some pussy. And once they get it, they keep you in the background or on the down-low. The same shit they do to you is the same thing they do to their wifey. The rings on their fingers don't mean a damn thing!"

"I wanna hear what he has to say, then I'm gonna move on."

There I was lying again; knowing damn well that it wasn't going to be easy getting away from the world I was now a part of. I was ready to confront Robert despite the risk and pain. Nevertheless, I wasn't going to let him embarrass and take advantage of me and get away with it.

"I need some time to myself," I told her.

"I understand take all the time you need. But like I said those trifling negroes need to check themselves. Don't let that shit get you down though. Remember that you still have school to complete and don't forget about your job. You can't afford to lose your head because of this mutha-fucka and his bullshit."

I nodded in agreement and hugged her and told her that I love her.

Jenny and I talked about our families, jobs, and some issues that were taking place in our lives before she began talking about her relationship with her two lovers. I certainly needed a laugh after all the drama I had been through and she didn't let me down. She then dropped a bomb on me.

"Girl, I had both of them in bed at the same time," she laughed.

"For real?"

How often does a person have both their lovers in the same bed? I bet it doesn't happen very often. Yet she pulled it off.

"I'm serious."

"How did you pull it off?"

"Who can resist all of this?" she asked as she stood up and spun around with everybody looking at her. "Look at this body. Look how gorgeous it is they couldn't help themselves. They both wanted this shit and I'm in charge. Like the Jamaicans say, 'me run tings, tings no run me'. And that's just how it is!"

We were laughing our asses off as the other patrons looked on.

"You're good."

"Matter of fact we're gonna hook up next weekend. Do you wanna hang?"

"A foursome?" I laughed.

"Yeah, or a threesome it's up to you."

"I'll let you know."

"Oh, before I forget what's up with the professor? The last time we spoke you said you wanted him to hit it. Did he?"

"You won't believe this shit."

"Try me."

"Energy and the professor are the same."

"Fuck outta here! The same person? Are u serious?"

"Yes, they are."

"I want details." I filled her in on all the details. "And you say I'm bad? Shit, you right there with me." We both laughed and headed out the door.

***

I kept avoiding Charles at every opportunity. On a few occasions, I saw him leaving the Student Union with his head held low. I guess he was hoping to see me. I ignored his telephone calls. He was a nice guy, and I didn't feel right treating him like I did. He was a good man who needed a good woman and I wasn't her.

I was angry and frustrated because I still hadn't heard from Robert. Jason would visit whenever he was horny, and I was constantly reminded to keep my mouth shut or else. The Playaz Club took over the responsibility of paying my rent and I was now driving a Lexus SUV. I knew Robert was behind it all.

When I finally heard from Robert, he claimed he'd been in the Bahamas ever since the raid in Queens. I wanted to know why he treated me like he did and why he hadn't returned my calls.

"What the fuck is up with you, Robert? Why did you play me?"

"What the fuck are you talking about? Do you mean all that shit with Jason? Don't worry; I'll talk to you about that once I get back in town. You know that you're my favorite girl, right? I'll see you soon. Love you."

"Fuck you, Robert!" I snapped.

"I'll do that too when I get back in town," he said, before hanging up.

I could not believe what I had just heard. He acted as if nothing happened. Then had the nerve to say that he loved me and that I was his favorite girl. When he had a wife and kids and told his best friend that it was okay to force himself on me.

Episode 9

$\mathcal{I}$ was home when Tara called and told me that we had to get to La Guardia Airport as soon as possible. Someone from the Playaz Club wanted us to pick up a black Cadillac.

"Whose idea is this?" I asked her.

"It came from Jimmy and guess who was with him?"

"Robert?"

"Yeah."

"You saw him?"

"No, we spoke."

"What did he say?"

"Nothing much, he just said that he was glad to be back in town."

"That mutha-fucka!" I snapped. "Anyway, let me get myself together. I'll see you in a minute. Meet me in front of my place."

We picked up the Cadillac like Jimmy ordered and called to let him know that we were on our way. As we drove back to the city, Tara and I began talking about the circumstances which led us down this path. We wanted to know how we allowed ourselves to get caught up in all this drama. She said our lives were similar and more alike than we could ever imagine because we both experienced a lot of hurt and pain. She had a serious look on her face as she quietly began talking.

"Things were cool between me and Marques. He was fucking me at first until one night we went out to Long Island. The next thing I knew Jimmy was pushing up on me. I told Marques thinking he would do something about it. Instead of getting upset this bitch ass nigga was down with the shit. Then the threats came when I refused to fuck Jimmy or anyone else for that matter. I held my ground and here I am. This is my job, Dana. I'm only in this for the money and for me to get it; I have to link up with the big dawgs."

I got the impression that Tara didn't mind her present situation because of the money she was making. She never gave anything a second thought after she met Marques. She did have a high school diploma. As crazy as that sounds at least she had something to fall back on.

Tara was twenty-three years old. She stood five-nine with long brown hair and a chocolate brown complexion. She was slight in stature and very pretty. She certainly had it going on. As I continued driving, she reclined her seat and began opening up about her life.

"I grew up in Chicago with an older sister and brother. Things were kind of fucked up for me and my family; you know what I'm saying? But maybe I had a lot to do with it. My mom and I used to get into it a lot. I was a badass. She always had some smart-ass shit to say. I remember one night I didn't come home and the next day she broke on me. Before I could respond she saw the bruises and scratches on my arms and legs. She went off saying, 'Which one of your sorry-ass lovers did this to you?' I was like come on Ma, you know I only have one boyfriend and that's Kaseem."

"So, what happened next?"

"She flipped. She said, 'Bitch, then you need to leave him alone. How in the world did you let him do this shit to you? I didn't give birth to you so that mutha-fucka could beat your ass. Where is your self-esteem?' I didn't know what the fuck to say to her," Tara explained in a calm tone as she lit up a Newport cigarette.

"You and those damn cigarettes," I said to her. They were making me nauseous. I opened the windows.

"I'm sorry but I needed one," she explained before continuing. "Whenever I tried to explain myself, she would cut me off and start cussing at me. My mom was bugged. 'What the hell is wrong with you?' she would ask. 'Shut up and listen. First of all, you're a weed head and you're fucking with that no-good Kaseem who got you selling your pussy. What the fuck did your father and I do to deserve this? What did we do wrong? Your older brother is a damn crackhead and a liar. Your older sister well, she turned out all right. But she thinks your father and I are unfit parents. That bitch doesn't stay in contact with us. Yet she has the most shit to say. I'm tired of all this bullshit. I want you and your brother out of my damn house.' Yo, Dana, I couldn't believe my mom was giving me the boot. She wanted me out and she was dead serious."

"Yeah, that's some messed up shit. But what did you do?" I asked, honking the slow-moving car in front of me.

"I was like Ma, why are you tripping? Why do you always gotta come out your face like that? You always gotta put me in shit with everybody else. I'm gonna get myself together. If only you would just get off my damn back. I'm tired of your shit too."

"You said that to your mom? Girl, you a snap," I remarked, as we laughed.

"I don't know what got into me, but my mom wasn't having it. She got all up in my face and said 'What? You little bitch this is my house. If you can't live by my rules, then get the fuck out.' I wasn't surprised at all. She had said this many times before but this time she looked like she meant it."

"What did you do?" I asked eagerly.

"I packed my gear and bounced to my sister's crib for a minute. But she was getting on my nerves, complaining about everything I did. So, I did the dip and went to Kassem's."

"How old were you?"

She looked at me as if she felt ashamed and said, "Fourteen."

"Oh, God!" I shrieked, as she bit her bottom lip and nodded her head trying to prevent the tears from flowing.

Hmm, I thought to myself, *she told me she lost her virginity at the age of twelve to Kaseem, who was twenty-five at the time. What in the world was a twenty-five-year-old man doing having sex with a twelve-year-old? He was a damn pervert. He was no different from my father.* However, I was shocked when she said that she was the one who wanted to sleep with him.

At the age of fourteen, she was selling her body for Kaseem on the streets of Chicago. She claimed he treated her well but at times would beat her. Being one of the youngest workers quite a few attempts were made by some of Kaseem's rivals who wanted her for themselves. And it eventually happened. I asked her how she got to New York City.

"Tyson, he brought me here."

"Who's Tyson?"

"Kaseem's friend, he was really cute and also a pimp. He was coming to New York and asked me if I wanted to come with him. I said yeah and here I am. When I first got here, I worked for a while in Hunts Point in the Bronx. I was young so Tyson had a friend of his hook me and a few other girls up with fake IDs. I worked in several bars. But after a while, the bar thing blew up in his face and he put me on the streets. Some of the girls were underage, but we were all making money. Then I started working in Queensbridge, Queens. But then I got tired of him and all that shit and got myself into a GED program and got my diploma. That's how I met Marques. I met him in front of the Long Island University campus in downtown Brooklyn."

"Oh, you were thinking about going to college?"

"Yeah, I'm still gonna go once I get outta this bullshit."

"How long have you been with Marques?"

"For like three years."

"Girl, we have to talk some more," I said, pulling into the underground garage at Thirty-Sixth Street and Third Avenue, where Jason and his favorite gal pal, Stacy, Jamal, and Larry waited.

Tara and I were given two yellow envelopes filled with cash and told to go home. Despite Stacy's presence, Jason couldn't keep his eyes off me. He knew my stuff was the bomb. He was desperate and always made it his business to let me know. Don't get me wrong, I wasn't trying to excuse Jason for what he did or give validity to it because it was wrong. He was less than a man as far as I was concerned. It's just that Stacy thought she was so hot, and I wanted her to know that I had it going on as well. She knew he had a thing for me and that he was also obsessed with Tara. The brother was strung out.

I was about to leave, and Tara told me she would give me a call. We got in separate cabs. I was exhausted when I got home. I took off my clothes, ran some bathwater, and had a glass of Hennessy. I didn't bother checking my phone messages or email.

I was lying on the couch naked after taking a bath, and it wasn't long before the Hennessy quietly worked its way into my system. I began thinking about Charles and slowly began to massage my coochie. I couldn't help myself. I opened my legs and inserted my fingers deep inside me. I was about to cum for the fourth time when I was suddenly interrupted by the ringing of my doorbell.

"Who is it?" I screamed, putting my robe on.

"It's me."

"Me who?" I asked, looking through the peephole.

It was Robert; he had a huge grin on his face. *It's about time this mutha-fucka showed*, I said to myself. I was thrilled to see him. However, I promised myself that I wouldn't show it. I still needed to hear his side of the story. I opened the door and there was my neighbor, Ms. O'Neal with her nosey ass self-looking to see who was entering my apartment.

"Hey, baby! How you doing?" he said, walking in.

"I'm fine." He reached out to hug me, which I wanted no part of. "How could you do this to me?"

"To be honest, I have nothing else to say. Jason already explained everything to you. So, what else is there to say, huh?"

"So, all that shit you told me about how you would explain everything once you got back in town was nothing but a bunch of bullshit, wasn't it? I trusted you, dammit! You didn't have to play me like that. But you know what?"

"What?" he asked, with a scowl on his face.

"I guess this is what I get for fucking with a nigga from a chat room."

"Come on now, the only thing that matters right now is that you're a member of the Playaz Club although you didn't do so on your own. And you're being taken care of, aren't you?"

"You must be out of your fucking mind. Fuck you, bitch!"

"I told you before that I'll fuck you soon." He smiled.

"You think I'm playing? You and your friends have put Jenny on y'all radar. I've been threatened, unknowingly used as a drug mule, raped by your lawyer and you have the nerve to say that I'm still around. What the fuck am I supposed to do now?"

"Don't flip on me. Nothing you've done so far is new to you. It's not like you're a virgin or anything like that. Look where I met you, in a fucking chat room. Come on now, you've been fucking and sucking your whole life. Given all the shit you've done do you sound like an innocent self-respecting person? Hell, no! Do you know what it sounds like? It sounds like you're a fucking slut, that's right, a fucking whore. Everything I've done for you has been a blessing. Nobody and I mean nobody, would do the things I've done for you. In other words, I saved your fucking life."

"You saved my life? What did you do for me?" I snapped.

"As I said, I saved your fucking life. I'm your goddamn guardian angel, your knight in shining armor. Kenny never treated you this good. He never respected you. He used to beat your ass and had you hooked on drugs. Don't look at me as if you're surprised. I know everything about you, bitch! Instead of beating your ass and taking your money, I did the total opposite. I gave you money, a lot more than you would ever make selling your pussy. Look at this fucking apartment, who gave you the money to buy all this shit, Macy's? Who pays the fucking rent? And you want to know what have I done for you? Bitch, you better recognize! Don't you know they wanted to play you out? But this fucking no good low life who doesn't give a fuck about you stockbroker saved your fucking life."

"I don't give a fuck what you say. Fuck you, Robert! Fuck them too! You're no different from Kenny and you both are a bunch of bitches and sorry asses. And you tell me you don't have a family, you're a fucking liar and stupid me believed you."

"As for my family, that's it they're just my family. Weren't you okay with our situation before you found out about them? Shit, I was spending more time with you than my fucking wife. Anyway, the marriage is over we're only going through the motions. But what the fuck am I telling you all this shit for? The best thing for you to do is to not stress that shit. In this organization we share…"

"So, they fucked your wife and had her sucking dicks too?" I yelled, cutting him off.

The scowl on his face returned as he shook his head from side to side and said, "You know what, I'm gonna act as if I didn't hear what you just said."

"Whatever," I countered.

"You need to shut the fuck up and listen. I was saying in this organization we share. What happened between you and Jason is nothing new. Shit like this happens all the time amongst us."

I knew I was in some really deep undercover shit. My life was in jeopardy and I didn't know how I was going to get out of this situation.

"What about the bust, Robert?"

"What about it?"

"You don't know?"

"No, tell me."

"I have to go back to court to face charges of being in a known drug house and being a member of the Playaz Club. I didn't even know I was involved with drug dealers much less being in a drug house and hanging with a crew. Fuck!"

"You don't have to worry about that court stuff. It will take care of itself."

"Oh, that's easy for you to say. Remember you got away."

"Will you listen, damn? None of the charges will stick. And like I said you're here now and you're a part of this whole thing so the best thing for you to do is to enjoy it while it lasts."

Chills overcame my body as I sat there listening to him. I realized that I couldn't walk away from my lifestyle so easily without others getting hurt maybe even killed and that included me. Robert disrespected me and he was aware of it.

Nevertheless, he felt I was convinced that I would go along with the program, and he was right. I dug deep within myself and decided I would see this through. Being the "bitch", I was and as he put it, I was going to be his "bitch". He pulled me close to him and this time I didn't resist. He was still fine and despite all the drama I was still attracted to him.

***

"Docket Number 0954896, the state of New York versus Gwendolyn Johnson, Dana Estick, Tara James, Tiffany Smith, and Barbara Davis!" a slim bleach-blond female court officer called out.

As we approached the judge, a robust gray-haired gentleman with his glasses fixed just below the bridge of his nose and wandering eyes I was scared. Tara seemed to be the strongest in the group. She looked straight ahead her head held high.

Her confidence was sky-high as she said to me, "Chill, it's gonna be a'ight."

The district attorney and our lawyers approached the judge. The men began talking. The courtroom was quiet. And although Tara had told me everything was going to be fine, I was extremely nervous. After their verbal exchange, our lawyers walked over and stood next to us.

The expression on their faces convinced me that everything would be fine. Only then did I manage a faint smile. Tara winked at me.

"Your Honor, we have decided to drop all charges," exclaimed the district attorney.

"Are you sure Mr. Folk?" the judge asked.

"Yes, Your Honor."

"Do you have anything to say, gentlemen?"

"No, Your Honor," replied our lawyers.

"Case dismissed," the judge said, as we hugged each other and left the courtroom smiling. I guess Robert was right, he did say that everything would turn out well and it did.

As we entered the courthouse hallway there stood Robert, Jason, Marques, and several of their associates. We greeted each other as if we were lifelong friends. I then noticed Tara glaring at Robert, Jason, and Marques with a nasty look.

We were leaving the courthouse when Tara asked, "Girl, what's up with you? You plan on doing anything?"

"Since everything went well today, and the bullshit is over with. I think I'm gonna head to class and then to work."

"Okay, call me when you get home tonight."

"Sure."

***

I had deliberately stayed away from Charles. But as fate would have it, I ran into him in the Sociology Department. I could tell he was glad to see me and I felt the same way. But I expected the worst despite his gentle demeanor.

"How are you?" he asked softly without a hint of anger in his voice.

"I'm fine. How are you?"

"I'm doing quite well. Can I have a word with you?"

"Sure." We walked to the McDonald's on Broadway and Sixth Street.

"Why are you treating me like this? I called you on several occasions and not once did you return any of my calls. What's going on? After that night together I thought we had something special. You said it yourself and then all of a sudden, you're giving me the cold shoulder. Something is wrong, and I want to know what it is."

"Well, if you must know I've been going through some shit with my father. Didn't I tell you about him?"

"Yeah, you did."

"He was here in the city stalking me and I had to stay away from my apartment."

"But what about your cell phone nothing was wrong with that, right?"

"I was staying with one of my girlfriends and I didn't want to be bothered. Don't take it the wrong way I just wanted to be alone and I didn't want to burden you with my problem that's all. I'm sorry I didn't return your calls, but I was stressed out. Try and understand will you please?"

"I understand but you should stay in contact and let me know how things are going. Do you have a problem with that?"

"No, I don't have a problem with it. I'll stay in touch with you," I assured him.

He held my hand and said, "I'm concerned about you."

Episode 10

*L*ike the other girls, Tara and I were making our usual deliveries. Things were going great. Jimmy, Robert, Jason, and several Playaz Club members bought new homes, speed boats; expensive condos and they were partying almost every weekend. They were living extravagantly. I thought only athletes and entertainers lived that type of lifestyle. No doubt I was misinformed because these brothers were living the lifestyle of the rich and famous.

Tara and I were constantly on the go and, on a few occasions, we traveled to Philadelphia and Hartford. However, we did most of our business in the five boroughs of New York City. Tara told me about the trips that a number of the girls made down south and some even traveled as far as Colombia, Venezuela, and Panama.

From what I was told Jimmy was the force and the man behind the organization. He was fifty-one years old. He was an old player with a booming baritone. He grew up in the West Bronx, where he was known as a number runner in his earlier years. Feared for his ruthlessness, the other number runners avoided him at all costs. Not only did he own a majority of the number joints, but he also owned several after-hour spots where dope, cocaine, and marijuana were sold. He catered to a rowdy crowd. He even had a few girls working the streets. Tara said he was enlisted in the army for several years and during that time he made a lot of friends in several Spanish-speaking countries.

"How the fuck you know all this shit?" I asked.

"Girl, I get all my info from Marques. Shit, all I have to do is whip this pussy appeal on his ass and I'll have him telling me his whole life story. That nigga will tell on his mother for this pussy." We fell out laughing.

"Anyway," she continued, "Jimmy got hooked up with some of those Spanish dudes once he got out of the army. He figured he wasn't gonna get rich driving a bus for a living."

"A bus?" I blurted out. "He drove a bus? This is unbelievable! I'm trying to picture that little big-headed mutha-fucka behind that big ass steering wheel."

"You'd be surprised at some of the shit these mutha-fuckas were doing before they became the Playaz Club. Oh, my bad, I mean the Playaz Organization," Tara said, as we mockingly looked at each other and fell out laughing once again.

"Marques said that shit to you too?"

"Yeah, he did but I don't pay that stuff any mind."

"Robert and Jason told me the same thing. But I ain't got no time for that nonsense either. My main goal is to get away from all this bullshit. These mutha-fuckas…" I suddenly paused.

"What?"

"Nah, forget it. It's nothing. Anyway, how did Jimmy meet Robert?"

"Wait, I'll get to that. You have to hear this shit!" She began telling me about Jimmy's wife and the woman he had on the side. "Jimmy supposedly was fucking some girl who was involved with a dude by the name of Big Red. Big Red was also involved in the same down-and-dirty shit as Jimmy. They were living grimy and running the Bronx like gangstas. Back in the day, they were tight until Big Red found out that Jimmy was fucking his girl. Big Red was pissed when he found out and cut all ties with Jimmy who still wanted to do business. But Big Red wasn't having that shit."

"I don't blame him. So, what happened?"

"This mutha-fucka Big Red flipped the script. He went to Jimmy's crib and merked his wife and two kids and left him for dead."

"Get the fuck outta here, word?"

"Yeah, the boys caught that nigga and locked his ass up."

"The boys?"

"The po-po. All the young kids say the boys. Po-po is getting played out."

"You're up on all the latest slang, huh?" I said, laughing.

"It's like everything else. You gotta go with what's happening. But like I was saying, Jimmy turned state on Big Red after the murders. They gave that dumb mutha-fucka three life sentences. Big Red was three years into his bid when he got jumped and stabbed to death by some mutha-fuckas in the rec yard. Marques said Jimmy paid off the correction officers to look the other way. I believe him because Jimmy got it like that. He's got connections."

"Damn, that's some fucked up shit. Jimmy turned state?"

"Yup, big time!"

"I still can't believe it."

"Tell me about it. After Big Red's death, Jimmy took control of the number game in the Bronx and went big time."

"This is some scary shit Robert got me involved in," I remarked. "Aren't you scared, Tara? How do you feel about all this shit?"

"As I told you before, I'm just getting mine, and then I'm gonna get as far away from here as possible, you watch. You should leave with me. Let me ask you something."

"What?"

"Why haven't you left?"

"I can't, not right now. I have to get some things together first."

"Okay, that's cool."

"Oh, you never answered my question."

"What was it?"

"How did Robert get hooked up with Jimmy?"

"He's married to Jimmy's niece. Her name is Jasmine, and they met in college. She's a school teacher. I believe she teaches high school in Westchester."

"Wow!"

"Yeah, they've been married for a while now with kids and all that shit."

"I knew about the wife and kids. Jason made sure of that. But I didn't know she was related to Jimmy."

"It's a family affair, Dana. I'm just here trying to get paid. You feel me?"

"What do you mean it's a family affair?"

"Girl please, Robert and Jason are cousins. You didn't know that?"

"Hell, no! It's a lot of shit I didn't know. That's how they planned on playing me. That's fucked up, but thanks for keeping it real with me, you are mad cool." I was pissed when she told me Robert and Jason were cousins. They did quite a number on my self-esteem.

"Look, whenever they call you to make a run let Jimmy know you wanna make it with me. Jimmy is mad cool like that."

"Okay," I said, as she and I hugged each other and said bye.

I headed to school to take my exams. I knew I was going to pull in an A. I was hoping and praying that I wouldn't cross paths with Charles and luckily, I didn't.

I was exhausted by the time I got to work, but I did my job, despite being fatigued and dealing with a bunch of smart-ass customers. Although it was difficult at times to find parking at New York University, I should have taken the chance and driven to school. Because the train ride home was noisy, exhausting, maddening, and slow.

Once inside my apartment, I ate some leftover lasagna with a glass of Alize. I took a quick shower and hit the bed. I turned on my CD player and lowered the volume as my favorite song put me to sleep.

***

Tara and I had been hanging out quite often and we talked about a lot of things. So, it wasn't a surprise when I asked her to tell me about the Playaz's Club and Marques. She was more than willing to enlighten me.

She said that Marques was a cold-hearted brother from the neighborhood. Thug was written all over him. He was six feet and weighed about one hundred and eighty-five pounds. He was reddish-brown in complexion and was a pretty boy, who kept his close-cropped wavy hair well-groomed. He grew up in the South, Bronx, where the only thing that mattered to him was the streets and the thug life he led.

He was a fixture in his Fox Avenue neighborhood, where he was well-liked, yet feared.

During the late 1980s crack explosion, he was a big-time player in the game. He led a crew who controlled Freeman and Simpson Streets and Southern Boulevard. They controlled the neighborhood and ruled it with violence. His workers were afraid of him. Many of the neighborhood thugs, along with his workers would get hyped whenever he showed up. They treated him as if he was royalty. There were even rumors that he shot and killed one of his workers, which I believe because I never trusted his ass. I hated it whenever he would stare at me with those evil-looking grayish eyes of his.

He was arrested for the murder of his worker. He took the case to trial and eventually was found not guilty. However, he was found guilty on several drug charges and after talking it over with his lawyer, he accepted a plea. He was sentenced to seven years in Federal Prison.

It was while in prison that Marques became familiar with one of Jimmy's cronies, who was doing a life sentence. He and Marques became fast friends and in no time, he told Jimmy about Marques. Jimmy, who was always looking for recruits to join his organization, told Marques to look him up when he got out.

Upon his release, Marques went back to his old stomping ground believing his reputation was still intact, and to reclaim the streets he once ruled. Instead, he was in for a rude awakening. His old neighborhood was being run by a group of young thugs. They killed with impunity. They were the new bosses of the neighborhood. Though they were mere babies when Marques went to jail, they were familiar with his name and knew of his reputation, but seven years was a long time. His time had passed and there was no way in the world he was going to reclaim it.

Once when Marques confronted several of the teenagers, they quickly set him straight. They had a reputation to uphold, and, in their minds, they weren't about to let an old-timer disrespect them. Furthermore, they were just as vicious as he was when he ran the neighborhood.

Instead of trying to work his way in, or take his old neighborhood back by force, he along with several of his most loyal friends decided to do business with Jimmy. Jimmy made it clear that his organization would not tolerate any senseless and random killings.

"This organization is about business first. The hype and all the other dumb shit that some mutha-fuckas like to do ain't happening here. We do things different here," Jimmy sternly warned Marques.

Jimmy eventually won him over by explaining that he was in a multimillion-dollar business and accountability was important. Marques understood once he saw the clientele and connections Jimmy had at his disposal. Jimmy was a cunning decision-maker and the head of a sophisticated organized drug empire whose membership included professionals and lowly foot soldiers.

Marques was more than eager to please not only Jimmy but Robert and Jason as well. Robert and Jason were pleased with the things that Jimmy said about Marques. They immediately agreed that he should join the organization as well. They saw him as an enforcer and his prison record spoke for itself. Marques and his buddies made sure that everything and everyone was on point.

Robert and Jason loved his approach. This didn't surprise me at all. It was a known fact that Robert and Jason were pussies. They didn't want to get their hands dirty, so to speak. They left things like that to Marques. He was ambitious and quickly moved up in the ranks, where he became an important member of the crew. Within a short period, the three were getting along like real-life brothers.

I also learned that they were the ones in charge of recruiting and picking up the girls from the internet chat rooms and high schools. They even did some recruiting at several middle schools as well. They made sure the girls were young and attractive so they could manipulate their asses as they did me. They knew the girls were hot in their pants, and to entice them and gain their trust they chauffeured them around in their luxury cars. They gave them money and bought them expensive gifts. Like me, quite a few of the girls were naive and they believed they cared about them. And not knowing any better they willingly carried their drugs. This was uncalled for and cruel. And what did Robert and the others do? They sat back and enjoyed the finer side of life in the Hamptons, Westchester, Connecticut, the Caribbean, South, and Central America.

Some of the girls were physically, mentally, and sexually abused. I knew the pain they experienced. Once you experienced something of that magnitude it stayed with you. On a few occasions, I sat down with several of the girls after Tara introduced us and we talked about a lot of things. Despite this, we never spoke about the physical, mental, and sexual abuse we all went through. I didn't know how to approach such a sensitive topic.

On the flip side of this were the girls who would give it up in a heartbeat without any remorse whatsoever. As far as those girls were concerned, they didn't mind the attention or the gifts that the men gave them. This was their dream and despite the drugs and violence they witnessed growing up, they didn't give a damn. Going to school didn't matter; the only thing that mattered was the money and the lifestyle that came with it. This was the lifestyle they craved.

Tara told me everything that she knew about the Playaz Club and some of its members. When I asked her about Stacy and Jason, she didn't hesitate in telling me about them. They first met while Stacy was in high school. But she wasn't in awe of him. Word is she didn't give a damn about his Mercedes Benz or his law firm.

"Stacy must have been going out of her mind or something because I certainly would have checked him out to see what he was up to. But I guess when you're young, you don't know any better," I said to Tara.

"I know, right," she said, agreeing with me.

"Who told you this, Marques?"

"No, Stacy did."

"She did? How did you get her to tell you all of this?"

"You know how I do; I'm cool with everybody. But she's cool though. For almost a year, Jason made it his business to cruise by Francis Lewis High School looking for her. He was also making his rounds, along with Robert and Marques at several other schools. But Jason was obsessed with her that she became his number one priority. He kept pursuing her until she gave in and gave him her phone number. Talk about obsessed, he was beside himself. All he wanted was some pussy. It never bothered him that she was only in the ninth grade. He even pretended to be her teacher when he called her house."

"Damn, he's a dog," I said, interrupting her.

"Isn't he?" she said, with a straight face. "He would take her to school every morning and return promptly at three o'clock to take her home. He called her every day. He tried his best to get her to his apartment and her answer was always no, but that didn't stop him. Instead, he took her shopping and began spending a lot of money on her, and bought her lots of expensive gifts and designer clothes. They were always at the movies and he even showed up with her at some of the Playaz Club parties. I thought I was a liar, but she constantly lied to her mother about her whereabouts so she could hang out with him."

"Word? She was that sprung?"

"Sprung isn't the word."

"I heard that, go ahead."

"She eventually introduced him to her mother. I believe she said it was six months into their relationship before she introduced him. But any way you look at it, it was a bad move. He was smooth and respectful. He gave the impression of being a nice guy. Her mom wanted to believe that she and Jason were only friends. It didn't take long for him to start scheming on sleeping with her mom."

"Damn, did he hit it?"

"Nah, he didn't get any at least not that I know of."

"Knowing him, it wouldn't surprise me."

"True that."

"Does Stacy's mom look good?"

"Yeah, she's hot and she looks young for her age. He eventually took Stacy's virginity and moved her out of her mother's apartment by the time she got to the eleventh grade. How he convinced her mother of this is beyond me."

"Wow! What kind of mother is that? I don't think she's all there."

"I don't know. Look what happened between me and my mom."

"You right. You went through some serious shit yourself, but damn!"

"It happens."

Tara said they have been an item ever since. It's demoralizing and sad when parents become so selfish that they would jeopardize the welfare and lives of their children.

Episode 11

*H*earing Jenny's voice on my answering machine made me realize how long it had been since we last spoke. I promised myself that we would talk more often.

Jenny's realty business was doing well. I was invited to her housewarming party on the east side of Manhattan. I called and asked her if it would be a problem if I brought a friend along.

"No, not at all, just make sure your ass is here."

"Of course, I wouldn't miss this for the world."

When Tara and I reached the coop apartment building located on Thirty-Ninth Street and Second Avenue, we were directed to the elevator by the doorman. *Damn, my girl is making her mark in New York*, I thought to myself. She was doing the damn thing and I was happy for her.

After making the rounds and being introduced to several of her friends and employees, Jenny and I sat down to chitchat. Tara sat down next to me.

"Jenny, this is Tara," I said.

"Nice to meet you," both women responded.

"Nice place," Tara said.

"Thanks," Jenny replied.

"I know you girls must have a lot to talk about so let me excuse myself and go get a drink," Tara said, walking toward the kitchen area.

"Is this the girl you were telling me about?" Jenny asked.

"Yeah."

I told her about Tara; however, I never went into details about the drugs, or the life we led. I told her that Tara was dating one of Robert's friends.

"Girl, things are going great for me." Jenny smiled.

"Shit, I can see that."

"My parents are visiting next week, and I want you to be here."

"I will. How are they doing?"

"They're chillin' and happy for me. My dad used his connections to get me in touch with several clients right here in the city."

"That's good. I'm proud of you."

"Thanks. I'm thinking about expanding the business. I need a larger place. Do you know what I'm saying? I was looking at a vacant storefront in Harlem on East One Hundred and Twenty-Fifth Street and Lenox Avenue. I'm gonna contact the owners and see what's up."

"Girl, when I graduate, I'm coming for a job and without a resume, so you better be ready. Honestly, though, I've been thinking about relocating."

"Relocating, where to?"

"I'm not sure as of yet, but definitely out of the city."

"Are you serious?" she asked, with a stunned look on her face.

"Yeah, I'm serious. But you know what?"

"What?"

"Now is not the time to be talking about stuff like this. It's about you tonight. So, forgive me for bringing up shit that I'm not even sure about, a'ight."

"Don't worry about it."

By now my curiosity had gotten the best of me. I wanted to know how my father was doing. Maybe I shouldn't have felt this way given our history together. But this was me and I couldn't help it. Jenny must have read my mind. I was about to ask her how my father was doing when she said, "My dad said your father is doing fine, and he wanted to know if he had heard from you."

"What did your dad say?"

"He said he hadn't heard a word."

"Thanks. Well, at least he's alright. Is he still with that young girl?"

"Yeah, they're still together." Jenny laughed.

"Your dad is something else."

"For real, you right."

"Okay, let's go and have some fun now. And bitch don't be taking so damn long to return my calls," she added, laughing.

"I promise I won't," I responded, as I bounced to Chaka Khan's *I'm Every Woman*.

***

The semester was over. I had taken my finals and I knew I had passed all my classes. It was just a matter of waiting for my grades. I was still putting in my hours at Macy's, but that was it. I now had a lot of time on my hands. So, when Tara called and told me that we had to pick up a package for Jimmy in Connecticut, I was more than eager because I needed the money. There was no way in the world that I was going to pass on that. I was starting to love the money. It paid the bills and allowed me to live a decent life.

When Tara and I arrived at the Connecticut mansion, we were searched by two buff-looking women who were with some guy named Andre. He was part Cherokee and black. He was about Jimmy's age, tall with a reddish complexion and dyed black shoulder-length hair. He was very handsome with dark gentle eyes which made me uneasy. I thought about avoiding them but then I thought, *don't do that because it will make it seem as if I'm hiding something.* I certainly didn't want him to get that impression. And so, I kept eye contact throughout our time there. On his arm was an attractive older-looking woman. She was dressed in the latest designer fashions and draped in diamonds to kill for.

We were led down a corridor where we were escorted by the two women to an awaiting elevator. Tara and I looked at each other dumbfounded. We couldn't believe our eyes. Jimmy's mansion was nice, but Andre's was like the ones you see on the television program *Lifestyles of the Rich and Famous.* When the elevator came to a stop, we were greeted by six men whose faces were meaner than twenty pit bulls. As we headed down a dimly lit hallway, we passed several rooms where the voices of several men and women could be heard. Finally, we were led into a room, and stacked on one of two tables were several briefcases filled with money. On the other table were ten neatly stacked rows of cocaine. I almost had a heart attack seeing so much money and drugs. Tara and I both looked at each other hardly believing what we were seeing.

We were handed two briefcases and Tara asked, "How much is in each?"

She was told not to worry about it. We were told the only thing we needed to do was to see to it that the briefcases were delivered without any problems.

Once we were back on the elevator, I realized that we were heading to another section of the mansion. One of the women had pressed a different floor from the one which we first entered. After getting off the elevator, we were led through a completely different section of the mansion, which led to an underground walkway, where we were led to our car. We hit I-95 and headed for New York City.

"Did you see that fucking house?" I asked Tara.

"Yeah, I've been there before but never inside."

I began to notice how quiet her responses were whenever I asked her a question. It was as if she was in a different world mulling over whether or not she should steal some of the money. She had an odd look on her face.

"What's wrong?" I asked her.

"Oh, nothin'. It's just Andre, he looks familiar."

"Don't sweat it," I remarked. "A lot of mutha-fuckas come around Jimmy. That's where you probably saw him."

"Yeah, you right. But you notice how that mutha-fucka made us leave from another section of the house?"

"Yup! Maybe he was trying to confuse us." We both laughed.

Although Andre kept a huge amount of cash in his mansion, its sole purpose and use were that of a transit unit. Tara and I agreed that it wasn't a smart idea. The drugs that she and I saw at the mansion were to be delivered elsewhere. The underground and elevators were built in case Andre had to haul ass.

"Dayum, that fat bitch was feeling all over my tits," I snapped.

"Word, that bitch almost touched my coochie," Tara said, her voice slowly rising. "I was about to drop kick her ass, but I chilled. I didn't wanna start any shit, cause both those bitches would have caught a beat down."

"You know that's a lot of cheddar we just picked up. These mutha-fuckas are making money," I said.

"Word, that's why we gotta get ours, but you know what?"

"What?"

"This shit, it ain't gonna last. One day all this is gonna crumble. That's why I wanted you to make this move with me. This is a big payday for us and that's what it's all about, you feel me? A bitch like me gots to stack my papers. We have to get as much out of this shit as we possibly can before it all ends because it's gonna end," she said, sounding as if she knew what she was talking about.

"Yeah, you right. That's word."

***

It was the day after Tara, and I had made our run for Jimmy when I suddenly felt the urge to see Charles. We hadn't spoken in days and I was quite sure he wouldn't mind seeing me. The telephone rang several times before he finally answered.

"Hi," I said.

"Hey! Sorry, I was in the shower. How are you?"

"I'm doing fine and you?"

"I'm okay, but even better now that I'm hearing your voice."

"Really?"

"Yes." He laughed. "Why don't you come by?"

"Are you sure you want me to?"

"Of course, I have something I want to show you."

"Hmm."

Laughing, he said, "Now I know you're curious, aren't you?"

"Yeah, but my curiosity won't kill the cat."

"Don't worry; I'll do the killing to your cat. "We both laughed.

I told him I would be there in an hour. There was something special about him, and I knew in my heart that he was the man for me. I was going to show him once and for all that he was. I was getting dressed when my cell phone rang. Thinking it was him; I answered it and blurted out, "I'm coming, give me a minute."

"Bitch, you going to get some dick tonight, huh?" the voice asked.

"Why are you trying to disguise your voice?" It was Tara; I couldn't help but laugh.

"The way you sound he must be special. Is he?"

"Yes, he is! I gotta get my groove on tonight."

"I won't keep you long. Give me a call later or tomorrow, I have some shit to tell you."

"Okay, I'll talk to you later."

I was dressed and looking fierce as I took another glance in the mirror before heading out the door to get the dick that awaited me. The ride to his place was quicker than I had anticipated because there wasn't much traffic. I quickly found parking after pulling up on the block. I hastily made my way to the building and called him. As I approached the door to his apartment, it was partly open. I entered, and there he was standing in his black silk robe in his dimly lit living room. In his hands were two glasses filled with Krug and Luther Vandross *Here and Now* was pumping softly through his Bose CD system. I took my jacket off and slowly walked toward him. He kissed me ever so softly on my lips.

"Baby, you're so beautiful. I must have been a fool to allow you to stay away from me for so long. I guess I must have waited too long to make my move," he said, sipping on the Krug.

I blushed. My knees trembled. I smiled and said, "You're not a fool and you didn't take too long to make your move."

"I think I did, but enough of that. The only thing that concerns me right now is that you're here and now."

"That's a nice way of putting it," I said, smiling.

He took my glass — placed it on the kitchen counter and began kissing me. It was exhilarating and exuding as our tongues slithered in and out of each other's mouths. I ran my hand over his bare chest. I could see his dick growing under his robe. He gently kissed my tits. Damn, it felt good! I loosened my bra so that he could get at them without any problems. Once he had free access to my tits, he began sucking, biting, licking, and rubbing his face all over them. We were all over each other. My skirt was on the floor. I stood in front of him in only my panties, which were soaked. He untied his robe. His dick was hard and jumping as if it had a mind of its own. He took my hand and led me to his bedroom. The walk seemed like it took forever. I was staring at his dick anticipating how hard he was going to fuck me.

He bent me over doggy style across his bed and began eating me out. I felt his tongue deep inside me. My hips began gyrating faster and faster. I pushed my ass onto his face. I spread my legs and held on tight. He ran his tongue over my fat ass. I could feel the damp sheets absorbing my cum as I lost control. I was in sexual overdrive. He was driving me wild.

"Fuck me, Charles! Give me that shit!" I moaned.

I straddled him and began bouncing up and down on his dick. It felt as if I was on a trampoline as I steadily kept pace with him. He flipped me on my back and put my legs over his shoulders. I felt it in my stomach. I was working overtime. He held onto me tightly, our bodies thrashing out of control as he exploded in me.

As we held each other soaked in our sweat, I told him he came too fast and that he needed to finish what he started. He agreed. We talked about taking our relationship to the next level. He was pleased but told me to quit the head games. I assured him I would. He wanted to know what I was doing with my free time now that school was out. I lied and told him I was working with Jenny at her realty company.

"So, what about your job at Macy's, are you still working there?" he asked.

"Yeah, but I only work part-time, remember?"

"Right."

"I work like twenty-one hours a week."

"That's cool. I just wanted to know that you're okay. How are things with you and your dad?"

"Who?" I had forgotten about the bogus story that I told him about my father.

"Your dad. Did something happen?" he asked, with a curious look on his face.

"Oh no, not at all, he's back down south. I'm so glad that is over with," I said, exhaling.

"I'm with you on that. He was making my life miserable. I couldn't see you whenever I wanted and that was not good," he exclaimed, laughing. "Dana, you know I love you very much, right? I only want to be with you and make you happy. I would never do anything to hurt you."

I was beside myself, because no one had ever cared about me, or said anything like that to me, except for Brian. He was the only person that ever loved me. I knew his love was genuine. But I felt Charles's love also, and it seemed sincere and genuine. I kissed Charles and told him that I loved him and wanted to be with him. The sun was coming up when we finally fell asleep in each other's arms.

Episode 12

"Dana!" Robert yelled as I made my way through the throng of co-workers and shoppers who were leaving Macy's.

"What do you want?" I asked sarcastically.

"Hey, I haven't seen you in a while and I was wondering how you were doing?"

"The last time I checked I had a cell and home phone. And you know where I live, don't you? I guess you only come by when you want some pussy. What's the matter, your wifey ain't fucking you enough? Or did she stop fucking you altogether?"

"Come on now cut the bullshit. Get in the car. Have you eaten?"

"Yeah, I did. I ate a few blouses, two pairs of shoes, and a scarf at work."

"Why are you acting like a…?"

"Like a what? A bitch, isn't that what you wanna say?"

"Hey, you said it I didn't. Enough of this nonsense, I didn't come here to fight or argue. Let's go get a bite, is that cool with you?"

After calming down, I gathered myself. I told him everything was fine. I got in the car and we drove to Tropical Blend, a Jamaican Restaurant on the corner of Fourteenth Street and Second Avenue. We discussed our situation and the things we needed to change to remain friends over a meal of jerk chicken and rice and peas. He also told me that Jason would no longer be a problem.

"So, he won't be bothering me anymore?"

"That's right."

"Did Jason tell you this?"

"No, I told him to keep his fucking hands off you."

"You told your cousin that? After you guys have been fucking the same pussy for years?"

"Shh, will you be quiet? Why do you have to be so damn loud? Who told you Jason was my cousin?"

"That's old news. Everybody knows you two are related." I was lying about everybody knowing, but he didn't know that.

"Everybody?" he asked, surprised.

"Yeah everybody, but you know what's fucked up about it?"

"What?"

"You didn't have the fucking balls to tell me yourself. You're nothing but a bitch ass."

"I'm a bitch what?" he asked, not understanding exactly what I said.

"Nothing."

"I guess I fucked up with you, huh? It shouldn't have gotten to this, especially with you. Sure, the members of the Playaz Club have been doing shit like this for a while. But some of the women are off-limits and I should have done that with you. All I had to do was say the word.

I fucked up and I'm sorry. I shouldn't have said those things and treated you the way I did when I came back to town. I care about you whether you want to believe it or not," he said, sounding sincere.

"Where did this revelation suddenly come from? Are you getting soft on me?"

"What the hell is wrong with you? I said I was sorry, and I do love you. I have always loved you. It's just that I was so caught up in the everyday operation of the organization, my wife, and the other nonsense that comes with all this bullshit."

I understood exactly what he was saying, but what was I supposed to do? Was I supposed to say, *I forgive you now let's get married*? Hell no, I was pissed. My life was being ruined by him and his associates. My hands were tied, but instead of untying me, he tightened the noose. I was the one who was sorry, sorry for ever meeting his dumb ass. I composed myself and reassured him that I accepted his apology.

Upon leaving the restaurant, he offered me a ride home which I accepted. We hardly said a word to each other during the ride. He pulled to a stop in front of my apartment building. He was about to drive off when I foolishly asked him if he wanted to come upstairs. Why did I invite him upstairs? I have always asked myself that question, maybe I was getting soft. He eagerly accepted the invitation.

Surprisingly, nothing happened, he never made any attempts, nor did he ask me for anything. The Robert I knew would have been on my ass in a minute. We ate some chocolate chip ice cream, snuggled up, and watched the Miami Heat beat up the New York Knicks. He must have been really tired because he fell asleep during the third quarter of the game.

I awoke the next morning to the smell of pancakes, sausages, and coffee.

After breakfast, he got dressed, kissed me on the lips, and said, "I have to get to work." To his legit job that is. I held the door as he walked to the elevator. "I'll see you later," he said.

"Okay," I replied.

After taking a bath and getting dressed, I headed to Tara's apartment. We had made plans to go shopping. I also wanted to know what she had to tell me that was so important. We stopped at Lord and Taylor, Bloomingdale's, and the Gucci and Prada stores. If I weren't a member of the Playaz Club, I certainly wouldn't have been able to shop at those stores.

"So, what was it you wanted to tell me?" I asked Tara.

"Remember the lady we saw with all the diamonds and shit in Connecticut?"

"Jackie? What about her?"

"That's Stacy's mom."

"Which Stacy are you talking about?"

"Jason's, girl."

"You're fucking kidding! Are you bullshitting me or what?"

"No, I'm not."

"Our Stacy, that's her fucking mom? Unbelievable! How did you find this out? Wait, let me guess, Marques?"

"You know it. You remember that time I was telling you about Stacy and Jason?"

"Yeah."

"Well, Jason used to fuck her mom on the down-low."

"Get the fuck outta here!"

"He did. Don't forget who we're talking about here."

"You're right."

"Her mom still looks good. I told you."

"Yeah, she does. But damn, he was fucking both of them? He's grimy."

"Yup. He's foul but so is her mom."

"You right because she knew that nigga was fucking her daughter. No wonder she let her move out of her apartment. Does Stacy know he used to fuck her mother?"

"From what Marques said she doesn't."

"That shit is gonna come out sooner or later though, you watch," I remarked, shaking my head.

"Look at how she acts. She's not acting as if she knows about it. Do you know what I'm saying? If she does then she's a damn good actress."

"You're right, Tara. But then again maybe she doesn't give a fuck."

"True that. But it was the money that got her mom open. Jason was flashing a lot of that shit and it caught her eyes. The bitch od on seeing so much gwop."

"So how did her mother get hooked up with that fine-ass old negro, Andre?"

"You a snap. He is fine with his old ass self! This is what happened. Jason invited Stacy and her mother to one of Jimmy's pool parties. Andre was there and he liked what he saw. That old nigga started to mack her ass, playa, playa," Tara said.

I was laughing so hard that I began to cry.

"For a while, both Jason and Andre were fucking her until Jimmy told Jason to back off," Tara continued. "The old playa wasn't having it."

"Wow, this is some shit. Are Andre and Jackie married?"

"No, but they live together. She's the one who takes care of the mansion, and she's the one who hired the female bodyguards including those buff ass bitches we saw."

"No wonder Stacy be acting like she's hot shit sometimes."

"She's cool though."

"We spoke a few times and she did seem cool. But sometimes she gets this attitude as if she's running things. She disses the other girls too."

"She does and I see it. But she knows who to fuck with. She's not stupid. You notice she doesn't bring any of that drama to me or you, right?"

"True that."

"Believe me, she's cool."

"I hear you, girl. But I still can't believe this shit."

"Well, believe it," she said, as she mockingly gave me one of Stacy's stares.

"Marques be telling you a lot of shit."

"I know. I told you that mutha-fucka would tell on his mother. This pussy got him whipped. Oh, there's more."

"Concerning who?" I asked as we entered McDonald's. I was exhausted and hungry from all the shopping we did.

"Jason. He's been involved with some dude name Platinum. And wanted him to join the Playaz Club, but I heard Jimmy wasn't having it."

"Why? What happened?"

"Jimmy doesn't like his ass. Word is he's a big-time playa in the prostitution game."

"But wasn't Jimmy into that lifestyle back in the day?"

"Yeah, but he ain't playing that shit now."

"Hmm."

"Platinum is notorious for beating his girls and getting involved with the boys and Jimmy doesn't want anything to do with that. He broke the jaw of three of his tricks and put them in the hospital."

"You know what I can't understand?"

"What?"

"Jimmy turned state and got Big Red murdered. Yet he acts as if he's some kind of religious guru, what the fuck!" Tara was dying of laughter when I said this.

"Girl, you're killing me," she said, trying to catch her breath as I continued.

"What's so special about a bunch of mutha-fuckas selling drugs? They're all hypocrites if you ask me."

"This is the game and it's a money game. You have a lot of brothas who started as armed robbers, murderers, pimps, players, small-time dope peddlers, and the like. They all dream about getting into the ultimate game and Platinum is no different. Take a look at how you and I live. We get paid thousands of dollars to deliver their drugs, right?"

"Yeah, you right."

"Where else could we make this type of gwop?"

"I know what you're saying."

"The million-dollar homes, the vacations, bitches, niggas, parties, the bling-bling, these brothas are big time and they love it. Jason, Robert, Marques, Troy, and all the other mutha-fuckas that we see day in and day out a lot of them are professionals making decent six-figure salaries. But they all have one thing in common and that's to get their share of the American pie and they will do whatever the fuck it takes. Trafficking drugs is their livelihood and Platinum is no different. They all want to shine and live like ballers."

"I know that's right," I said, nodding in agreement.

"They ain't thinking like me and you. We wanna get the gwop and get the fuck up outta here and move on with our lives. But not these mutha-fuckas this is their livelihood and Jimmy is not about to let Jason and Platinum fuck his shit up. None of these negroes want to get out. The bitches they with make sure their asses stay in there."

"You are crazy. You got me laughing and this stuff is serious.

"It's true, they ain't doing jack to get out. You feel me?"

"No doubt."

"Jimmy isn't with that prostitute shit. But you never know he might wanna put the move on us."

"For sure and we've been there and done that already," I cracked.

"I believe Jason is supposed to meet up with Platinum at the Robinson's tomorrow afternoon. If you roll by you might get to see what he looks like. I've never seen him either so here's your chance to see the one and only Platinum."

"Fuck that! I've got too much shit to do already. Are you gonna be there?"

"Yeah, I'll be there for a hot minute. Marques is supposed to hook up with him and Jason."

"I'm not gonna promise anything but if I have the time I'll drop by. If not, I'll give you a call."

"Okay, that's cool," she said, changing the topic to Andre. "Do you know that Andre is having his birthday party tomorrow night?"

"Where?"

"I think in White Plains."

"Oh, but I don't know if I can make it."

"Are you out of your fucking mind? Do you know who Andre is?"

"No, but…" I began.

"You have to be there. Everybody will be there. That's how it is. Plus, I need you there to keep me company," she said, cutting me off.

"That's how they do it?" I asked, with a scared look on my face before she reassured me that it wasn't that bad.

"Yeah, that's how they roll. Once you're in, you're in, and you know how they feel about the Playaz Club." We laughed before saying our goodbyes.

Episode 13

I guess Robert was true to his words. He showed up at my apartment later that night. I sat him down and asked, "What is it that you want? Is it a quick fix you're looking for?"

He shook his head and replied, "No, I'm looking for something long-term and permanent. "I was confused now more than ever. "Everything I said to you last night I meant. My feelings for you are genuine and it's all love. You're the one I want to be with. My divorce is almost finalized and as soon as it is, I want to marry you."

"Do you believe I want to marry you?"

"Yes. Although I've put you through a lot of drama, I honestly believe you love me. Have you forgotten all the good times we had? Weren't they wonderful? You know they were and that's something you just can't throw away or act as if they never happened."

I started crying not because he wanted to marry me. But because of all the things I had been through, here he was doing it to me all over again. I couldn't think straight. I was on the edge not knowing whether I should jump or not.

I wanted to get away from everything. It was frustrating. I knew I had said before that I needed to get away from the Playaz Club, but I just couldn't. I continued to cry as I thought about what they could do to me. I knew they were capable of doing anything they wanted. I was in a dangerous environment so basically, I was screwed.

"Robert, I need to think. Why are you pressuring me?"

"Dana please, I'm telling you the truth this time. You're the one. I'll wait for you. I'll do whatever it takes. Take as much time as you need. My kids are with their grandmother. If you think I'm lying you can ask Jimmy. He knows what's going on. He knows my marriage is over. He's pissed because she's his family, but he understands."

I sat there listening to him. I could tell he meant every word. But I knew where my heart was, it was with Charles. *I can't keep doing this shit to him. What the fuck was wrong with me,* I kept repeating over and over to myself.

I gave Robert the bed and snuggled up on the couch while listening to my favorite song. After he left for work in the morning, I called Charles. I could hear it in his voice that he was upset with me because I didn't show up as promised. However, he never said a word about it. I told him that I would stop by his apartment after running a few errands.

"No problem, I'll be here," he said.

***

It was funny how Robert never said a word about Andre's party, but I figured he would tell me later that evening. I then got a call from Jimmy. He told me to get to Kennedy Airport as soon as possible.

"Tara, Jimmy just sent word that he needs me, you, Babs, and Tiffany to get over to Kennedy Airport right now," I told her on the phone.

"Pick me up in thirty," she said.

"Thirty? He said right now. I'm on my way."

"Okay, I'll be ready."

Upon arriving at the airport, we were told to wait for American Airlines Flight 1107. The flight arrived within minutes of our arrival. The mules that were carrying the drugs were unknown to us. Under peering eyes, we checked out our surroundings while observing the passengers from Flight 1107, before noticing two Latino men and a young Latina woman in a wheelchair. Our eyes locked upon making eye contact and as they got closer the woman in the wheelchair said the password.

As they handed me the bags the police appeared out of nowhere and were on our asses. The young woman in the wheelchair was the first to make a run for it. She got out of the wheelchair so fast, that I couldn't believe my eyes. I thought she was confined to the damn wheelchair. Jimmy had used physically challenged workers before so it's not like I was surprised. What surprised me was how fast she got up and hauled ass. They all ran in different directions except for me and Tara.

"Give me the bags," she said, as I handed them to her.

"Where are you going?"

"Look, it doesn't make sense if we all get busted. You ain't ready for that shit. Let them follow me, and you get outta here, you hear me?" she hollered at me, running with the bags.

"Yeah!" I yelled. "Be careful!"

"I will."

I took off in the opposite direction and jumped over three metal rails before hitting the street. I was running so fast that I swore I outran several cars. I was looking wild and crazy as I flagged down a yellow cab. I got in and quickly lowered myself into the backseat.

The driver, an African glanced at me at least three times in his rearview mirror before asking in a deep accent, "Why do you run? Who chase after you?"

"My boyfriend, he's crazy and he wants to beat my ass."

"Aaaah, he does sound crazy. Where do you want to go?"

I saw several signs: Belt Parkway East, Belt Parkway West, and Verrazano Bridge. I told him to just drive and get me as far away from the airport as he possibly could. He put the pedal to the metal and sped toward the Belt Parkway East before heading to the city.

Once in the city, I called Jimmy. My phone kept ringing while Jimmy and I spoke. It was Robert, Jason, and Marques. I told them I was talking to Jimmy and I would get back to them. Jimmy knew what happened. He told me that Babs, Tiffany, the woman in the wheelchair, and one of the Latino men were arrested. I asked him about Tara.

"She got away with three bags," he said.

I was relieved knowing that she was safe. "Where is she?"

"She's on her way over here. Meet us in the Bronx. You know where right?"

"Yeah, I'll be there."

My SUV was at the airport. And I wasn't going to ride all the way home with the African driver. You don't take chances like that in this game. So, I flagged down another cab and headed to my apartment, took a shower, changed my clothes, and rode the train uptown to the Bronx.

***

"Hey, listen up. As some of you know some shit went down not too long ago," Jimmy said to several of his top-level members.

The group was quite small. There were other members from the Playaz Club present. However, they were not allowed in the room. The faces of those in the room were unfamiliar to me except for Tara, Robert, Jason, and Jimmy. Their eyes penetrated my body like sharp knives as they glanced at me. The room was quiet as they listened to Jimmy.

"We lost three of our six parcels. But let me digress for a minute here," Jimmy said. "We are not about to use this situation as an excuse to not show up at Andre's party later tonight. As I was saying, Babs, Tiffany, and two of our connections were apprehended. We won't know their situation until tomorrow. Dana and Tara were the only two who got away and they are here. If they weren't on top of their game, the shit could have been much worse. They did what they had to do to get away. Something went wrong. I don't know if it was on our side of town, or our connection. I say this because the Drug Enforcement Agency knew what time the flight arrived and who the players were. They were waiting at the airport for the transaction to go down. This was not NYPD, this was bigger. Whoever leaked information and allowed this to go down, we will find the mutha-fucka or mutha-fuckas and deal with them accordingly as only the Playaz Organization can."

Tara smiled at me when he mentioned the organization. I had to hold in my laughter so I wouldn't interrupt him.

"Okay, I will see y'all later tonight at Andre's," he finished up.

"Girl, I'm so happy to see you. I'm glad you made it," I said to Tara, hugging her.

"Shit, I never ran so fast and so far with so many bags before," Tara exclaimed. "If it weren't for some brotha driving a limousine I wouldn't have gotten outta that bitch. This dude was hitting me up for a date and

I was trying to dodge those mutha-fuckas. Can you believe that shit? How did you get away?"

"Girl, I almost ran across the highway. There were two mutha-fuckas behind me and I hauled ass. They must have gotten tired or something because they were on my ass when all of a sudden, they just stopped. I flagged down a cab and got my ass outta there. Did you see how fast that little bitch got outta that wheelchair?" I asked, with a smile on my face.

"Oh God, that shit was funny. She ran like Marion Jones on steroids," Tara said, laughing. "That bitch bounced outta that wheelchair as if she heard a starter gun."

"It's fucked up what happened to Babs and Tiffany," I expressed.

"Yeah, I know. But they know the rules, run, run, run, and keep running. But they stopped and tried to play it off."

"You saw them?"

"Yeah, I saw them. They stopped at a Budget Rent-A-Car thinking the boys didn't see them. But they rolled right up in that joint and put them under locks."

"Dayum! Did they see you?"

"They saw me. I was praying they wouldn't keep staring. But it was all good because I got away."

As we continued talking, Robert approached us. "Excuse me, ladies. Tara, can I have a word with you?"

"Sure, what's up?" she asked.

They stepped aside and began talking. I was somewhat surprised that he approached us and only asked to speak to Tara. I thought he was coming to comfort me because of what I had gone through earlier. Nevertheless, I knew he wasn't Tara's type, so I immediately dismissed the thought.

I was chatting with several of the girls when I felt a tap on my shoulder. It was Robert. Tara by now was quietly snacking on some potato chips and smiling at me.

"What do you want now?" I said, with an attitude.

"I want you to know that I'm glad you got away. I don't wanna see or hear anything bad happening to you. I'm just concerned that's all."

"Well, thanks. It was scary but I got my ass outta there."

"Thank God. I know you must be wondering what I said to Tara, right?"

"No, I don't want to know." I was lying.

"I asked her if it was cool if Jimmy changed her partner. I know that you guys are tight and y'all usually make runs together. But it's just that I don't want anything happening to you. Tara is experienced and knows how to take care of herself."

"Okay, what did she say?"

"She said it's up to you and it's whatever you say."

"That's my girl, she's got my back and I've got hers. How am I going to get the experience if I'm not out in the field?"

"It's just that…"

"It's just nothing. You just wanna be overprotective and controlling and there's no reason for it. But thanks for your concern once again, it's cool. By the way, when were you going to tell me about Andre's party?"

"I was gonna tell you tonight, but Jimmy beat me to it." He laughed.

"You're lying."

"No, I'm not lying. Let me tell you this though, everyone here sees your potential and they all believe you're going places along with Tara. You guys are high on everybody's list. It looks like it's just me that's worried about you. Guess I've got too much love for you, huh?"

"You do know the word love is not a word to play with? It's a serious word that signifies feelings and emotions and it connects people who feel the same way about each other. You do know that don't you? Because if you don't then I think you should find another word."

"Why should I when it's from the heart? But I'm gonna let you mingle with the crowd until you're ready to leave because I don't want you to get loud on me, remember the restaurant?"

"Good for you," I said, as we both laughed. I walked over to where Tara was sitting. She had her eyes on Robert as he shook hands with several of his associates.

"Did he tell you what he wanted to do?" Tara asked me.

"Yeah, he did. But it's gonna be me and you like Whitney and Bobby back in the day."

"Ha, ha, that's a good one. He was gonna ask Jimmy to split us up because he's in love with you and he doesn't want anything bad happening to you."

"He said that? Stop lying."

"He did and those were his words. He sounds serious, I can tell you that much."

"Yeah, he told me, but that's for another time in another world on another planet. It ain't gonna happen in this lifetime."

"I hear you. You know what's best for you and you know that whatever decision you make I've got your back like Whitney and Bobby. It's not what he says it's what we say."

"No, you didn't go there." We were laughing as several of the guests stared at us.

"But it's true."

"I know."

"So, are you ready?"

"Yeah, I'm ready to get outta here. I've gotta get myself prepared for later. My ride is still at the airport."

"Jimmy got that covered."

"But he ain't got my keys."

"Don't worry they got it."

"Okay, sis!"

Jimmy then stood up and reminded everyone that he expects to see them at Andre's party, period.

"Let me roll with you," I said to Tara.

"That won't be necessary," Robert replied, walking over, and taking my hand.

"I'll see you later, Dana." Tara smiled at me trying to hold back her laughter.

"Bye, talk to you later."

Episode 14

The ride to Andre's party was noticeably quiet and subdued. Robert was trying to convince me that he did love me without being too aggressive. I respected that. Something must have gotten into him; this certainly was unlike him. I could tell he had been to Andre's Westchester home before. He knew exactly where he was going pinpointing every curve, right and left turn like a damn compass. The mansions on the tree-lined streets leading to Andre's home looked stately and majestic with the grass neatly manicured. The driveways were filled with several late-model luxury cars and SUVs. Robert turned right onto Commonwealth Drive, a meticulous and spectacular-looking street filled with some amazing jaw-dropping mansions. Andre's Westchester home stood out like a sore thumb. As we got closer, I could see several men dressed in their red valet outfits taking care of the fly-ass cars pulling up one after the other.

The mansion was immaculate, to say the least. At the entrance were two gold lion head statues with a plush red carpet leading up to the walkway. It was awesome. Several lights illuminated the front of the mansion perfectly. Andre certainly went the whole nine yards to pull this off. I guess that's how you do it when it's your birthday, especially when you've got it like that.

Andre's party was teeming with an abundance of handsome men and beautiful women. They were both gorgeous and sophisticated looking as they mingled with each other. They were dressed rather tastefully and elegantly. I felt as if I were in the diamond district in Manhattan with all the bling I saw. I was dressed in a black Versace dress which showed off my figure in all the right places. The shoes and bag were also Versace. I made sure I showed up looking like a star.

Tara wore a confident expression on her face and looked elegant in a light beige Prada pantsuit with shoes and a bag to match. Her confidence was sky-high as she sashayed across the room like a movie star and approached me.

Stacy quickly caught our attention as we observed the interaction between mother and daughter. They were staring at me. The other partygoers, who were unfamiliar to me, were also checking me out. However, the karma coming from Stacy and her mother, who kept glancing over at me gave me a bad feeling. Stacy was dressed to kill in a black hugging Versace dress with slits down both sides. It wasn't one of those raunchy-looking dresses that made her look like a whore. The dress was tasteful as far as I was concerned. I was thinking, *who knows, I just might get one of those bad boys but in a different color.*

"Don't pay them any mind. The hater aid is in full effect tonight," Tara said.

"I can see," I replied, as a young couple I was familiar with walked over and said hi.

R. Kelly and Jay-Z's *The Best of Both Worlds* was playing when the deejay flipped the script and started playing the black dancing anthem…the electric slide. The dance floor got crowded as several of the old and young players started doing their thing as well as the man of the hour.

I wasn't about to be left out and neither was Tara. We started to boogie-woogie to the electric slide. Out of the corner of my eye, I spotted Jason eyeballing me. He hadn't said a word to me ever since Robert told him to leave me alone. I began scanning the room to see where Robert was. I spotted him talking with Marques through the glass doors which separated most of the partygoers from those who wanted to relax away from the loud music. I knew Jason was up to no good because he continued staring at me. The next thing I knew he was in my face.

"Let me tell you something," he snarled, as I tried to get the attention of the young man serving the drinks. "I don't give a fuck about Robert and what he told you. You're gonna give me the pussy whenever I want it. That's how it's going down, bitch! Your pussy doesn't mean a thing to him. He fucks bitches like you a dime a dozen. You're just another fucking trick!"

"So why the fuck you all up in my face wanting to fuck this trick then, bitch? The last time I checked, let me see, isn't that your trick Stacy over there? For someone who has fucked two tricks from the same family you sure have a lot of nerve. You're a fucking pussy, Jason! Do you think I didn't know you were fucking Stacy and her mom? You grimy mutha-fucka!"

"You fucking little bitch! I guess you must have forgotten about Professor Charles, huh? Does New York University ring a bell?"

"You mutha-fucka, you better leave him alone. I can't stand your fucking ass!"

"How long have you been fucking your professor? Forget it, it doesn't matter because you'll be fucking me whether you like it or not. Before I leave let me say this. If anything happens to Charles, you'll only have yourself to blame because a slut is a slut of course."

"You pussy ass mutha-fucka!" I yelled as several of the guests turned to see what all the commotion was about. I threw my drink on his ass and tried to bust him upside his head with a Moet bottle. He had a menacing look on his face. He was about to take a swing at me when Robert and Marques pulled him away.

"Don't let that nigga stress you. He's gonna get what's coming to him," Tara said, taking me aside.

"I know, I know," I answered, not fully comprehending what she meant.

I was mad as hell. Tara tried her best to get me back into the vibe. My Versace dress was a bit damp from the Moet but other than that everything was fine.

I was wiping the Moet from my dress when Robert said to Jason, "What the fuck is wrong with you? I can't believe you would do some shit like this at Uncle Andre's party. Did you want to hit her? What the fuck is up with that?"

"Fuck that! That bitch is disrespectful!" he shouted.

"She's not a bitch and you need to tone that shit down. I told you once before to leave her alone and I'm not gonna say another word about it to you!"

"Funny how you weren't saying any of this shit before now all of a sudden she's not a bitch, huh?"

"I told you don't refer to her as a bitch!" Robert snapped.

Marques, who was watching the whole thing unfold grabbed Robert who was about to throw a punch.

"I'm cool," Robert said to him.

"You sure?"

"Yeah, I'm good. You know what Jason?" Robert said, turning to him. "I'm done."

"Whatever man, whatever you say," Jason scoffed.

"Is the shit squashed? Are you cool Jason?" Marques asked, and Jason nodded his head.

"Damn, I can't believe this fool would start some shit over some pussy. You know what I'm saying, Marques?" Robert remarked. "He's doing all this shit in front of Uncle Andre, Jimmy, and their clients and connections, come on, man."

"Fuck you, Robert!" Jason snapped.

"Calm down Jason," Marques retorted, as he walked him outside.

"Maybe some fresh air will wake his dumb ass up," I said to no one in particular.

Nothing spectacular happened after the run-in between me and Jason. Andre cut his cake as a bunch of professional drug traffickers clapped, drank, and danced their asses off. Quite a few of the young men had their eyes on me and Tara, but I guess they respected Robert and Marques, and that put a stop to them taking it any further. The old players were another story. They were flirting at every opportunity and the women they were with acted as if they approved of their behavior. Andre made eye contact with me on a few occasions and those were eyes I wasn't going to mess with, especially at his party. I certainly didn't want to get Jackie all riled up.

It was about four-thirty in the morning when the party ended. I was more than thrilled because I was tired, bored, and ready to take my ass home. As I finished my last glass of Krug, I noticed Robert having a lengthy conversation with Andre, Jimmy, Jason, and three other men. The two Latino men doing most of the talking weren't familiar to me. I knew the other guy was a Jamaican, who went by the name King. I could tell they were discussing some really important business because they were sitting in the farthest corner of the room away from everyone else.

As I sat talking with Tara about that fool Jason, she told me to keep an eye on Robert.

"Girl," I said, "I've told you the deal. Although I'm ripped right now, I'm just going with the flow."

Tara was sober and was trying to get Marques's attention. He was busy making sure that both Andre and Jimmy had their usual number of bodyguards before noticing Tara whom he waved at and nodded.

"Are you and Marques leaving now?" Robert asked, after the conversation between him and the men ended.

"Not yet, but we'll be outta here in a minute," Tara answered.

"Well, Dana and I are about to get up outta here."

Before we said our goodbyes, Tara pulled me aside and said she had overheard Jimmy earlier telling the Latino men that somebody in the crew could be trusted and would be a great addition.

"So, did you hear their response?" I asked.

"They said they could use somebody like that. That's the last thing I heard because they lowered their voices when they noticed me. They had to be talking about Robert, Jason, or Marques."

"I guess somebody is about to get paid."

"I hope it's Marques so I can get paid too."

"Hey, what's up with y'all long-ass conversation?" Marques asked, approaching us. "Let's go!"

"See you later. Call me," I said, hugging Tara.

The ride back to the city was quick, which was good. I was feeling tipsy and all I wanted to do was get in bed. It must have been the alcohol because Robert drove right by my apartment and pulled up in front of his place. The funny thing was I didn't mind one bit. It had been a while since I was at his apartment.

As I entered, I began checking every crevice and corner to see if there was anything, I should take notice of. Unfortunately, I didn't find anything unusual that caught my attention. You know how guys are; they tend to get rid of their mistress's pictures, clothes, and other females' paraphernalia before inviting another girl over.

He still had the pictures we took together in Central Park. Two were on his dresser in his bedroom. The others were on his bookshelf in his living room. Was I impressed by this? Yes and no. Yes, because I thought he had gotten rid of the pictures. And no, because he could have put the pictures up earlier that night knowing he was going to try and convince me to come over.

I was in bed tipsy and horny. He wanted to make love. But I wasn't in a loving mood. The alcohol was in my system and all I wanted was pure unadulterated fucking and that's what I did. He was putting it on me with that magic stick of his. I wasn't holding back either. We were all over the bedroom. I gave it to him in every conceivable position that you can imagine. He had me going out of my mind and I surrendered my pussy to him like a captured soldier. We finally came after an hour of wild sex and fell asleep.

He drove me home later that afternoon. He was being nice, and I knew something was up, but I just couldn't put my finger on it. He was a bit upset that I wanted to go home. Nonetheless, we got in bed and fell asleep once we got to my apartment. I slept most of the day and I certainly wasn't in the mood to go anywhere that Saturday night.

Jenny called and said she wanted to hang out at the new nightclub called the Dome. It was located on Fourteenth Street between Ninth and Tenth Avenues. I heard the Dome was the place to be because it not only had a chic crowd but the Timbs, sneakers, hoodies, and baseball hat-wearing crowd wasn't allowed. I lied and told her that I had been hanging out with several of my co-workers until five o'clock in the morning and that I had a hangover. She started making fun of me and said I sounded like Barry White.

"Sure, you right," I said, laughing.

"I guess I'll just kick it with Ebony and Greg then." She chuckled.

"Oh, y'all three were going? Hmm, you're a bad girl."

"I know. You know that offer is still open, don't you?"

"What offer?"

"The one to come and hang with me and my peeps."

"No doubt, I will," I said, giggling.

"Bitch, you better. Ever since Ebony saw your picture, she's got the hots for you. She's got it bad like Usher."

"She does?"

"Yeah, so don't forget to come by and do the damn thing."

"I will boo, don't worry."

"Take care and get some rest. I'll get back to you. Love you," she said, hanging up.

"Love you too."

When I finally got my lazy ass out of bed, lying on my dresser was a note from Robert. I had been snoring like crazy when he kissed me on the cheek and said something about, "I'll call..." That was the last thing I remembered.

"Baby," the note started, "I have to make a run to Virginia with Jimmy. I'll be back on Friday. I'll call you. Love you."

I still didn't know what to make of Robert. But I felt somewhat special that maybe things would change for the better. But I quickly dismissed the thought. After washing my ass, I ordered a medium pizza with extra cheese from Pizza Hut. I certainly wasn't in the mood to do any cooking. I devoured several slices in a matter of minutes. I then began thinking of an excuse to give Charles for not showing up on Friday. I had promised him I would. I thought about showing up at his door. But at the last second, I decided against it. I figured I would see him the next day. I was going to try and be honest with him. At least that's what I thought.

Episode 15

The next day as I drove to Charles's apartment my mind was working overtime. Several scenarios and endless stories flashed through my mind as I thought about what to say to him that would make sense. After a while, none of the stories made any damn sense to me, and as I pulled up on his block, I was surprised to find a parking space in front of his building. Normally, I would have to circle the block a few times before finding parking. After stepping off the elevator on the third floor, I heard the soulful voice of Jaheem singing I Should Be Your Lover. *Cool, maybe he's in a good mood*, I said to myself.

I knocked on the door and there was an eye peering at me through the peephole. I couldn't believe he hadn't opened the door. *He's got a bitch in there, that's why he won't open it*, I thought.

I knocked even harder, and the eye appeared once again at the peephole. "Who is it?" he asked.

I was tempted to say a lot more than my name, but I held back. "It's me, Dana."

"What's up, babes?" He opened the door and gestured for me to come in.

"Nothing," I remarked, my eyes roaming all over his apartment.

"Give me a minute; let me turn the music down."

"Yeah, I think you need to. I guess you had company before I got here, huh?" I sarcastically asked.

"No, not at all, I've been waiting for you along with Jaheem since Friday. What happened to you on Friday? I thought you were supposed to stop by. Isn't that what we agreed on? I canceled all my other engagements and waited on you for several hours. You never showed up, nor did you call. What happened?"

"It's just that some unexpected things came up. I was wrong for not keeping my word."

"You know what? I'm not even gonna ask what the 'unexpected' things were. All I'm gonna say is that it's time for you to keep it real. Don't look at me as if you're surprised, I used the word 'real'. I can tell you wanna laugh, so go ahead."

"You're changing on me," I said, giggling.

"How is that?"

"The last time I was with you, you were using words such as dayum, waddup, and other slang. And now you want me to keep it real? You're losing it!" I said, turning on his plasma television.

"Hey, you're the one who grew up in wealth, not me. I grew up in the hood. I'm more hood than you."

"Yes, you are. You're all hood and it's big and long, so it's all good." We both laughed.

"See," he said, "you're always making me laugh. But I'm serious though babes. We need to keep it real. Do you love me?"

"Yes, I do. I love you."

"So, if you do why do you carry on the way you do?" he asked, as I looked on clueless.

"Okay, I'm having some problems with an ex-boyfriend of mine. He's obsessed. He's been threatening me, and my friends and I just didn't want it to become your problem. This guy is crazy and jealous. He's even tried to hurt several of my friends in the past, especially the guys. I didn't wanna bring all this drama into your life."

"So why don't you call the cops?"

"I've tried that," I replied, lying through my teeth but I had to. At least some of what I was saying were half-truths. "He's never actually hurt anyone, but I wouldn't put it past him."

"I hope he didn't follow you here."

"No, I made sure of that. But from now on I'm gonna keep it real as you said."

"Good, come here."

I slowly walked over to him. He held me close and gently kissed my lips. It was so refreshing, unlike the deep throat tongue-twisting kisses that I was used to. This kiss was soft and smooth. There's a time and a place for everything and being in his arms as he held me certainly was the right time and place and it was sweet.

He took a shower and got dressed. It was a rather brisk day, but we decided to walk to Central Park. We held hands and talked about how beautiful life is when two people are truly in love. I was so in love with him, that I wanted to cry. I knew I didn't want to lose him. However, I needed some closure from the Playaz Club, and come hell or high water, I was going to get my man. I sure wasn't going to let them deny me my true love, something that I had been looking for most of my young life.

I wanted this moment with him to last forever. I dreaded going back to my apartment and the lifestyle of being a drug mule.

The whole day was fun. We went to the movies and ate at Red Lobster. We kissed, laughed, and hugged. It was simple and romantic, and I loved that. He was so irresistible I couldn't stop myself from playing with his dick at the movies and in Red Lobster.

Robert and I used to do things like this before I found out who he was. He was trying and it did seem genuine, but something was missing. I didn't get that spark that feeling inside like I used to. It's a special person and a certain touch that will have your coochie, tits, and mind in sync all at the same time.

The only time my coochie jumps when I'm around Robert now is when he gets me horny and wants to fuck. He has a big dick. He is bigger than Charles. However, I need more than a big dick to satisfy me and Charles certainly offered me that and more.

I stayed the night with Charles and although I wanted him, I held back and so did he. The great thing about Charles was that he never acted as if he was upset if we didn't make love every time, we were together. Not once did he push the issue or make any attempts to pressure me.

The chemistry between us was sky-high. I guess we both realized that holding, kissing, and caressing each other sometimes bring out certain hidden emotions that go well beyond the sexual act itself. When the emotions are combined with the sexual act, damn, you wind up doing things out of character. And it's only after you've done the act that you ask yourself, *did I do that?*

***

I got back to my apartment sometime around mid-afternoon the next day. I didn't notice anything unusual as I walked toward my bedroom. However, a strange feeling came over me. I had a gut feeling that something wasn't right. I nervously tried to make my way back to the living room when I suddenly heard a voice and felt a fist smashing into my face. I screamed at the top of my lungs but was hit in the back of the head and told to keep quiet. I feared for my life after hearing several other voices and as I fell to the floor, I was momentarily stunned. My vision was blurred but I desperately tried to see who my attackers were.

"Bitch shut the fuck up! You know you a dead bitch, right?" snarled the man whom I believed punched me in the face. Whenever he spoke you couldn't help but notice his platinum-filled mouth. He spoke aggressively as he helped me up off the floor.

"What did I do?" I managed to ask, sobbing.

"It's not what you did, it's what you didn't do, bitch!" he angrily said.

"Let's get this shit over with. Kill that bitch!" yelled one of the other men whose features I couldn't make out because he wore a nylon stocking over his face as did his two partners. I did notice that he was the tallest of the three.

"Please don't kill me!" I kept repeating, as I felt my swollen face.

"You a pretty little bitch ain't you?" the man with the platinum-filled mouth asked. "You probably think you all that, don't you?"

I was at a loss for words. I tried to speak but it seemed like I had lost the ability to do so.

"I like to slice pretty bitches' faces," he continued.

The tall brother grabbed my face. I felt the cold steel from the blade in his hand. He then rubbed the blade slowly against my cheek.

"Oh God, please don't do this to me!" I begged.

"Yo, don't fuck with her face," said the shortest of the three men. He hadn't said much up to that point. His demeanor exuded an authoritative presence. His tone of voice was calm, yet firm. I was scared. I thought I was going to die.

"Help me! Help me, please!" I wailed.

"Bitch, there's no help for you!" warned the brother with the fake ass platinum in his mouth.

He began tying my arms and legs as snot ran from my nostrils. He was about to remove my pants when I started yelling. "This bitch!" he angrily said, viciously slapping me across my face. He was about to rape me, and I was powerless to prevent it. My panties were off. He removed his underpants with his dick dangling in my face.

"What the fuck you doing?" yelled the short brother who seemed to be in charge. "What the fuck is wrong with you? This ain't about raping her. Put her shit back on."

"Fuck that let her put that shit on herself!" the brother with the platinum grill snapped. That was the last thing I recalled. They beat me and left me tied to a chair.

I awoke two days later in Lenox Hill Hospital, lucky that nothing was broken, nor was I raped. However, I was in a lot of pain.

I guess somebody did hear my screams after all. Minutes after my attackers left me bloody and beaten my inquisitive neighbor, Ms. O'Neal called the cops. This was one time when her being nosey paid off and it probably saved my life. The cops found me naked, tied up, and unconscious.

Robert was at my bedside immediately. Tanisha, India, and Monique showed up as well. Jenny and Tara always showed up together. Despite my ordeal, I was praying that Robert and Charles wouldn't show up at the same time, and thank God they never did.

While I was in the hospital, Robert found me a new apartment on Fifty-Fourth Street and Seventh Avenue. There were a lot of questions to be asked and I wanted them answered. I wasn't going to tolerate the bullshit. I almost died and Robert was the first on my list of suspects.

"What do you know about this shit?" I asked him. "Who did this to me? You do know, don't you?"

"How would I know who did this to you, was I there? Why would you say that? I'm trying to figure this thing out myself."

"You were the only one who had keys to my apartment."

"I would never do that to you. Sure, I have a set of keys, the keys that you gave me. How many times have you been home alone? A lot, right? So why didn't I do this to you a long time ago? Come on Dana it makes no sense. Do you think I would do some shit like this? Then go out and find you an apartment? Come on now!"

"Anything is possible. You keep saying you wouldn't do this, and you wouldn't do that to me. Yet I can't leave this fucking organization! You mutha-fuckas have…"

"Oh, now I'm a mutha-fucka?" he asked, cutting me off.

"Yeah, you're a mutha-fucka! You and your drug-dealing friends have threatened me and my friends. You Robert! Yeah, you, you've put me through a lot."

"Dana, I'm telling you the truth. I had nothing to do with this. I love you. Goddamn it! Why the fuck would I do this, or have someone do this to you?"

"Yeah, right, just like you told Jason he could fuck me."

"Damn, must we go through that again? I told you before that I was wrong for doing that."

"I bet it's Jason."

"You're delirious. Calm yourself down."

"Delirious? Calm down? Fuck that! It's him, isn't it? Answer the question!"

"I don't know. But I'm gonna find out although I doubt it."

"Why do you doubt it, because he's family?"

"No, that's not it. This is not his style. He doesn't roll like that. In all the years that I've known him, he would rather be ghost than do some shit like this to you."

"I don't give a fuck what his style is or him being ghost. He's gonna pay big time if he did this to me, believe that," I said, meaning every word.

After several hours of talking and making a few calls, he managed to calm me down and convinced me that he doubted it was Jason. He went as far as to contact Jimmy, who said he would call a meeting to get things straightened out.

A few days later the girls came to visit and right away they blamed Robert for my hospitalization.

"Leave that man alone. You need to get the fuck away from him," they would say. They knew that I was sleeping with him and that he was the only one besides me who had a key to my apartment. So, they figured it had to be him who set me up, which made a lot of sense. I wasn't angry at them for taking that position.

"Robert got me a new apartment. Doesn't that mean something?" I asked them. They stared at me and rolled their eyes.

They knew nothing about the Playaz Club, or that I was an involuntary drug mule because of the threats made against me. Jenny didn't even know that our lives were at stake and Charles' as well. They didn't understand and there was no way in the world I could just walk away, not now.

Somehow, I managed to calm everybody down after telling them that according to the police my apartment was forced open without a key being used. They used a special tool to jimmy-lock my apartment door. This was quite troubling to me. *How could that be,* I asked myself.

I used my key to let myself in that afternoon and I certainly didn't notice anything unusual at all. The door didn't look as if it had been tampered with. I guess I was so overwhelmed with Charles and the way he treated me that night that I overlooked something as important as my safety.

It was only after getting out of the hospital and returning to the old apartment that I realized that someone had tampered with the door. I was glad that no one had purchased my apartment and fixed the door, or I wouldn't have seen it with my own eyes.

Robert was upset at Jenny and the others. I convinced him not to pay any attention to what they had said because they were only looking out for my best interest.

I said to him as we spoke on the phone, "How would you react or feel if your friends from the Playaz Club didn't support you in your time of need? You would be pissed, right?"

"Yeah, I guess you're right. But damn, you make it sound as if they wanted to beat my ass and I don't even know them."

"Don't sweat it. I'll call you later, bye."

I called Charles. He was angry at the way things turned out. "It's that mutha-fucka that you told me about, isn't it? That crazy ex-boyfriend of yours," he snapped.

"I don't know," I retorted. "It could be, but I'm not sure. I couldn't see their faces. But I'm quite sure he wasn't one of them."

"So, who else could it be? Do you have any other enemies?"

Kenny came to mind but knowing him, he would have certainly wanted me to see his face. So, I never bothered mentioning his name.

"I'm not gonna stand by and watch all this bullshit and not lift a finger to help you. This is ridiculous!"

"I know the cops are working on it, so hopefully they'll catch whoever did this to me," I said, hoping that would calm him down.

"Good. I hope they do. So how have you been feeling lately?"

"The swelling and the pain are gone. I believe I'm back to my old self. I think I'm in the mood for some dick right about now. Oh, let me rephrase that, I'm in the mood for your dick."

"Yeah, I need you too."

"I'll be over later tonight. If you play your cards right, you just might hit the jackpot."

"I love what I'm hearing."

"Hmm," I said. "Oh, let me call you back."

"What happened? Is it something I said?"

"No, I have to go and deal with these snotty ass people from the Coop Rent Board."

"Okay, you do that and call me once you're through."

"I will boo, love you."

"Love you too."

Episode 16

$\mathcal{A}$ fter my conversation with Charles, I met up with Tara at her apartment. We were glad to see each other as we hugged.

"I hope they find out who did that shit to you. I was kicking it with Marques, and he says he doesn't believe Jason had anything to do with it," Tara said.

"Robert pretty much convinced me that Jason had nothing to do with it and he said that he was gonna prove it. I guess this is the reason why he set up this meeting with Jimmy."

"Wow, Robert called a meeting for you?" Tara had a stunned look on her face. "You're going places, huh?"

"Should I be happy about this?" I was trying to make sense of what she said.

"Damn, this negro is open. I don't think he's playing you. Just remember what I told you, okay?"

"Yeah."

"Just don't sleep, but it looks like the brotha is for real."

Hmm, I said to myself, reaching for one of her Newport cigarettes.

"Bitch, you don't smoke. I ain't giving you my cigarette. These shits are expensive." We both laughed.

"I need something," I said.

"You might be right, but it doesn't sound like you need a cigarette. What you need is some dick."

"Girl, you're so right." I laughed.

Tara suddenly got serious and said, "Don't worry; the boys will get those bitches."

"I know," I exclaimed, as we left for the meeting.

The faces at the meeting were unlike the smiling jovial ones at Andre's birthday party. They were seated in Jimmy's spacious living room chitchatting when I walked in. The stern looks etched on their faces were visible. I was rattled. My nerves were getting the best of me. Nevertheless, Tara told me to remain calm, before telling me who they were.

Although she didn't know all of them personally and she wasn't familiar with their faces, once their names were called, she knew who they were because Marques had mentioned their names on numerous occasions.

The living room was decorated with some of the finest paintings I had ever seen. They were paintings of African, Asian, Caribbean, European, and Latin American lifestyles, and faces, which adorned the walls. Jimmy also had some of the finest Italian furniture along with wall-to-wall carpet.

"This is nice," I said to Tara. "Is this his place?"

"Yeah, one of four."

"Get the fuck outta here!" I said looking around.

There he was sitting next to Stacy as I walked by. I purposely kept eye contact with him to see what his reaction would be when he suddenly got up from his seat. My first reaction was to run in the opposite direction fearing another beating.

Instead, he walked over to me and said, "Dana, I'm sorry about what happened to you. I wanted to visit you at the hospital, but I was advised not to. I'm sorry about your ordeal and I do hope you're doing well."

"Thank you," I replied, feeling uncomfortable.

He was eloquent and charming, yet it scared me. I was surprised at how pleasant and soft-spoken he was. He sounded sincere but I thought it was all a ploy. The majority of those at the meeting greeted me and wished me well. However, I got the impression that Stacy was pressured into saying hello. Her acting skills weren't up to par to start with. It was a charade, a facade. But like I said things like that didn't bother me. What did was how after saying hello, she waltzed right over to Jason and cuddled up next to him as if they were Siamese twins. It was as if she wanted to make me jealous, please.

"Dana, there goes Ms. Jackie, but where is Andre? I don't see him," Tara said, through pouted lips.

"Oh, yeah," I said, as Jackie waved at me with her fake-ass hello and blew me a kiss.

I immediately had a flashback to the stares that Andre would give me. I was paranoid. *His stares didn't mean a thing. Why he would want to kick my ass or threaten me?* I thought, trying to convince myself. It just didn't make any sense, so I downplayed the thought.

While Tara and I continued with our conversation, the topic turned to Babs and Tiffany.

"It doesn't look like Babs and Tiffany will be hitting the streets anytime soon," Tara said.

"Word?"

"Yeah, they ain't got no bail and this is like their third arrest for the same shit."

"Damn, that's fucked up. I hope they don't get an ass-hole full of time. What about Jimmy and them?" I asked, but I was abruptly cut off by Jimmy's booming voice.

"People, we have some serious fucking issues to deal with!" he blurted out with a serious look on his face. Jimmy had a way of getting people's attention with that voice of his. Everyone was attentive as I looked around the room. "Now, Dana was...where is she? Okay, there she is. A few people here believe there was a conspiracy behind the unfortunate incident that led to her hospitalization. Let me say this. This is my fucking organization. I'm the Grand Puba, the boss, whatever the fuck y'all wanna call it. I don't like the idea of shit going down without my knowledge if it did.

What happened to Dana should not have happened especially when there are allegations that members here might be involved. What the fuck y'all think I'm running here, a fucking circus? Do I or anyone here look like Bozo the fucking clown? Huh, tell me?" The place was strangely silent as Jimmy continued. "Dana, Tara, Babs, Tiffany, Stacy, and a few others have contributed mightily to our organization. And though there are some things that we tolerate and y'all know what the fuck I'm talking about, threatening, beating, or trying to kill another member is not and will not be tolerated in this mutha-fucka. Do I make myself mutha-fucking clear?"

Everyone nodded in agreement as Jimmy carried on. "I will personally deal with the mutha-fuckas who did this to Dana when they are found. Oh yeah, you will be found. If anyone of y'all set that shit up there's no getting around it."

The reaction from Jackie and Stacy didn't surprise me at all. They had a slight smirk on their faces as Jimmy finished up. Overall, Jimmy addressed the situation in its entirety, and I knew some of the members were furious that he called an impromptu meeting on my behalf and that they had to cancel their other commitments to be there. From the looks I was getting, I could tell they thought Jimmy was sleeping with me.

"This fucking meeting is closed! Now get the fuck outta my house!" Jimmy barked.

He then approached me and reassured me that any inkling I have of Jason being involved in something like that was way off base and out of character. He added that he would personally find my attackers.

"I know him, Dana," Jimmy remarked. "And he would never do anything like this. He and Robert are like my sons. I will go as far as to say that he has done some dumb things but who hasn't?"

"I understand. I believe you."

With that said he kissed me on the cheek and told me that Tara would fill me in on our next assignment along with Stacy. I told him it wouldn't be a problem. He then approached Robert and whispered something in his ear. Robert smiled, nodded, and shook his head. Whatever he said it must have been all right with him. I could tell that Robert was relieved from the look on his face.

"How are you?" Robert asked, smiling as he approached me.

"I'm cool."

"See this is how we do things around here. If there's a problem we get together sit down and try and resolve whatever it is. I wanted you to know that I supported you. I didn't want to give you the wrong impression in your time of need. This is a serious matter, and this is how things are supposed to work. We take care of our own and as Jimmy said, whoever did this will pay. If they were here tonight this certainly gave them something to think about. To be honest, I believe you. Someone set you up and I think it's someone here."

"Thanks, Robert. I don't know what to say. You went out and did the damn thing."

"What can I say? But what you can do is start treating me better with your fine-ass self. I know I shouldn't say this, but when you were in the hospital you looked damn hot. And although you were tore up from the floor up, I wanted to do you."

"You're crazy. You are." We laughed. "I have some unfinished business to take care of downtown. I'm gonna ride with Tara. Is that okay with you?"

"Sure, just hit me on my cell when you're done."

"Okay," I said, as Jackie almost bumped into me.

"Bye, Donna. Oops, I mean Dana," Jackie said in a sarcastic tone.

"Bye," I uttered under my breath. I wanted to slap her. But being the lady that I am, I left it alone.

"Dana, where did Tara go?" Marques asked, looking around.

"She was just standing here."

"You tell her to wait right here," he said, walking away.

"Tara," I yelled from across the room, "are you ready? Marques said to wait for him here."

"Yeah, I'm ready. Give me a second. I need to know what this fool is gonna do later," she said, shrugging off most of what I said.

"That was quick. What the fuck did y'all talk about?" I asked her when she returned.

"Dang, you a nosey ass bitch," she said, laughing.

"I ain't nosey. He was asking for you as if he had something important to tell you."

"Come on, let's get the fuck outta here," she smiled, blowing Marques a kiss.

Episode 17

C harles was waiting for me in the hallway of his apartment complex when I stepped off the elevator. I felt like a child as I ran into his arms sobbing.

"It's okay," he consoled me. "It's going to be alright."

I heard every word he said. However, I was so out of it emotionally. My emotions had taken full control of my mind, body, and soul. He walked me inside the apartment, and we cuddled for several minutes before removing our clothes. We were standing naked in his living room holding each other. Our lips locked and he began kissing me slowly. He stared into my eyes as his tongue danced its way over my teeth and into the farthest corners of my mouth. I reciprocated by sucking his tongue. His hands slowly began to explore my body.

I felt his hard dick between my legs. I moved my hips and he eagerly entered me. He moved in and out with powerful strokes. He held my ass in his muscular hands as I tried to balance myself. My legs were tired and shaky as we moved at a rhythmic pace. It felt so good. I ran my hands over his bare chest.

Then in one motion, he lifted me off the floor. I held him tight around his neck with my legs wrapped around his waist and began meeting his every stroke as hard as I could. His dick was deep inside me. We were sweating profusely. I felt another orgasm as I screamed his name and came all over his dick.

What he did next absolutely freaked me out. With his dick still inside of me, we walked to the kitchen. He would stop, gyrating his hips, and start walking again. He kept doing this until we were in the kitchen. How we got there, I don't know. It was awkward but we got it done.

Once inside the kitchen, he told me to bend over next to the glass table. It was thick and strong enough to support our combined weight. He slid his bulging "anaconda" inside me from behind like the Reggae dance hall star Elephant Man calls it and began humping, pumping, and stroking me at a fast pace. I held on for dear life. I grabbed the sides of the table, arched my back, and pushed back as hard as I could. He was moaning. I turned to look at his face which was writhing in pleasure as he exploded inside me. We lay on the table for several minutes before making our way to the living room couch, where we fell asleep.

The next morning after making breakfast he called me into the living room and spoke in a soft voice as he got on his knees, "Dana…" My head was spinning out of control and my mouth was dry. I was in shock as Charles with a beautiful diamond engagement ring in his hand continued. "You know I love you and you mean a lot to me. I want to cry every tear that you cry. I want to try every task that you try. I want to keep every memory that you have kept. I want to love you and be with you until death. Dana, I have wanted you from the first time I laid eyes on you. Will you be my wife?"

"Yes, I will!" I said, crying.

My whole life suddenly flashed in front of my eyes. Through the abuse, drugs, ass-kicking, lies, and deceptions, my life had been an uphill climb and now Charles, a college professor wanted me to be his wife. It was hard for me to grasp the moment.

I was crying and smiling all at the same time as my song kept playing over and over in my head. I believed that this was the start of things getting easier, brighter, and better. I couldn't keep my eyes off the ring. The two carats sparkled. I stayed another night with him. He wanted me to give up my apartment and move in with him. I told him that I would eventually. I reminded him that I was still a student at New York University, and he was still an instructor there.

"I'll find another teaching job. New York University isn't the only school," he remarked.

"You're right, but I wouldn't let you do that. If it comes down to it, I'll get a transfer."

"Don't worry everything will work out. I'm just wondering what you're going to say when your friends see the ring."

"None of your damn business, that's exactly what I'll tell them if they start getting too personal. Don't worry Charles, you said for both of us to keep it real and that's exactly how it's going to be. I love you and I want to be with you."

We did the nasty before I left that morning. There's nothing like getting a good hard dick in the morning before going to work or school, or in my case home. I had a lot on my mind as I drove home that morning. I knew I had to put things in perspective. The embellished stories and outlandish behavior had to end.

For one, Robert was still in my life. For God's sake, we lived together, if you could call it that because his ass was always at my place. But I was going to do whatever was necessary to keep my damn sanity, life, and man. *I'll hide my engagement ring from Robert. He won't know a damn thing about this. Once I get away from him, I'll be fine,* I told myself.

Once inside my apartment, I checked my home phone and cell messages. Jenny and Tara had left several messages along with Robert, who wanted to know where I was and for me to give him a call. I hadn't seen Robert in two days, and I could tell from the tone of his voice that he was frustrated. I wasn't going to be a fool anymore. After moving into the apartment, I changed the damn locks and refused to give him a key. Sure, he was angry, and he complained but I wouldn't budge. He was in love and love will make you do some foolish things. Despite everything I said about him, I returned his call. I told him that I was going to meet up with Tara and Stacy.

"Sure," he said. "Just make sure you hit me when you get back."

"Okay," I answered.

***

I met Tara and Stacy at the Robinson's home. We were greeted by Hally Robinson, who gave us the information we needed.

"Why would a corporate lawyer be involved in all this illegal stuff?" I whispered to Tara.

"Greed. It makes no sense and they got mad connections," she uttered with a straight face.

The tension between me and Stacy had reached its boiling point. I tried to be nice to her the whole time we were together because I didn't want to make a scene. But she had an attitude. Why I don't know. I said to myself, *I'm not gonna let her fuck up my money or my day. I'm just gonna do my part and leave the bullshit alone.*

We were driven to Kennedy Airport in separate vehicles and booked on the same flight to Texas. We were cautioned by the Robinsons to resist the temptation of talking or making eye contact with each other.

When the plane landed, I was whisked away in a taxi. Tara and Stacy left in two separate SUVs. I was a bit apprehensive and terrified because this was all new to me and it seemed dangerous.

I was driven to a hotel and taken to a room. Inside were Derek Robinson and Jamaican King. Within minutes, Tara and Stacy arrived. Derek Robinson and Jamaican King were doing most of the talking but they had a look of uneasiness on their faces as the minutes ticked away. Suddenly there was a knock on the door. Three men walked in dressed as if they were in a fashion competition with Sonny and Tibbs from the television series *Miami Vice.*

I quickly recognized one of the men. He was one of our contacts who were arrested by the Drug Enforcement Agency at Kennedy Airport. Tara and I immediately made eye contact and we both nodded in agreement that it was indeed him.

"Mami, how are you?" he asked, smiling at me and Tara.

"Fine," we both replied.

"Ahhh, that's good. My name is Ramon, what's yours?" he asked, focusing his attention on me.

"I'm Salt and this is Pepper," I said, pointing to Tara and completely ignoring Stacy. Derek and King looked on trying to make sense of the friendly chat between the two of us and the names I gave.

"Nombres bonito," he bellowed, snapping his finger.

After briefly talking to Derek and King, one of the men walked towards the window. He whispered into an earpiece. There was another knock on the door and in walked three Latina women with several briefcases. The men took the briefcases and opened them. Inside were several pounds of crystal-looking white powder secured in huge sandwich bags. Derek and King handed over three briefcases filled with cash to the men. Neither man bothered checking the product nor counting the money.

Damn, they didn't even check the product that's how they living, I said to myself. I certainly would have taken a look at my product and the cash. But I guess after years of doing business they trusted each other. The men took the briefcases and headed out the door with their small entourage.

"Adios Mami," Ramon said.

"Adios," Tara replied.

The drugs were transferred from the briefcases into suitcases which were specially built for this kind of transaction. We stayed the night and the next morning we were handed the suitcases and driven to the airport. Where we were placed on three different flights which were to arrive in New York City, give or take an hour or two apart.

I didn't notice anything unusual once we arrived in New York. Jimmy and Andre had paid a hefty sum to their airport connection and they made sure that things went as planned. Everything went well and I hopped in a cab, which was sent by the organization.

Stacy was already at the Robinson's home along with Derek and King when I got there. Several minutes later Tara showed up. We handed the suitcases over. Hally then handed us three yellow envelopes. As we left, Stacy's attitude still hadn't changed. She started making subtle remarks about me as if I weren't there.

Maybe she's upset because Ramon never paid any attention to her, I thought to myself. She was cool with Tara, but evidently, she had a problem with me. This was it; I wasn't going to put up with her bullshit any longer.

"Bitch, if you have something to say, say it!" I barked at her.

"Fuck you, bitch! I ain't got no time for you. You're trying to get where I'm at bitch!" Stacy said.

"Y'all need to stop this shit!" Tara yelled.

"Fuck that! Did you hear what this bitch said? I'm trying to get where she's at. This bitch is crazy!" I snapped.

"Crazy? Do you think I'm crazy? You're the one who was looking at my man, bitch! And when he refused you, you blamed him for the beat down you caught," Stacy scoffed.

She had said enough. I grabbed her and started throwing punches from every conceivable angle. I hit her with a bruising uppercut that snapped her head back. She got a few blows in. She hit me with a stinging left but it was nothing compared to the ass whipping she got from me. It wasn't funny but I beat her ass like Kenny used to beat mine. I was on her like a crackhead looking for a hit. She started crying and pleading for Tara to get me off her.

As Tara pulled us apart and calm me down, I hit her with a hook flush on the jaw. Stumbling, she didn't waste any time at all as she got in her BMW X3 cursing and calling me all sorts of names before driving off. Tara was laughing.

"You're crazy," she said holding her stomach from laughing so hard. "I've wanted to kick her ass for a long time. I'm glad you did. Shit, you were throwing down like a brotha. You went Sugar Shane on her ass." I couldn't help but laugh. I was tired of Stacy and the nonsense.

"Her mom is next that bitch is always staring at me," I exclaimed to Tara. "But enough of that, I have something I want to show you." I extended my hand to show her the ring.

"Oh, my God, that ring is off the chain! Don't tell me that negro Robert gave you that shit?" she asked, with a look of disdain on her face.

"No. It's from my secret lover the one from school. He's a cool brotha. We've been seeing each other for a while now and he loves me, and I love him. Girl, he went down on his knee and said the magic words."

"Really?"

"Yes, he did."

"So, when do you guys plan on getting married?"

"Maybe next year, that's what I'm working on right now because it's not gonna happen anytime soon."

"What about Robert? What are you gonna do about him? He still comes by, right?"

"He does but he doesn't have a key. I changed the locks."

"Good, you did the right thing. But what about the ring isn't he gonna be angry when he sees it?"

"Who says he's gonna see it? I'm gonna keep the shit on the down-low until I bounce."

"I'm with you on this. Do what you gotta do. Damn, that ring is hot."

"I know," I said, getting in my car and telling her to call me later.

Episode 18

I hadn't spoken to Jenny since I returned from Texas and instead of calling, I decided to visit her.

"What's up?" I said, entering the apartment.

"Nothing much, how have you been?"

"I'm fine."

"That's good. Oh, let me introduce you to my friends," she said, introducing me to Greg and Ebony. I had never met Greg before being introduced but she must have forgotten that I had met Ebony on two previous occasions. We were sitting on the couch talking when I noticed Greg and Ebony making out on the loveseat. You could tell they were seasoned exhibitionists as Greg kept staring at me.

As I sat there watching them explore each other, I was getting turned on. I had never watched another couple getting it on before. I was so caught up in their lovemaking that I didn't hear a word Jenny said.

"What did you say?" I asked, snapping out of my inner sexual thoughts.

She wanted to know if the police were still on the case and whether they had apprehended anyone.

"No, they haven't. Girl, I came to hang out with you. I don't want to discuss that right now."

"Okay, you right. What else is going on with you?"

"You don't notice anything different on me or about me?"

"You're smiling a lot. Your clothes are hot."

"Nope, not that!"

"I don't see a damn thing," she said, smiling.

"Look good," I remarked slowly shoving my left hand in front of her face revealing my engagement ring.

"Oh, shit! Is it what I think it is?" she asked excitedly.

"Yeah!"

"Dana, that is hot. I hope it isn't from that married dawg?"

"Nope, it's from Charles."

"Charles? Isn't that the professor?"

"Uh, uh."

"Oh, my God, this is great!" she screamed.

Greg and Ebony heard the screams and ran out of the bedroom naked wanting to know what all the commotion was about. Greg had some nerves as he stood in front of me with his big ass dick dangling in my face and pretending as if I wasn't there.

"My girl is engaged! Y'all look at that ring. Why don't you guys put on some clothes and stop running around here as if my place is a nudist resort or something," Jenny snapped.

As Greg headed into the bedroom with his fine self, I saw the disappointment on his face. He probably felt this was the perfect opportunity to invite me into his world of sex, toys, and freaks. From what Jenny told me, I knew he was dying to sleep with me, and it was written all over his face. Ebony didn't display as much sexual overture toward me as Greg did. Yet she made her feelings known by smiling, sticking out her tongue, and licking her lips whenever our eyes met. I thought about going into the bedroom and joining them, but I resisted the temptation.

"How do you put up with all that shit?" I asked Jenny.

"What shit? Them?" she asked, pointing at the closed bedroom door.

"Yeah, those two and the other things that you're going through like your business and the people you deal with every day."

"As for those two, they are what they are. You know I just take them as they are and pray for them." We both laughed. "When it comes to my business and those people, I deal with them just like you. I know when to go hood and when to keep it proper. Remember what Bradley said about you? He loved it when you switched from Ebonics to Standard English, and how it turned him on." I couldn't help but smile.

"Wasn't he something? I switch up all the time. I don't see anything wrong with going hood when you have to."

Greg and Ebony were now dressed, and they both agreed that the ring was fabulous.

"Thank you," I said, as they headed to the kitchen.

Jenny started messing with me. "I guess I won't be getting that coochie anymore, huh?"

"Who knows maybe you will and maybe you won't but never say never!"

"Yeah right, once you settle into married life, you'll be getting so much dick you won't remember this phat pussy," she exclaimed, laughing.

"You a nasty heifer, don't you have enough of both worlds?" I asked, trying to hold back my laughter. "You've got Greg and Ebony and you're still greedy."

"Oh no, you didn't just say that did you?"

"Yes, I did."

"You ain't right."

"I'll let you come and hang out with me and my husband but on my terms."

"Okay." She chuckled.

"I'm gonna go now. We have to do lunch. We need to talk."

"Sure, give me a call this weekend."

"I will," I said, as I hugged her and left.

***

On my way home I decided to make a quick stop at the corner deli. I bought a six-pack of Corona, some cold cuts, bread, and tampons. I was walking to my apartment when I noticed a white Cadillac Escalade parked behind my ride. The engine was still running. The windows were tinted, and it was dark which prevented me from seeing who was behind the wheel. As I fumbled with my door keys, I glanced across the street only to see Jason stepping out of the driver's side of the Escalade.

"What's up, Dana?" he hollered.

"Hey, what's up? What are you doing on this side of town?" I asked, with some anxiety.

I quickly entered the lobby hoping the door would slam shut on his ass. But he took several long strides entering before the door slammed shut.

"I figured why not stop by and see how you're doing." He grinned.

"I'm doing great," I exclaimed, praying my answer was good enough and that he would leave.

"I never got the opportunity to visit while you were in the hospital. I didn't want you to hold that against me," he said in a calm voice.

"Of course not! I'd never hold that or anything against you," I said, taking a deep breath. I was trying my best to remain calm. I didn't want him to see how nervous and scared I was. I pressed for the elevator and acted normal. "Well, as you can see, I'm fine, no pain, nothing. I'm feeling great."

I knew he wanted me to invite him up to my apartment. *What if I scream and he gets upset and pulls out a gun and shoots me right here in the elevator or the hallway,* I asked myself.

I decided to play nice. I began fumbling with my keys as we got off the elevator.

"Let me get that," he said, reaching for my bag of groceries. "Isn't this much better?"

"Yeah." I giggled, scared as ever.

I felt so uncomfortable with him inside my apartment. Luckily, he didn't notice my ring.

"Excuse me," I said, walking to the bathroom and hiding my engagement ring under some towels in the linen closet. I didn't want him to see the ring because I knew he would go running back to Robert.

"That was quick," he said when I returned.

"You know how it is sometimes. You think you wanna pee and then you get there and then you can't."

"Sure, that happens to me all the time."

He sat watching television as I made myself a sandwich. I thought about having a Corona but after thinking it over, I realized it wasn't a good idea. I feared it might lead to other things, which I wanted no part of.

"Care for a sandwich?" I asked.

"Yeah, extra mayo, thanks."

"Okay," I barely muttered.

"Aren't you gonna offer me a drink? How rude," he said, with a sigh.

"It depends on what you want to drink."

"What do you have?"

"I have orange juice, beer, milk, water, Alize, and Remy, which one do you want?"

"I'll have a beer."

I gave him a Corona along with his sandwich. He was doing most of the talking as I ate. I wished he had kept his mouth shut, eaten, and gotten the hell out of my apartment. I got an eerie feeling that my worst fears were about to come true. I dismissed the thought and remained optimistic that he would leave after a while.

"You know why I'm here, right?"

"You said you wanted to see if I was okay and I am."

"There's more to it than that."

"There's more? Why are you here then?"

"You forgot that quickly?"

"No Jason, come on. What about all that stuff you said at the meeting?"

"All of it was true; I had nothing to do with that."

"So, it's like that?" He didn't answer.

He slowly put the remaining half bottle of Corona to his head and guzzled it down. He had a menacing look on his face as he bit his bottom lip. I knew what his intentions were. I told him I didn't want to sleep with him and that my period was about to come at any minute.

"What, you're kidding, right? Until it gets here, I want some," he snarled.

I shook my head and replied, "No!"

"Bitch take your clothes off!" he said in a commanding and forceful tone.

Although I was used to the routine I began to cry as I stood in front of him naked. "Noooo, Jason, please don't," I pleaded.

"Get your ass over here on your knees!" he shouted.

I walked over to him and got on my knees. He unbuckled his pants, took out his dick, and told me to suck it. My whole body cringed as I began doing it. The worst part of it was that he kept staring in my face. He called me some of the nastiest names and slapped my face. I felt his member getting hard in my mouth. The name-calling was turning his freaky sick ass on.

"Suck my dick!" he kept repeating whenever I stopped. Then he yelled, "Get the fuck up bitch, and lie on your stomach." He said it in an eerie and twisted voice almost as if possessed. It scared me.

I begged him to use a condom, but he would have none of it. I couldn't bear to look as he forced himself inside me. My vagina was not only dry, but it was painful. I grimaced in pain as I was being raped. He was humping me fast and hard. He was sweating profusely.

"This is my pussy isn't it, bitch?" he asked, with wild-looking eyes. I was lying there speechless. He slapped my face every time he asked, "Whose pussy is this?" The tears began welling up in my eyes. "You like this don't you slut?" he smirked.

"No, I hate you!" I said, through the tears.

"Shut the fuck up! Does Robert fuck you like this?" he grumbled, slapping me even harder and pulling my hair. I said nothing. He then began choking me.

"Why, Jason? Why? What did I do for you to treat me like this? Why?" I begged, hoping he would stop.

"Does Robert fuck you like this? Say he doesn't."

"He doesn't. He doesn't!" I sobbed.

"Does the professor fuck you like this?"

"No, he fucks me better," I said, through clenched teeth.

"What? You little slut," he remarked, biting me all over my back. "He fucks you better, huh? Better than this?" He was like a wild man.

By now I was bleeding. He was bucking and rocking as he was about to release. He was breathing and sweating all over me. I thought he was finished after he came.

Believing he was satisfied and that he would leave I screamed, "I hate you! Get the fuck out of my apartment!" Only to end up on my back looking up at him from the slap he gave me.

"Shut the fuck up! I'm spending the night!" he barked at me.

My home phone rang several times, but he wouldn't let me answer it. He also had me turn my cell phone off. I was praying that Robert would show up, but that prayer was never answered. During the night he raped me repeatedly and violated me in every way possible.

Every once in a while, he would begin ranting. "If I had set your ass up, I would have killed you, bitch! I'm dead serious, but that's not my style. Do you wanna know why?" When he realized that I wasn't going to answer him he slapped me on my ass and said, "I love fucking you. You're a pro at what you do best and that's being a ho. Shit, you do me much better than that bitch Stacy. Besides, a little blood ain't gonna hurt you."

I was in a morbid state, physically I was conscious but mentally I wasn't. I gathered myself, grabbed my tampons, and ran to the bathroom. The whole thing was humiliating.

The rising sun found me sitting on the floor in my living room staring at nothing in particular. I couldn't recall what time he left. The only thing I remembered was him reminding me about Jenny and Charles's well-being.

Episode 19

I immediately called Charles after Jason left my apartment. I told him that I was going to fill in for one of my co-workers on the morning shift. He wanted to know if I was going to work my normal evening shift also. I told him yes. I lied once again. It seemed as if I couldn't stop lying to him. He said that he understood and for me to call him after work.

I called Jenny and canceled our weekend get-together for later that evening. She was fine with it. I also called Tara. I never mentioned Jason to her. Instead, I asked her if we had any runs to make. She informed me that we did have a night run to make in Jamaica, Queens.

"Cool," I said. "Holla at me later."

I was cleaning my apartment and nursing my wounds when I heard a knock on the door.

"There's a bell use it!" I yelled as I looked through the peephole to see who it was. It was Robert and I was somewhat hesitant about opening the door. However, I relented and let him in.

"Whaddup, girl?" he asked, with his usual trademark smile. "What are those marks on your face?" he asked, staring at the bruises.

"Nothing, me and India got into a fight with some girls."

"I'm telling you; you need to stop it. You're too old for that shit."

"Aren't you supposed to be at work?" I said, cutting him off.

"Yeah, but I called in sick. I had some unfinished business to take care of."

It was on my mind to tell him about Jason, but I didn't. I didn't want everybody to know what was going on in my personal life. And I certainly didn't want him to bother Jimmy any more than he had to. Moreover, I couldn't take the drama of having another meeting.

"I'm hungry. What do you have to eat? Aren't you gonna make some breakfast?" he asked.

"Nope."

"Why not?"

"Because you have two hands, and in case you didn't notice this is a broom, that's a vacuum cleaner and that's the window cleaner. I'm in the middle of cleaning, duh."

"Okay, okay, I got it. I'll make it myself. Do you want some?"

"No, but a cup of coffee would be nice."

"You got it."

Within minutes my apartment was filled with the smell of coffee, bacon, eggs, and sausages.

"Here you are," he said, handing me a cup of coffee. "Are you sure you don't want some of this great-smelling breakfast?"

The temptation was too much for me to resist. I fixed myself a plate and took a seat next to him at the kitchen table. As I sipped on the coffee there was some uneasiness on his face; his fingers slightly trembled as he softly tapped on the kitchen table.

"What's wrong?" I asked.

"Nothing. Okay, here." He handed me an envelope and then walked into the living room, sat down, and turned the television on.

I was curious as I slowly opened the envelope. Inside was a neatly folded sheet of paper filled with the smell of a fragrance which I couldn't distinguish, but it smelled great. I turned and glanced at him, but he refused to make eye contact with me. I quietly began reading.

Dear Dana,

I hear your voice in every sound that the wind makes. I see your smile even when I can't see your face. I hear your laughter in every step that you take. I can touch the expressions on your face. I can feel the warmth and love as we embrace. I will always remember the tenderness of your soft kisses whenever we caress. Whenever I'm with you, I pray the day will never end. You always greet me with a heart of warmth, kindness, and charm. Just to see that smile on your face brightens the sun, which illuminates the place.

I think of you every night and day. I have become so confused, not even B.B. King's lyrics can cure my blues. If I had the chance to love you again, I would fill your heart with joy and smiles instead of pain. You are love and love is my friend. Dana, I want you, all of you, from beginning to end.

Loving you forever,
Robert

I was flabbergasted, amazed, flattered, and suspicious.

"You wrote this?" I asked, walking into the living room.

"Do you like it?"

"It's nice, but the part that says, 'If I had a chance to love you again,' isn't it from Luther Vandross *Forever, For Always, For Love* CD?"

"Why? You heard that line before?" he said, laughing.

"Is it?"

"You don't believe I wrote it? But I did."

"You're a liar. Stop playing. You didn't write that part maybe the rest of it, but not that part."

"Okay, okay, you got me. It's from Luther's song. But damn the shit sounded cool, so I thought why not," he said, laughing even harder.

"You almost got it by me, almost."

"I know."

"Don't you know I'm one of Luther's biggest fans if not the biggest? Anyway, since you got busted what is this all about?"

"Everything that you read on that sheet of paper, I meant. I do care about you. I don't wanna come into your life and fuck it up and then be 'ghost like these young brothers like to say. I think I've done enough to you already and all I want to do now is to make amends and prove my love to you."

My first thought was to say no but after thinking it over, I said, "Alright." I wanted to see how far he would take this.

He then reached into his jacket pocket and pulled out a diamond ring. The diamond was the size of a baseball. It was at least five carats. It almost blinded me.

My eyes were transfixed on the bling when he turned and said, "Dana, I love you. Will you marry me?"

Surprised, shocked, and flabbergasted weren't even the right adjectives to describe how I felt. I thought to myself, *this must be a fucking joke, because nobody, I mean nobody will ever believe that two different men have proposed to me weeks apart.* I felt as if I was having an asthma attack. I hurriedly opened the window to my living room. I began inhaling the cool New York morning breeze trying to gather my thoughts.

"Are you serious, Robert?" I asked, my voice trembling.

"Yes, I'm sure. Is there a problem?"

"Maybe." The look on his face was one of disappointment.

"Then explain."

"It's not that I don't want to, but this is all so sudden. I need to think about this. This is a serious commitment, and I'm not quite sure if I'm ready."

"No, we don't have to get married right away. We can do it next year or the year after. Tell you what, you think about it and let me know. In the meantime, here, take the ring. I want you to wear it."

He took the ring and put it on my finger. Luckily, I still had Charles' ring hidden. I had the utmost respect for Charles, but his ring was nothing compared to the one that Robert put on my finger. Granted my boo was only making five figures and I didn't want to sound ungrateful or unappreciative. Nevertheless, the diamond Robert gave me was worth several thousand dollars. He could afford it; he was making six and seven figures, maybe even more.

This shit is da bomb, I kept repeating to myself.

As we continued talking, he began touching my ass and breasts. I wasn't turned on and it wasn't working. The rape was still on my mind. He put his hand between my legs and started rubbing my vagina.

"No Robert, not now."

"What's wrong?"

"I've just been thinking about school and my job."

"What about them?" he asked, with a puzzled expression.

"I didn't get the grades I expected. I thought I had done well on my finals, but I guess not. Also, they've cut my hours at work and this bitch ass supervisor of mine is behind it."

"You make enough money from the organization why do you put up with that job?"

For a second, I thought he had caught me lying, but I quickly responded by saying, "Like you, I need a real job, you know what I mean? You haven't left your stockbroker position, have you? Well, I've got to cover my ass too. Although I'm only a manager at Macy's I have to protect my interest."

"No doubt. Yeah, you're right." We laughed.

"No, I'm serious though. The shit that happened to me has left me scared. I'm still taking my medication and it makes me drowsy."

The lies were coming one after the other. He believed every word I said. He listened intently before adding, "It's cool." And he told me to take it easy and not stress myself out. He then went into the bedroom and fell asleep while I finished cleaning.

Later that afternoon, I made some steamed red snapper fish, salad, and brown rice. I ate, took a bath, got dressed, and waited for Tara's phone call. Robert was now awake, and he reminded me to be careful.

"Although you'll only be a decoy your pretty face and demeanor will come into play. If you happen to get pulled over by the police you must remain cool and assertive. But if shit doesn't look right get the fuck out there don't wait around or try to be a hero. This run is basically about poise and using your head."

"I got you," I replied.

He always knew the location of where the transactions would take place. He also knew who the mules were and the number of drugs or money that would change hands. Though they normally canvassed the areas where they did business things sometimes got out of control. As we left my apartment, he advised me to listen to Tara whose experience he thought would be helpful.

***

I was told to take a taxi to One Hundred and Twelfth Street and Eighth Avenue where I was supposed to meet up with Tara. I was somewhat surprised to see Troy when we arrived at our destination. I was under the impression that this run would only involve me and her. I was glad that Stacy wasn't there.

We were driven by a handsome young man whom I had never seen before to Hunts Point in the Bronx. There were several warehouses and junkyards strewn throughout the neighborhood. The place looked the same. Nothing much had changed since the last time I was there.

As our car pulled up on the block, which was dominated by several huge tractor-trailer trucks, we were met by a tough-looking Puerto Rican who looked like he hadn't shaved in days. Pretty Boy, the name I called the young man who drove us to Hunts Point said something to Tara that I couldn't make out. When I asked her what he wanted she said he mentioned something about Troy. I didn't pursue the matter beyond that. He gave us the thumbs-up sign and then drove off. The tough-looking Puerto Rican then led us inside this huge cold warehouse. There were stacks of meat all over the place. It smelled like a slaughterhouse for animals. Several men began lifting and loading a few crates which supposedly contained meat onto a black truck that had its engine running.

"Is there meat inside those crates?" I asked, Tara.

"No," she said, softly.

"Damn, that's a lot of drugs," I said under my breath.

"Yeah, this is a huge shipment. They've been waiting on this for a while now."

"So Troy is gonna drive this truck?"

"Hell, yeah!"

"What are we supposed to do?"

"Ride with him."

"That's it?"

"It sounds simple, right?"

"Yeah."

"But it's not we're his decoys. The organization has lost several shipments because some of the girls couldn't handle the intense pressure after being stopped by the boys. Stacy doesn't fuck with this part of the job. Many of the girls feel the same way."

"Why us then? Shit, this sounds dangerous, "I said, nervously.

"You know how they feel about you. They think you're fearless and you know how I roll already," she said, with a smile.

"But damn, I don't know."

"Our role is to be upfront in the truck to play it off. We have to get it through the tolls and the checkpoints that the boys set up along the way."

"Dressed like this?"

"You'll see."

"It sounds as if you've been through this before?"

"Last year we did two runs like this."

"Damn girl, I'm just gonna do whatever you do."

Troy was busy with the men, and now and then he would ask how I was doing. No sooner than the truck was loaded, Tara and I were led inside a storage room and handed two old white overcoats splattered with blood and some dirty-looking galoshes.

"Eww!" I yelled. "This overcoat is filled with blood and it smells, and these boots are uncomfortable. Couldn't they have given us some better shit?"

"Tell me about it. Come on, let's get back out there so we can get the hell outta here," Tara said.

Troy was dressed and waiting for us. When we got in the truck the stench was unbearable. We were about to drive off when the tough-looking Puerto Rican said something to Troy. As the truck rumbled out of the warehouse, it felt great as a rush of fresh air greeted us. We were on the highway heading to God knows where.

"I thought we were going to Queens?" I said to Tara.

"I guess they must have changed the plan. They do things like this all the time, don't worry about it."

"Okay."

As we pulled up to the Triboro Bridge toll booth, my legs began shaking. Since the 911 terrorist attacks, the police presence has been a constant. Their main objective was to safeguard the city highways and bridges and be a deterrent. Why we were taking such a risk was beyond me, and on this particular day, a large number of tractor-trailers were being stopped. I figured there was no way for us to get around such a large police presence. But as we got closer one of the police officers who had his eyes on our tractor-trailer smiled at me. I nervously returned his smile as Troy glared at me. At any second, I expected to hear the words, 'Open the trailer and get out.' I felt his eyes on me as we waited for the trucks ahead of us to go through the toll. I felt like he was deliberately trying to scare me out of my wits to have a reason to stop us.

Tara was calm and relaxed as Troy took care of the toll. We slowly began moving inch by inch. Once we were through the toll, I took a deep breath. I thought it was my beautiful smile that got us through, but Troy later explained to me that we were lucky.

"What do you mean we were lucky?" I asked, curiously.

"Didn't you see all that backed-up traffic? There's no way in the world they could have checked everything. Chalk it up to luck and being at the right place at the right time," Troy said.

We passed through three other checkpoints without any major problems as we headed to the Long Island Expressway. Matter of fact, two of the five officers I spoke to gave me their phone numbers without their sharp-eyed supervisors knowing. Boy was I glad when the truck finally turned off on exit 65. We then turned onto a deserted-looking street with several railroad tracks where we pulled into what looked to be another warehouse. I was so glad that everything went well. As crazy as this sounds, I have always felt we had a guardian angel watching over us.

Inside the warehouse were several vans and a group of men who immediately began unpacking the crates from the truck onto the vans. Once the vans were fully loaded, they were driven off the premises.

"Where are they taking them?" I asked Tara.

"Either to Connecticut, Westchester, or right here in Long Island. All this stuff will be distributed throughout the city."

No sooner had Tara answered me, I heard the familiar voices of Jimmy and Robert which startled me. Robert was with me the whole day and he never mentioned a word about showing up there. Yet there he was, and he got there before us.

"Great job, ladies," Jimmy gushed, as Robert nodded in agreement.

"Thanks," Tara and I smiled.

We then headed to the bathroom where we removed the filthy overcoats and galoshes. Jimmy, Robert, and Troy were laughing, smiling, and giving each other the thumbs-up sign when Tara interrupted them.

"I think it's time for us to leave you, gentlemen, alone," she said.

"Okay, there's a car waiting for you guys. The driver will also take care of you," Jimmy said.

"Cool, Jimmy," she replied. They were staring at her ass as she headed towards the door.

"Good work, Dana," Jimmy added, smiling.

"Thank you."

"Dana, I'll holla at you later," Robert said, with a serious look on his face.

"Sure."

Tara and I hopped into the waiting car. At the wheel was Pretty Boy who handed us two yellow envelopes. I could smell the scent of the crisp hundred-dollar bills as they traveled up my nostrils.

I could have sworn I saw Pretty Boy staring at Tara through his rearview mirror. It seemed as if she was trying hard to avoid his eyes. Maybe it was just my imagination, but I thought he had the hots for her.

Instead of having him take us home, we decided to catch a movie. We stopped at McDonald's to get something to eat as we contemplated which movie we were going to see. I called Charles to let him know that I was okay and that I would stop by his apartment later.

"I guess I was wrong," Tara said.

"About what?"

"Well, remember I told you they were either going to take all the drugs to Connecticut, Westchester, or leave it here in Long Island?"

"Yeah, what about it?"

"When we were leaving the bathroom after taking off those smelly ass overcoats, I overheard Jimmy telling Robert and Troy that the shit was going to Bathgate. I don't know if he was talking about the Bathgate in the Bronx or somewhere else."

"Who gives a fuck where they take it?"

"I was just curious that's all."

After the movie, we caught a cab and began discussing our roles in the Playaz Club, when Tara revealed to me that she was thinking about leaving Marques and the organization.

"How you're gonna do that and why now?" I asked.

"It's just that time, girl. Do you remember what that old female Civil Rights leader use to say back in the day?"

"Which one?"

"The one who said she was sick and tired of being sick and tired."

"Oh yeah, that was Fannie Mae. I remember that saying."

"Well, that's me and I'm sick and tired of this shit."

"You starting to sound like me, but you got to do what's best for you. I guess me and you are on the same page," I said, as the taxi sped up Broadway.

Episode 20

I was late for my appointment with Jenny. So instead of meeting her at Junior's, I called and told her that I was on my way to see her. I hadn't gotten enough sleep from the events of the day before and what Tara said. I was hoping that Jenny didn't have any company and thank goodness she was home alone.

"What's on your mind?" she asked, as I began crying. "What the fuck happened?"

"I was raped."

"Raped? By whom?" she asked, with a shocked look on her face.

"Jason."

"Who the fuck is Jason? Wait, isn't he the lawyer?"

"Yeah, Robert's cousin."

"That son of a bitch, I'm gonna get that mutha-fucka, you just wait."

"No!"

"What do you mean? Fuck that bitch, let me handle this shit."

"This has trouble written all over it, and I don't want you to get in any trouble."

"Did you call the cops?" she asked, clearly upset.

"No."

"No? What the hell is wrong with you? This is too much. First, you were assaulted and ended up in the hospital. You could have been killed and now this? This shit is starting to look and sound like the same kind of drama you went through with Kenny."

She was right, but I had to calm her down. I didn't want the cops getting involved. The timing wasn't right. Can you imagine if I had told her about the whole intricate plot with the Playaz Club and all the other things associated with it?

"Dana, this has to stop. You can't let these niggas use and abuse you. Fuck that either you call the cops, or I will."

"Noooo! I'll call them."

"I know you're not gonna call them. Why are you being like this?" she snapped.

"It's not that trust me. Will you please? He won't get away with it."

"I hope you're right. How long ago did this take place?"

"Recently."

"How long is recent?"

"I answered you," I said, with some annoyance.

I could tell she didn't like the body language I gave with my answer. I was not being rude, nor did I think I was being disrespectful. I just didn't want her to underestimate me. I knew I was going to take care of Jason but on my terms and I wanted her to understand that. For years, she had been my backbone; she had always been there for me. But this time it was all on me.

She wanted to know if I had spoken to Charles about the rape. I explained to her that I hadn't because I didn't want to put any added pressure on him. She said she understood. But knowing her as I did and for as long as I had, I knew she wasn't fully buying it. After finally convincing her that I would take care of everything she relented. It was only then that we changed the topic to our parents.

"I'm thinking about visiting my parents," she said.

"Are they okay?"

"Yeah, they're fine. You know that you fucked up, right?"

"What are you talking about?" I asked, with a puzzled look on my face.

"Your ass was supposed to be here the last time my parents visited me. What happened?"

"Oh, damn girl, I forgot about it! Why didn't you remind me?"

"I kind of figured you were busy with school and trying to get yourself together. That's the only reason why I didn't bring it up."

"You should have reminded me. I honestly had forgotten."

"Why don't you come with me?"

"Hmm, that sounds like an idea. Are you going anytime soon?"

"In about three to four months."

"Cool, I can deal with that."

"Are you sure? Don't front on me, bitch!"

"Nah, not this time! You know I was thinking about visiting myself."

"Okay, so it's a date."

"Yeah," I said.

As for my father, he was still with his young sweetheart and going through a lot of drama. He wanted to know if Jenny's parents had heard anything about me and as usual the answer was no. The time I spent with Jenny was quite helpful and fulfilling. The conversation and the whole atmosphere helped ease some of my problems. It was always like that whenever she and I were together. It seemed as if she knew which button to push to release my tension. I left her apartment feeling much better than when I arrived.

***

I called Charles to let him know that I was on my way. The ride over to his place was quiet and serene. I had the driver's window slightly open and the cool New York night breeze gently massaged my face. There wasn't a stir, no music, nothing; just me, the car, the night, and my thoughts. Charles was there to meet me in the hallway as usual. I felt safe as his powerful arms wrapped around my shoulders, holding me in a loving and caring way.

"What's wrong?" he asked, immediately sensing that something was amiss.

"Nothing, boo. I've just been wondering why life has dealt me such a bad hand."

"Don't say that, life has dealt you some wonderful things."

"Like?"

"You're here, right? You're living, breathing, working, and going to school. You're engaged and you have me and despite many of the setbacks that you've experienced, you have come a long way. You've removed many of the obstacles that were blocking your path. You're a work in progress, a bright light, a true achiever that's going to shine even more, just wait and see."

"That's so nice of you, you're so caring," I said, trying to downplay all the things he had said.

Whenever I visited Charles, I made sure that I was wearing his engagement ring and not Robert's. However, for the first time in my life, I could honestly say I felt dirty, guilty, remorseful, and sad. Sure, I had said many of these things before but this time they stung. I felt everything. It was tearing me apart.

"You know what I want you to do?"

"No, what?" he asked.

"Take off your clothes and come to bed. I want you to hold me tight and never let me go," I said, as tears filled my eyes.

"Sure," he whispered.

We made our way to the bed, where I fell asleep in his arms as he gently stroked my face. I got up bright and early the next morning and made breakfast. I then showered and got dressed.

"Baby," I said, "I have to go. I made breakfast, talk to you later."

"Okay, close the door behind you. I love you," he said, as I aroused him from his sleep.

"I love you too," I said kissing him on the cheek.

I was exhausted from all the running around the previous night. I took my ass right home after leaving Charles' apartment. I was glad that I left him in a good mood so he wouldn't have to worry about me. I felt better knowing that for one night he wouldn't have to worry about my many personalities. At least that's how he put it. Quite a few people have told me over the years that I should see a doctor. When I asked them why they said I displayed a lot of bipolar symptoms. According to them, I was always moody, hyperactive, and depressed. One minute I was up and the next I was down. I told them they were entitled to their own opinion. I should have gotten in touch with Robert, but I forgot. I was surprised that he hadn't called. Tara called wanting to know what I was doing.

"I'm staying home today," I said.

"I'm gonna stop by."

"No problem."

I had a lot on my mind and Charles was at the heart of it all. I felt what I was about to do was the right thing. And although my judgment was clouded, I decided to write him a letter via email telling him how I felt.

Dear Charles,

As I sit here drowning in sorrow, I remember how good it felt to hear you say, I LOVE YOU. This has got to be the hardest thing for me to do, but I have to. It hasn't fully been a day and already I'm missing you like crazy. You are my first true love and that's why it's so hard for me to let go. Part of me is saying not to give up, but then again, I'm not worthy of your love. So why bother?

You deserve someone who will be there for you one hundred percent and you and I both know that has not been the case with me. You need someone who'll be a mother to the children that you yearn for and someone who is the opposite of what I represent. Go on with your life. It's not worth wasting your time on me. You'll find that there's a world of joy awaiting you and all the things you need in life. I won't be able to give you happiness.

Just remember, Dana will and forever LOVE YOU. You'll forever be in my heart and thoughts. There is never a day that goes by that I don't think about you. Yes, it's going to be difficult but in my heart of heart, I believe it's the right thing to do. You, the man of my dreams, I love you sweetie, but I must go now. My love for you is unconditional…it is. Maybe someday we'll be together.

Love Always.

Dana

I must have been sitting at the computer for quite some time. It was the ringing of my doorbell that woke me out of my stupor.

"Damn, your place is a mess!" Tara said entering the apartment and taking a seat on the living room couch.

"So, what's up?"

"Girl, I was bored in the apartment by myself after Marques broke out with those fools Jason and Platinum."

"Platinum? Isn't that the dude Jason wanted to bring into the Club?"

"Yeah, that's him."

"That's how they are rolling now? It looks to me as if he's already a member."

"He's trying and Jason is working twenty-four-seven to get it done."

"Did you ever see what Platinum looks like?"

"Remember that time when I told you they were supposed to meet up at the Robinsons?"

"Yeah."

"I left because he was taking too long so I never saw him. And when he came by today, he stayed downstairs in the ride."

"Oh, I see."

"He runs with Jason permanently now. He's like his right-hand man but he keeps that nigga clear of Jimmy and the Club."

"Shit, maybe he was one of those bitch ass mutha-fuckas who assaulted me."

"I thought about that too. But he's one of those player types. He's strictly about his tricks and his gwop. But Jason is foul like that, and I can see him using Platinum to do that shit."

"I've been thinking about hiring a private investigator with some of the money I've got saved up. It looks to me like the cops are dragging their feet because I haven't heard a word from them so far."

"Let me tell you something keep your money. You don't need a private investigator. Believe me, the boys are working on it they aren't dragging their feet. This was an assault, not a parking ticket or misdemeanor. This is a felony case. They'll get those fools and if Jason had anything to do with it, he'll go down too."

"Damn, Tara!"

"What?"

"You always find a way to explain things to me. Are you a freaking lawyer or something? Because the last time I checked you were an undercover ho."

"Bitch, you're crazy." She laughed. "That's what I'm here for to support you, you forgot?"

"What?"

"We've got something in common," she sang, stuffing one of my pillows under her shirt imitating Whitney Houston as she danced towards me. I was dying of laughter because it was so funny.

"Finish your story!" I said.

"Okay, like I was saying, Jason came up with some wild shit. He asked Robert to let him use several of Platinum girls to make a few runs for the next two months."

"What did Robert say?" I was taken aback by what I was hearing.

"He was just nodding his head as he listened. He then asked Robert to limit some of our runs."

"Our runs?" I snapped.

"Yup, our runs."

"Come on now, Robert must have said something?"

"He did. He told him that shit wasn't happening. Then he added that he spoke to Andre and he flat out said no."

"It's funny how Robert never mentioned any of this to me."

"Girl don't sweat it. I had to work on Marques to get this information."

"The nerve of that mutha-fucka!"

"That's what I said."

"Damn, he's trying hard to get this guy in, huh?"

"I know. But you know what? Jimmy and them ain't that stupid. So how are things with you and Charles?"

"It's good, but..."

"But what? What's going on? Where's your ring? Talk to me, what happened?"

I knew she wouldn't stop pressing until she got an answer. So, I deliberately tried to change the subject, but she wouldn't leave it alone. It's not like I didn't want to talk about it because I did, but I didn't know where to start. Then I thought, given the type of environment and lifestyle I was surrounded by and though I was hesitant to come clean to her, I felt it was okay. We both were involved in the Playaz Club and were living the same lifestyle so why not? One thing I was quite sure about was that I would not mention the rape. Besides, Tara wasn't like Jenny whom I had to constantly keep things from. Jenny was the type who once she hears something, immediately wants to deal with it.

"I don't know where to start," I said to Tara.

"Start somewhere, like why you're not wearing your engagement ring?"

"I broke it off with Charles. I wrote him an email telling him it was over."

"You wrote the man an electronic letter? Am I hearing you right, you broke it off through an email? What is wrong with you? Why didn't you do it in person or over the phone? You don't do shit like that! What did he do?" she asked, sounding like Jenny.

"Nothin'."

"He did nothing, and you broke it off, why?"

"Okay, this is why I broke it off with him," I responded, walking into my bedroom, and returning with the engagement ring that Robert gave me.

"What the fuck! Dayum, where did you get that shit from? That ring is at least 4.1 carats," she bellowed.

"Robert gave it to me several days ago."

"Robert?" she asked incredulously.

"Uh uh, and he proposed."

"Girl, I don't know what to say. What did you say? Did you accept?"

"I told him no. Well, not exactly."

"What do you mean by that?"

"I told him I wasn't ready, but he kept insisting. And when he realized that I wasn't gonna change my mind he told me to wear the ring until I'm ready."

"Wow and because of all this, you decided to break it off with Charles? I guess neither one of them know about the other, huh?"

"Nope."

"Fuck Robert! What's up with that?"

"I know, but..."

"But what, you're telling me that the man you love doesn't mean a thing to you? But a negro who has played you once before and may even be doing it now means something to you? Dana, we're around him most of the time. We both know what he does. Come on. Does he mean that much to you?" Tara had a rather interesting look on her face.

"Of course not."

"Do you want to hear what I have to say?"

"Yeah."

"Look, you're beautiful, in college and you've met a brotha who thinks the world of you. You guys are in love with each other and the brotha is a college professor. And you wanna throw all that away just because you still have feelings for a brotha who is still married? Though he will swear he's working on his divorce, or better yet says he's already divorced. Yeah, he's a stockbroker who works on Wall Street but he's a drug dealer. He's no different from all those bitch ass niggas we see selling that shit on the street corner. You don't even know if he's been involved in any other shit. People are dying in this game, Dana. It's just that we don't see it, but it does happen. Mutha-fuckas be getting ghost believe me."

I remained quiet as she continued.

"He's played you more than once and has put you through a lot of drama more drama than Mary J. Blige." We both laughed at that one. "Fuck his ring and all that other shit!" she continued. "Have you ever thought that he might have been behind the assault on you?"

"No, why would he? What purpose would that serve, and he wants me to marry him?"

"I'm just saying. You don't know and neither do I, but anything is possible. I think you're making a big mistake by leaving Charles. Robert only wants to have his cake and eat it too, that's all."

"I know I've said it a million times, but I'm confused. I am," I said, sadly.

"I can tell but don't lose your head. You can't allow your emotions to blind you. From what you've told me about the professor, he's been good to you, unlike this fool Robert. I think you should go and clear the air with him. Sending an email is not the way to go about doing this."

The more she spoke the more things became clearer. I had to admit the things she was saying were cutting through me like a sharp knife. I began to wonder what Charles's face must have looked like as he read the email. The little voice inside of me was hoping that he hadn't checked his email. *Maybe he's like me,* I thought. *You know the type that allows the emails to add up until you get a warning.*

"I think you should give the brotha a call because, in my opinion, you owe him an explanation." She sure was making me feel guilty.

Episode 21

"Hey,"

"What's up?" Charles asked, not sounding like his normal self. I could tell that he had already read the letter. "Are you calling to find out if I read your email? If you are, I already did," he added before I could respond.

I felt terrible as I blurted out, "I'm sorry. I wasn't thinking."

"And this is how you go about it?"

"Please forgive me. I was confused. Please hear me out. We need to talk," I said, trying to explain myself as Tara looked on with a curious look on her face.

There was a pause that seemed like an eternity before he finally answered, "Come on over, I'll be here."

"No, you come over here."

"No problem, I'll be there in an hour or so."

I said okay and hung up the phone. Tara by now had her jacket on. She held my hands and said, "You did the right thing."

"You think?"

"Yeah," she said, calmly.

"I hope so."

"Girl, you better give me all the dirt later. Make sure you call me. I want all the details don't leave anything out."

"I won't."

"We can hang out next weekend," she said, hugging me.

"Bet, but make sure you take care of the drinks," I added, smiling.

Tara left me on a high note. I was feeling upbeat; however, I still had some doubts. The knock on the door awoke me from my guilt-ridden thoughts. As I walked toward the door, I questioned whether or not I had done the right thing. But when I opened the door and saw him, I knew I would be crazy to let him go. He stood there like a black God and he belonged to me.

"What's up, baby?" I coyly whispered under my breath.

"I'm good," he said, with a look of skepticism on his face.

"Come in, have a seat."

It was obvious that my sexy cat woman snarl wasn't working. He sat down and pulled out a printed copy of the email from his pants pocket.

"I've been reading your email for the better part of the day, and I'm truly hurt and disappointed. I couldn't believe what I was reading. All you have shown and displayed is your lack of maturity and selfishness."

"Can I see that?" I asked as he handed me the paper. I glanced at it before tearing it to shreds. The look on his face with his lips slightly open made me realize what a fool I had been. The brother was fine as hell. He loved me and wanted to marry me and instead of seizing the moment, I was messing it up.

"I thought this was all a big joke. I kept asking myself over and over what did I do, and I still couldn't figure it out."

"Baby, I'm sorry. There's no excuse for what I did. Please forgive me."

"What motivated you to write this email? Was it something I did?"

"No."

"Are you afraid of getting married?"

"No."

"Then what is it? Now I'm confused."

"What I did was stupid, and I admit that. I do love you and I want to be with you."

"Are you sure?"

"Yes, I'm sure."

"So, are we on good terms now? Are you still my fiancé?"

"Yeah, but I should be the one asking you that."

"Do you want to be?" he asked, staring into my eyes.

"Of course."

"Well, you have to promise that you won't write another email like this. If there's a problem let's sit down and talk about it."

"I promise and it will never happen again."

I smiled at him and playfully stuck my tongue out at him. We were all over each other in a matter of seconds. I really couldn't tell whether it was the excitement of him kissing and feeling on me or the water I had drunk earlier. All I know was that I had to pee badly. He didn't miss a beat as he pushed me up against the bathroom door as soon as I finished. My panties were below my knees as he began kissing my nipples, my belly, and between my legs. He was teasing the hell out of me as he deliberately avoided my coochie. He knew I needed some lip service badly. I held onto his baldhead while I worked my hips. His tongue finally stopped at my pleasure spot. As usual, my legs gave out. So, I sat my ass on the bathroom sink with one leg on the side of the bathtub and the other on top of the toilet bowl cover.

My legs were now spread wide apart, and he drove me wild with his tongue. We then got in the shower where I returned the favor as the hot water and steam filled the bathroom. I was sucking him good as the water drops fell from my forehead onto his hard member. Pulling out, he entered me from behind and began hitting my love canal. The water seemed to hit my body with every stroke. I could feel his dick swelling inside me. It jolted me into a moment of stupendous pleasure and excitement. He then arched his back and pushed forward. I turned and looked at him as he smiled and continued working my pleasure spot. We were speaking in another language as he began gyrating at a frantic pace. I was about to cum. He quickened his pace and exploded in me. We fell to our knees in the tub as we continued to yell, groan and moan like wounded animals. Damn, it was so good! He held onto me and filled my hot pulsating pleasure spot. The excitement, feelings, and companionship were mutual between us once again. The sex was great as always. It had been a while since I had any dick and Charles did not disappoint me. He spent the night with me and of course, we did our thing throughout the night. Things were back to normal between us, which was great. I slept my ass off after he left. Shit, I had nowhere to go and I was fucked out.

***

The telephone must have rung at least four or five times before I answered it.

"Hello," I said, groggily.

"Dana!"

"Oh, what's up, Nisha?"

It had been a while since I last heard from Tanisha. I figured she had something juicy to tell me, but this was not what I expected. She was like the National Enquirer, Extra, and Wendy Williams. She always knew what was going on. I guess she got her information from an anonymous source because I could never figure it out. If you wanted to know what was happening on the streets, or on-campus she was the one to go to.

"Dana, I've got bad news!"

"What, what kind of bad news?" I asked eager to find out what it was.

"Jamel just got shot!"

"Jamel? Big Jamel?"

"No, Lil Jamel," she said, crying.

"Oh, my God! No! Oh, God! Please don't say that. He's okay though, right?" I frantically asked.

"He's dead!" she bellowed, as her tear-filled voice rambled on. "He got shot in the neck. He was only six years old."

"Where is Monique?" I screamed.

"She's with her family at the hospital."

"Where are you?"

"At my sister's house."

"What's the address? I'm coming to get you."

After getting the address from Tanisha, I got dressed and headed to her sister's place. Luckily, the traffic flow on the Queensboro Bridge was moving smoothly. In a matter of minutes, I was at her sister's front door.

"How did it happen?" I asked Tanisha, my voice rising as she let me in the house.

"You know Big Jamel sells that crack shit, right?"

"Yeah."

"Well, this stupid mutha-fucka got into an argument with some niggas supposedly from Guy Brewer Boulevard. He was arguing with them while Lil Jamel sat in his car."

"That's a dumb mutha-fucka!" I screamed as Tanisha continued.

"He left Lil Jamel and walked into the lobby of some building to discuss a dispute over money and territory. The dudes he walked inside the building with got nervous when two other dudes entered the lobby from a first-floor apartment. There was a lot of shouting and cursing and then a scuffle broke out and that's when shit got crazy. The dudes who came into the lobby began firing and Big Jamel hauled ass outta there. Instead of running away from his ride, this negro ran toward it and Lil Jamel was hit. Three people died including Lil Jamel."

Tanisha said that last statement like it was some sort of consolation as if it was going to ease the pain of losing Lil Jamel. I knew its intent and her purpose for saying it. I understood what she was saying but it annoyed me.

"He's dead!" Tanisha exclaimed as she began crying.

"Damn! Damn!" I hollered, as I too began crying. "He was only a kid, a child, it's not fair!"

I wiped the snot from my nose and called Monique. "Meet me at the apartment," she said.

"Okay," I told her, me and Tanisha were on our way.

As we got closer to the apartment, the sound of crying and moaning emanated in the hallway. The apartment was filled with family members and friends. We made our way through the crowd before spotting Monique's parents in the hallway. We hugged and kissed her mother and stepfather. I waved and said hi to Big Jamel who was talking with his friends in one of the three bedrooms.

At first, I refused to say anything to him, but I felt I needed to only because of Monique. If it was just him, I wouldn't have said shit, dumb ass bastard! I could hear the continuous eerie wailing the closer I got to Monique's room. She looked terrible. She was hysterical. Tanisha and I immediately began crying as we hugged each other.

"Oh God, Dana! They took my baby! Why! Why did they take my baby? Dana, Why? It hurts, it does!" she cried, barely able to stand on her feet.

"It's gonna be alright. You have to be strong; you have to! You have to be for Lil Jamel," I struggled to say.

There were several people in the room, and they too began crying. This was too much for me. I was devastated. The only good that came from all this if there is one and that is the shooters were quickly apprehended. That was the least that fool Big Jamel could have done. He was the one who provided the police with the information and pointed the guys out. I could see the hurt and pain on his face. But damn, how stupid can one person be?

I somehow pulled myself together despite the emotional outburst from the family. I needed some privacy and the only place I could get it was in the bathroom. Once there, I called Charles.

"Hi, baby. What's going on?" he asked.

"A lot."

"Hey now, why are you crying? Why the tears? What's going on?" he asked, in a concerned voice.

"It's Monique."

"Who?"

"Monique. We took your class together with India and Tanisha."

"Oh yes. Is she okay?"

"No, her son was shot earlier today and he's dead!" I said, crying hysterically.

"Oh my God, that's terrible! Dana relax I can barely hear you. I know it's hard but give it a try."

"I'll try," I said, trying to compose myself.

"How old was he?"

"He was only six years old."

"Damn! Where are you?"

"I'm at Monique's apartment."

"Please give her and the family my condolences," he said.

"I will. I'll stop by on my way home."

"Don't worry about coming over. I believe she needs you more than ever right now. She's in a terrible situation and your support and companionship will mean a lot to her. Take your time."

"Thanks, boo. I'll get back to you. Love you."

"Love you too," he responded, before hanging up.

Bishop Clarence, the pastor of Abundance Grace Deliverance Church was talking to Monique and her mother when I walked into the kitchen. I took a seat next to Tanisha, as Bishop Clarence began telling the family that God was a fair God, healer, deliverer, and comforter.

"God now has Lil Jamal," the Bishop said.

Realizing the Bishop had made a mistake, one of the brothers that accompanied him and who was standing next to him said, "Lil Jamel, it's Lil Jamel, Bishop."

"Yes, Lil Jamel is now with God," he said correcting himself. "He's in good hands now. He might not be here with us but he's looking down on us all. And he's saying Mommy, Daddy, Grandma, Grandpa, I'm alright. I'm alright, glory to God!" Bishop Clarence said, wiping the sweat from his face.

Monique, her parents, and most of the people who were in the kitchen had their eyes closed as they spoke under their breath. I was staring at Bishop Clarence as he continued. "We're running for our lives. Guns and drugs are killing and destroying our children, and this has to stop. God knows we're running for our lives." As if on cue, the others joined in as they began singing, "We're running for our lives, we're running for our lives. If anybody should ask you what's the matter with me…" It wasn't long before the kitchen sounded like church.

Bishop Clarence was backed up by some of his church members as they continued singing, "Tell them I'm saved, sanctified Holy Ghost filled . . . I'm running for my life."

It was unbelievable. As people drifted toward the kitchen there wasn't a dry eye inside the apartment. Although Lil Jamel was dead there was a serene calm oozing from the lips of Bishop Clarence as he accentuated every word. The atmosphere changed from one of sadness to one of happiness. The only person missing was India. She was in Florida but would be back in time for the funeral. Nonetheless, she was missed. Tanisha and I spent the night with Monique and her family.

***

Luckily enough, the days leading up to Lil Jamel's funeral were very favorable for me. Robert was out of town and I didn't have to make any runs. I called my job and explained there was a death in my family. I did however speak to Jenny and Tara. I told them about the tragic death of Lil Jamel.

Lil Jamel had a beautiful funeral. Several local elected officials showed up as well as community leaders. Surprisingly enough, none of Big Jamel's friends showed up. The church was filled with strangers, who were there to pay their respect. Charles was there along with India and several of Monique's former and present professors.

When the funeral procession finally got to Heavenly Green Cemetery in Long Island, Monique, seeing her son's coffin being put in the ground began to wail uncontrollably. It wasn't long before Big Jamel, Mr. and Mrs. Livingston, and other family members and friends, including me, Tanisha, and India, began crying. Overwhelmed with emotion, I tried to grasp how a person so young could be taken away in the blink of an eye. I guess Charles must have seen the glazed look in my eyes because he held me so that I wouldn't fall.

The ride back to Charles' apartment was a somber one. He did his best to engage me in several conversations. I was just not responding because I was so out of it. Once we got to his apartment, I quickly poured a glass of Moet

"You know," he said, as he made himself an Apple Martini, "a lot of our young brothers and sisters don't understand that they are slowly destroying themselves by getting involved in the drug trade."

This was a rather interesting subject as far as I was concerned. He had never spoken about drugs before and I wanted to hear how he felt about the whole thing.

"Growing up, I saw what drugs can do if one allows them to take over and control one's life. I saw what it did to a lot of my friends and family members. I know a lot of brothers who believed that the only way to make it out of the 'hood' was to sell drugs, become gang members, and glorify the thug life as if it were something worthwhile. Do you know what it did? It ruined them."

"You're right."

"It's a misnomer on their part and their whole outlook is to romanticize the thug life. At the center where I volunteer, I oftentimes ask the kids what are their thoughts on education. The responses I get from them are unbelievable," he said, cringing.

"What do they say?"

He let out a faint laugh. "They say it takes too long and that it's a waste of time spending all those years in school when they can go on the corner and sell drugs. It's not only the boys who feel this way; the girls all say the same thing too. I'm telling you it's crazy. There's this kid by the name of Duane, his thing is to always say, 'It sounds good Mr. Anderson but that was back in dah day, shit is different now!' I told him and the others that this is still the same day we are living in. 'What you talking about Mr. Anderson?' they said, sounding like Arnold Drummond from the television series *Different Strokes*. I told them you guys are dropping out of high school. You don't want an honest job. As for those who remain in school, they are constantly harassed and ridiculed as nerds as if something is wrong with being smart. I let them know that it was the same way when I was growing up. So, they need to stop that 'back in dah day' nonsense and make something of themselves."

"That's true. I see a lot of teenagers all the time in Washington Square Park doing all types of shit when they should be in school."

"It's a damn shame that these guys don't get it. They don't realize some powerful people in high places allow a lot of the drugs to move freely throughout our communities." Charles was taking this to another level, and it was enlightening. I poured another glass of Moet.

"I know."

"All these so-called brothers that you see selling drugs on the street corner they're not the ones bringing it into the community. They are supplied by those who have the planes, boats, and even ships." I immediately thought about Jimmy, Andre, and the Latino brothers. "The brothers in the neighborhoods then purchase the drugs and start their genocide in their communities against their families and friends. It gets even deeper once they start making a profit. They then have to get some form of protection and that's when the violence starts. Then you have the damn crackheads, when they need their drugs and they can't find the money to buy them they will steal from their mothers and family members. The situations that you and I see such as Lil Jamel's death are nothing new. It happens all the time and what do the politicians do?"

"I don't know," I said, anxious to hear his answer.

"I'll tell you what they do, they show up at the funerals and call for a few marches and that's it. My uncle used to always say the only time a politician showed up in the tough section of Riverdale is when a child is killed, or at election time. A lot of people don't realize that Riverdale had its ghettos and I'm a product of that community. However, I decided to do something with my life. It's sickening, Dana. There are no winners in the drug game. They're all losers."

I knew exactly what he meant but I asked anyway, "Chuck, what do you mean when you say they're all losers?"

"The dealers either wind up dead or in jail," he said. "Many of our young promising sisters who aspired of becoming doctors, lawyers, and productive citizens, get caught up in a downward spiral infested with all sorts of negativity. And eventually many of them end up sucking-dicks, pulling tricks, and getting their asses kicked by some degenerate male chauvinist. Others get pregnant and strung out at an incredibly young age. They also have to deal with sexually transmitted diseases and if that's not enough, yes, quite a number of them do wind up dead or in jail. Their loved ones are then left with only the memories of their sons and daughters. They need to wake up; it's similar to what I call the Project Syndrome."

"What the fuck is that?"

"The Project Syndrome relates to those families who choose to remain in housing projects for many years where they seemingly never want to leave. The apartment is then passed from one generation to the next. I wasn't about to let that become a constant in my mother's life. That's why I worked and studied so damn hard to help my mother and end the cycle before it got started. By the way, the term 'Project Syndrome' is mine."

"I figured that."

Charles was on point. I guess I was getting to know my man. He was reading me and calling me a loser. It stung me, especially with the death of Lil Jamel. How many Lil Jamel's and young sister's lives had I singlehandedly destroyed by making all those runs for the Playaz Club? The conversation that I had right after Lil Jamel's death put me in a transition phase, it made me take a long look at my life and what I wanted to do with it. Did I want to continue with my present life? Did I want to share it with Charles? What I did know was that I needed to make some changes and the first person I needed to start with was me.

Episode 22

Robert had just gotten back in town when my phone rang. My instinct told me it was him and boy was I right. He didn't say much other than to let me know that he would stop by my place later that night or the next day. The bottom line was that Robert still had some unfinished business to take care of with me. He never gave me an explanation as to where he was although I knew. Not that I gave a damn. But let's just say what if I had agreed to marry him is this the way how he would have treated me? Several other issues needed to be dealt with and I felt that I needed to get them done and stop procrastinating. Although the semester was about to start, I figured I could use an extra week. I called Tara and informed her of my plans to visit my hometown.

"Did you speak to Jimmy or Andre about it?" she asked.

"No, I didn't. Am I supposed to get their permission or something?"

"Yeah girl, they don't like it when they're not informed about members going out of town, especially when it doesn't have a thing to do with making money."

"See, it's bullshit like this that pisses me off!"

While she continued talking, I had a flashback to what Jason had said to me about the Playaz Club wanting to know the whereabouts of its members.

"They'll think you're a snitch. I'm telling you if you go without letting them know it might get ugly and believe me, I have seen it."

"Is that right?"

"That's how they do it."

"Okay, I'll ask Jimmy. If he says it's cool, then what? Who will cover for me?"

"Cover for you? It's not like that. They have people working twenty-four-seven. Don't worry about it."

"So, you think it's a good idea to call him now?"

"Yeah, as soon as we get off the phone. How was the funeral?"

"He had a nice send-off, but it was sad. My girl is going out of her mind."

"I'm so heartbroken. I can't imagine how his mother is feeling right about now," she said, sadly.

"And to make matters worse not one of Big Jamel's friends showed up."

"That was fucked up. I hope your girl pulls through. Was he her only child?"

"Uh uh."

"Damn!"

"That's the same shit I said."

"How are you holding up?"

"I'm doing well. I'm handling it trying to be strong for my girl."

"Well, I'm gonna let you go. Call me."
"I will."

***

I had decided who I would call, and Robert seemed the obvious choice. I wanted to know how he felt about me visiting South Carolina.

"I need to ask you for a favor," I said when he picked up the phone.

"Why didn't you ask when I called a minute ago?"

"You seemed as if you were in a rush that's why."

"Don't worry about it and you can ask me anything. You're my fiancé so go right ahead."

"I know."

"So, what is it?"

"My aunt is sick, and I need to know from Jimmy or Andre..." Before I could say another word, he cut me off.

"Is this true, or are you just making things up?"

"Seriously, she's sick," I said in a sincere voice.

"How did you find this out? I thought you told me you didn't have any family here in the city?"

"I don't. My girl Tanisha told me. She has family from South Carolina also. Negro please, she was the one who got me hip to the chat room. If it weren't for her I would have never met your inquisitive ass," I said, lying.

Laughing aloud, he replied, "Oh yeah, I do recall her. Sure, you can go."

"Don't fuck with me because I certainly don't need the Playaz Club following me all over the country."

"What did I say? I said don't worry about it. I got you covered. Just stay in contact so I can know when you're back in town. When are you leaving?"

"The weekend."

"Do you need any money?"

"No, I'm cool. But if the offer is still there when I get back then I'll take it."

"It'll be here. Just make sure you're back on time. Are you wearing your ring?"

"Of course, what's wrong with you?"

"I was just checking that's all."

"So how is business?"

"It's good but there are a few loose ends that need to be straightened out."

"Just be careful."

"I will."

"I'll call you."

"Sure, babes, and like I said I'll take care of everything with Jimmy."

"Love you, bye."

He certainly had me thinking. Jenny was the only person in the city that I knew from South Carolina. And both he and Jason knew about her. I got the feeling that he knew a lot more than what he said. Was he going to investigate me? Perhaps, but all I wanted was his approval and I got it.

***

I could see the light emanating from Jenny's apartment window as I pulled up in front of her building. She looked tired as she let me in.

"What's up, girl?" I asked.

"Tired. How have you been? How is Monique doing?"

"So far so good. She's devastated but I'm praying for her," I said, as she plopped herself down on her couch.

"That's so sweet. So, what brings you here this time of night?"

"Dang, you make it sound as if it's late."

"It's not that it's just that I've been noticing a black Mercedes coupe and a silver Escalade parked a few feet from my building for the past week. I don't know but it seems strange to me."

"Maybe they're visiting one of your neighbors. Look where you live. Money, girl! You live around a lot of it and it probably ain't got nothin' to do with you," I suggested. "Anyway, it's early and I came by to take you up on your offer of going to South Carolina for a visit."

"You're kidding, right?"

"No, I'm not."

"Why now though? I believe I told you I was gonna go sometime in the summer, or in a few months."

"Yes, you did but I've been thinking why not this weekend?"

"Are you serious?"

"I sure am."

"This weekend? Did I hear you right?"

"Yeah bitch, you heard me right," I answered, as I playfully shook her.

She looked at me and then asked, "What about school? Aren't you supposed to be starting the semester soon?"

"Yeah, but I would only miss the first few days of the semester if that much. We don't do shit in the first week anyway."

"Dayum, you aren't playing. You got that shit all figured out, huh?"

"You damn skippy."

"I could have Norman and Jean look after the business for a few days." Norman and Jean were two of her most trusted workers who on numerous occasions ran the business while she was out of town with her two lovers.

"Okay, I guess we can do it this weekend." I was so happy. I grabbed her and spun her around several times.

After leaving her apartment, I headed to Charles' place and told him that I was planning on visiting South Carolina. Not only was he supportive but he felt it was something that I needed to do. I agreed with him and informed him of my desire to quit my job. He didn't like this idea at all. However, after explaining to him that I would find a much better-paying job once I got back to New York, he relented.

***

Jenny and I boarded Flight 2004 from Kennedy Airport to Columbia, South Carolina. I was anxious and apprehensive, yet happy to be going back home. My mind was racing back and forth as I thought about Brian. Was he still in Crisppen? Was he married? Does he have any children? I couldn't help myself as I stared at the blue and white sky. Jenny seemed so calm and relaxed and here I was all tensed. God, I wish I were like her. Despite her calm demeanor, I knew she was looking forward to seeing her family and friends. We chatted a bit before falling asleep.

When the plane finally landed at Columbia International Airport it was as if my whole body had transformed. I felt as if I was a little girl all over again. My heart was pounding. I had goosebumps all over. There wasn't a drop of saliva in my throat. I began to feel lightheaded as if I were about to pass out. However, the fresh country air revived me, and I began to feel much better. Hearing the familiar southern drawl of the people made me feel at home. Seeing Jenny's parents especially brought a smile to my face.

"Hi Dana, how are you?" Mrs. Thornton asked.

"I'm fine Mr. and Mrs. Thornton,"

They hugged and greeted me as if I were one of their children. Jenny was beaming with a huge grin on her face. It was one of those sentimental moments. I didn't notify anyone from my family that I was coming. So naturally, no one was there to meet me. The deal was for me to stay with Jenny and her family which I objected to. But the Thorntons would have none of it and eventually, I gave in.

As we drove to her parents' home I began reflecting on my father, and as I passed the many familiar places that brought back so many childhood memories, I got teary-eyed. I was gone for some years and being in New York had suppressed many of those memories. So, seeing them once again rekindled a lot of feelings that I had kept hidden. I wanted to see my father despite all the traumatic heartache he had put me through. Nonetheless, I wasn't sure how I would react and what kind of reception I would receive in return. Then again, it didn't make any sense for me to travel this far and not visit his sorry ass. The weather was wonderful compared to New York's which was a relief.

The Thornton's home was beautiful. They could have been on BET's *How I'm Living*. I was glancing at the huge volume of books in their library when I noticed Jenny and her mother talking and pointing in my direction.

"Dana, can I have a word with you?" Mrs. Thornton asked. "I know this is none of my business and I don't want you to get the impression that I'm intervening. I know the relationship between you and your father has been strained but…"

Dayum, I thought to myself, *Jenny must have told her.* Mrs. Thornton must have been reading my mind because she shook her head to let me know that Jenny hadn't said a word.

"Yes, Mrs. Thornton," I replied.

"Your father used to come by now and then wanting to know if we had heard from you. If you do feel like visiting him, he's much closer than you think," she said, as we walked out to the front porch.

"He is?" I asked, trying to downplay my concern.

"He lives several houses away," she said, pointing in the direction of a huge off-white brick house at the end of the block.

Episode 23

A s I approached my father's house, I immediately noticed the manicured lawn and the colorful flowers that adorned the front of the house. It certainly brought back memories of my parents on their knees doing their gardening. I could only smile as I slowly walked toward the front door and the soulful voice of Al Green singing *For the Good Times* momentarily took me back to when I was a little girl. I knew it was my father playing the music. Anything from Motown, Stax, Atlantic, and the Philly Sound was great music. He and my mother loved it. Two black Mercedes Benz and a maroon-red Jaguar were parked in the driveway and as I took a closer look the license plates read ALICE and DANA. Tears welled up in my eyes as I tried to collect myself.

Upon reaching the door, my hands began to tremble as I pressed the doorbell. An elderly black woman opened the door and after telling her who I was, she gestured for me to come in. There she was the hot young girl who was living with my father. She stood at least five-ten. She was slender with a light complexion. She had dark brown shoulder-length hair. Her brown eyes were slightly slanted, and her soft features made her look younger than her twenty-five years. She was extremely attractive. She wore a gray Gucci sweatsuit and loafers. Despite the gray sweatsuit, she was wearing, you could tell she had a nice figure.

She walked over to me and introduced herself. "Hi, my name is Tanya and you must be…"

"Dana," I quipped. How she reacted at the mention of my name not only surprised me, but it was quite charming.

"Wow, you're Richard's daughter?"

"Yes, I am."

"Dana, Richard talks about you all the time."

"He does?"

"Yes, very often." She spoke very eloquently in her South Carolina drawl, sounding more mature than I expected. "Did he know you were coming?"

"No."

"That's all right. He'll be happy to see you. He's inside the study, go on," she said, pointing me in the direction of the study.

My father was sitting in a wheelchair with his back turned. I walked toward him to get a better look at his face. I noticed a feeding pump with a bottle filled with beige liquid, which led to his abdomen. As I stood in front of him, the man I was staring at looked nothing like my father. I knew it was him because his features hadn't changed, but he looked nothing like the strong well-built man I last saw. His once-massive body and muscular arms, which used to hold me as a little girl looked like several strings of spaghetti under his oversized pajamas and robe. His hair was in patches and his complexion was a dark discolored spotty looking tone. His head was hung, and his chin rested on his chest, just below where his neck ended.

"Dad," I said, "how are you doing?"

He slowly raised his head as his eyes found my face. "Is that you, Dana?" he asked.

"Yes Daddy, it's me."

"How are you doing?" he asked, in a gravelly voice.

"I'm doing fine. How are things with you?"

I knew something was seriously wrong. However, I dared not ask, seeing the condition he was in.

"I'm hanging in their sweetheart." Cough, cough, cough.

I couldn't believe what I was seeing. The man I knew as my father was no more. He was a shell of his former self. His voice was weak, and he looked fatigued and withdrawn. I gently held his hand, as he began to cry.

"Dana," he said, "can you ever forgive me? I'm so sorry for all the things I did to you. I know I wasn't a good father, much less a man, as far as you are concerned. I have a lot of difficulty speaking." Cough, cough, cough. "But I want you to know that I'm sorry. And although you may not forgive me for what I did, seeing you here and holding you mean a lot to me."

I too began to cry. In a crazy and twisted way, I wished he hadn't brought those things up. I could tell it was eating away whatever strength or hope he had of recovering. I told him that I forgave him, although it was difficult for me to say those three words. Nonetheless, I did it through the tears and the recurring memories. He then picked up what looked to be a small microphone and spoke into it. I couldn't hear exactly what he was saying, however, I did hear Tanya's name.

As Tanya approached us, she had a metal box in her hand. She opened it. He pointed at several envelopes, which she handed to him.

He then opened one of the envelopes, looked it over, and handed it to me. Not only did it say I had full access to my trust fund, but he also assured me his lawyers would deal with his final will, which would take care of me.

"Final will?" I shrieked.

As if on cue, he fell right back into the condition he was in when I first arrived. While he rocked back and forth his nurse came in to check on him. Tanya then called me into the living room, where she began explaining everything to me.

"Is he dying?" I asked.

Tears began to fall from her eyes as she replied, "Yes, he has throat cancer and it's getting worse. He'll be going back to the hospital sometime next week, where he'll remain for a while."

"Oh God, no! He's gonna stay there until he dies?" We cried as I thought about the years of cigarettes, cigars, and drinking that he did. *I guess it all caught up to him*, I said to myself.

It's funny how I never wanted to visit him until I had that conversation with Charles after Lil Jamel's death. He must have seen something that I didn't see. I remember him also saying that taking the trip would do me a world of good and that it was something that I needed to do.

Although I had come intending to confront him and to get some answers, seeing him like that tore me apart. Maybe some things are better left unanswered or unsaid. Maybe I was supposed to be there and to make amends despite the incest, rape, and physical, mental, and psychological abuse. This I never expected.

"Do any family members visit?" I asked.

"Once in a while," Tanya said.

"And how long has he been like this?"

"For quite some time, and from what your father told me, he was diagnosed with cancer before you left for California."

I couldn't believe what I was hearing. He was sick all that time. Yet he was acting as if nothing was wrong. I do recall the late-night alcohol binges and the private conversations he would have with himself. This was unbelievable as I tried to make sense of what Tanya was saying. Jenny was always insisting that I visit. She had to know he was sick. No wonder her parents had reacted the way they did at the mention of his name. Everyone at least had an idea of what was going on except me.

Tanya told me they were married and had both agreed upon and signed a prenuptial agreement. The ring she wore was expensive. I guess he was in love. Tanya spoke and acted as if she genuinely cared about him. If this was the case, I was quite sure he cared for her also.

I went back to the den, kissed him on the cheek, and told him I would be back to see him. I also informed him that I was living in New York City, and was a student at New York University.

He smiled and gestured for me to get closer. He hugged me and said in a whisper and hoarse voice, "Be the best person that you can be and make your mother proud. I want you to promise me one thing and that is whenever you have children, please don't mention me to them." I looked at him with a puzzled look on my face. He kissed me on the cheek and said, "Promise me now before you leave."

I was crying as I replied, "Yes Daddy, I promise."

I said goodbye to my father and Tanya and headed back to the Thornton's house. I had a stoic look on my face as I entered their home. I could see they were concerned and worried about me.

"How are you holding up?" Mr. Thornton asked, motioning for me to have a seat.

"Not so well," I softly replied.

"It will be alright, Dana. God is alive and well. He's a miracle worker. God will make the impossible possible, you just keep praying," Mrs. Thornton interjected.

At first, I thought, *what the hell is Mrs. Thornton talking about? Doesn't she realize his condition is terminal? But who knows, maybe she's right.*

"Where is Jenny?" I asked.

"She's upstairs," Mrs. Thornton answered.

"I know you saw him," Jenny uttered, as I entered her room.

"Yeah, he looks terrible. He doesn't look good at all. He eats from a tube hooked to his abdomen. He can barely speak and when he does his voice is hoarse."

"I'm so sorry, Dana."

"But why didn't you tell me?"

"I know I should have but I promised my parents I wouldn't say a thing. The whole idea was to get you here on your own without saying too much about your dad. I knew he was sick, but I didn't know it was cancer."

Fighting through my tears, I barely whispered, "He's going into the hospital next month. His cancer is terminal."

"You mean a hospice?"

"Is that what it's called? Tanya said, the hospital."

"I think she meant to say hospice. Oh, my God! Dana, I'm so sorry!" she cried.

"He and Tanya are married. They even signed a prenup."

"She loves him."

"That's what I said."

"If she only wanted him for his money, she would have dipped a long time ago."

"Yeah, you're right."

"It's cool that she's standing by him. What does she look like?"

"She's pretty. I thought she was one of those hot girls but she's far from it. I like her. He's got himself a dime piece." We both giggled.

I knew Jenny had made plans for us to hang out with Kim and her friends, but she must have sensed that I wasn't in the mood. I was quite sure she was looking forward to it and I didn't want to ruin things.

"Don't worry about it," she said to me, "we can party or whatever another time."

I went back a few times to see my father and his wife. I showed him my engagement ring and invited him to my wedding, pretending as if I wasn't aware that his cancer was terminal. I told him that I would be back in a few months to visit him. I wished Tanya the best and told her I would stay in touch.

***

I did a little investigation of my own to find out Brian's whereabouts. I was surprised when I found out that he was married and had a baby on the way. I was a bit jealous of his wife because I knew she had a good man. Men like Brian don't come a dime a dozen. They are ridiculously hard to find and so far, I had come across two, Brian and Charles.

The few days that I spent with the Thorntons were wonderful. I thanked them for their hospitality and the love and affection they showed me. They wished me well and reminded me not to forget their invitation to my wedding.

Jokingly, Mrs. Thornton said, "I have this fabulous dress that I need to show off."

We all laughed, and I promised I would make sure she gets to show off her dress. Jenny had her moment with her parents as she hugged and kissed them. Several of her relatives had stopped by and tried to convince her to relocate her business to South Carolina. But she would have none of it.

"I sell enough houses in New York, I don't need to move my business here," she said sheepishly to me.

Jenny's father and uncle drove us to the airport. Naturally, we didn't get to party or do anything outrageous because of my father's health. But I must say, it was worth it going home. The flight back to New York was long, boring, and tiring. We had to make a stop in Maryland. When the plane finally landed in New York, I was glad to get my ass off. My butt was hurting like hell from all that sitting. Greg and Ebony were at the airport to meet Jenny. Charles was there also. He looked shocked when he saw Greg, Ebony, and Jenny hugging and kissing each other. After saying bye to Jenny and her small entourage, Charles and I headed to his apartment.

"Damn, baby!" Charles said.

"What now?"

"I saw those two…"

Giggling, I asked, "What about them?"

"They were at the airport the whole time kissing and hugging each other. I thought they were a couple. You know, like a real couple? Never in a million years would I believe they were waiting for you and Jenny." We both were laughing when he asked, "Do they all live together?"

"No."

"But are they lovers?"

"Yeah," I responded, laughing like crazy.

"I admire that man. When I grow up, I wanna be just like him. He's my hero," he said, smiling. We were coughing from laughing so hard.

"You like shit like that don't you? I bet that's one of your fantasies?"

"I can't lie, what man doesn't? What man wouldn't want to be with two fine-ass ladies?"

"Oh, do you think Jenny is fine?" I said it with a smile.

"Um, well, yeah she is."

"So, you would wanna do it with two fine ladies, huh?"

"Only if you were one of the fine ladies in my fantasy."

"Yeah right, you're just saying that."

"So, what about you, wouldn't you want to be one of the fine ass girls in big daddy's fantasy?" He laughed.

"Now where did that come from? What's up with the big daddy talk?" I asked, giggling.

"Ooh, I see there is a case of amnesia going on here. The last time we were getting busy, I distinctively remember a certain young lady screaming and hollering, 'Yes, big daddy, right there, big daddy. Don't stop big daddy'. Didn't you?"

"So, I did so what?" I said as the laughing continued.

Neither of us could take it any longer. The heat inside the car was getting under our skin. He was feeling my tits and coochie with one hand, as he maneuvered the car with the other. I reached for his crotch and gripped his hard member. I undid his zipper and began massaging his pulsating ebony dick as he stuck his finger in my coochie. Shit, I was cumming and I wanted more. I leaned over and began sucking his dick as he sped along the parkway.

"We're almost home," he managed to utter as I let his dick slide out my mouth.

As the car pulled upon his block, he quickly parked. He snatched up my bags and headed upstairs. I pulled his zipper open and slid my wet coochie on his dick as we rode the elevator.

"Dana, there's a camera in here. What if we get caught?" he kept repeating.

I pretended as if I didn't hear a word he said. I was giving him a taste of what he was about to get. Lying there with him that night made me realize how committed he was and how hard he was willing to work on our relationship. I was consumed by guilt as the thoughts rattled my mind. The only obstacles that were preventing me from giving one hundred percent in the relationship were my baggage and the lies. While I sat there looking into those dreamy eyes of his, I felt it was time for me to clear the air and share with him some of my life experiences. I started by telling him that my father was dying from terminal cancer and that I had to fly back to South Carolina in a matter of weeks.

"I'm sorry to hear that," he said.

"Thanks."

"How is your family taking it?"

"Not too well, especially my father's parents."

"What kind of cancer does he have?"

"He has throat cancer."

"Damn, that's terrible!"

"I know, but…"

"But what?" he asked, inquisitively.

"My dad, he's given me access to my trust fund."

"I never knew you had a trust fund."

"Yes, I do. It's just that my dad and I weren't on good terms. So, I just stayed away from him because of all the shit he did to me."

"What did he do?"

My reality had set in, as I began telling him how my father had molested and raped me from the age of nine until I was eighteen years old. His demeanor was unsettling as he tried to make sense of what I was saying. As I continued talking, he became more relaxed, composed, and attentive. He understood how difficult and painful it was for me.

"Was that the reason why you moved to New York?"

"Yes, but there's more to it."

I explained everything to him, beginning with my father and how I ended up in New York City. There was silence, and he got up and poured himself a glass of Moet and gulped it down. I thought, *this is it, the relationship is over.* I was ready to swallow my pride and give him back his ring. The look on his face betrayed him. It was as if things were spinning out of control. He shook his head and gave me a slight smile.

"Well, it's about you and me now and no one is going to come between us. What your father did to you was wrong. However, it takes a strong and decent woman with morals; love, and understanding to forgive as you have done. You refused to lie down and die, and I respect that. You're as beautiful inside as you are on the outside. Perhaps not telling me at the beginning of our relationship might have been a blessing in disguise."

"What do you mean?"

"Maybe I would have reacted differently back then as opposed to now, who knows? You telling me now and the way I feel about you prove that our love for each other is where it ought to be. People say that things happen for a reason. Maybe they're right. Because there have been numerous instances where I've crossed paths with women who wanted to be with me, but something was missing, I moved on. I knew what I was looking for and I know now that I've finally found it."

"Are you serious about everything you've said?" I asked. He looked me in the eyes and said yes.

I didn't know what to say. I was tongue-tied. I started crying. I had always felt that any man with a conscience wouldn't want to be with me much less marry me after hearing how I was abused and raped. Whenever people hear the word incest, it paints an ugly picture. A stigma that is unparalleled and it certainly made me feel ugly. With guys like Kenny, Robert, Jason, and even Bradley, it never bothered me because I knew what they were about.

I couldn't say the same when I was around Charles and some of the decent and respectful men, I had crossed paths with. Once in their company, I would feel shy, yet comfortable. I thank God every day for Charles and although I didn't tell him about my involvement in the Playaz Club at that moment, I knew eventually I would have to.

***

As Charles drove me home the next day, we spoke about the upcoming semester, which had already started. After getting out of the car, I told him if I need an override from his department to get into a closed course, he will have to use his connections, to which he said it wouldn't be a problem, smiled, and drove off. Once inside my apartment, I called Tara. She was about to give me the update when my home phone rang, it was Robert. I told her I would call her back.

"What's up, Dana? How was your trip?" he asked.

"It was good."

"How is your aunt?"

His question caught me off guard and I hesitatingly replied, "Oh, she's still not feeling well but she's coming along."

"How come you didn't call? Is this the way to treat the man you're about to marry?"

"No baby, I was just busy running back and forth trying to help the family out that's all. The place was chaotic and mentally I was so out of it, that I didn't have time for anyone. Can you forgive me? I'm so sorry."

"It's cool, but next time call even if it's just to leave a message."

"Okay."

"Are you gonna be there later?"

"Yeah, I'll be here. I'm tired."

"Alright, I'll talk to you later."

"Bye," I said, about to hang up.

"Hold on. Umm, Tara will give you a call. There have been a few changes since you've been gone," he added.

"You mean in that short time shit has changed? What the fuck is going on?"

"A few changes, you know what I'm saying? Tara will explain everything, don't worry. I'll fill you in later, bye."

"Girl, how was your trip?" Tara asked when I called her back.

"It was great other than my dad's health problems."

"I hope he gets better."

"It's much more serious than that."

"Oh wow, I'm sorry to hear that. Would I be asking too much if I stop by your place? I know you just got back in town and you must be tired."

"It's okay, you can come on over. I need to know what went down."

"See you in a minute then."

While I waited for Tara, I fell asleep. It was the ringing of the doorbell that woke me up.

"What's up, baby girl?" Tara said as she entered my apartment smoking one of her stink-ass cigarettes.

"Nothin' much, it's just my dad."

"You were saying that he's sick?"

"Yeah, he has throat cancer, and it's terminal."

"Damn, that's messed up. How are you holding up?"

"I'm just hanging in there doing what I have to. So, what's going on? What's all that shit Robert is getting so hyped about?"

"Girl, money, and drugs have been missing and Jimmy thinks there's a snitch in the organization."

"Word, damn! Do they have any idea who did the shit?" I asked, shocked.

"Nah, it's just a lot of lip service, but nobody knows for sure."

"How much gwop and drugs are we talking about?"

"Over half mil and ten kilos."

"Get the fuck outta here! You're bullshitting, right?"

"No, I'm not. Somebody hit Andre's crib."

"The mansion? This is unbelievable. I thought his security was tight. What happened to those big ass Amazon bitches weren't they doing their job?"

"Somebody fell asleep."

"I knew that shit was gonna happen sooner or later."

"Everything is on lock now. Everybody is being watched. Mutha-fuckas are being searched at the drop of a dime. Whether it's a pick-up or a delivery or going from one stash house to the next, your ass is getting searched."

"You're fucking kidding? It's like that now?"

"Hell yeah, these niggas ain't playing. Did Robert tell you we have to make a run?"

"No, he didn't. He just said that you would explain some shit to me. What is it this time?"

"Jersey, we have to do a pick-up."

"Drugs or gwop?"

"Both, and it's next week."

I felt a sudden uneasiness in the pit of my gut, as I thought about doing another pick-up. Although I had my trust fund, I had to be careful in more ways than one. I couldn't afford to let anyone from the Playaz Club know about it, including Tara. I knew I had to use my smarts and wits if I wanted to get away from all the chaos around me. *I had come this far*, I thought to myself, *so I might as well see this shit through and stick to my plan.*

"It's no problem, I'll do it. But I'm telling you, this is it. Like you, I've had it and I think this might be my last run," I said, meaning it.

"I'm glad you feel that way because a lot of shit doesn't look right. Do you know what I'm saying? Niggas are getting robbed, mutha-fuckas are snitching and it's crazy."

"Tara, I'm tired. Do you hear me? I need to do something productive with my life and this isn't it."

"You're still in school, right?"

"Yeah, I have classes tomorrow."

"Cool, you just go ahead and do what you have to. Don't sweat it."

"What's up with Jason and that brotha he be rolling with?"

"You mean, Platinum?"

"Yeah, what's up with him?"

"He's still running around with Jason."

"What's up with Jimmy?"

"Jimmy is still the same. He's still acting as if he's some big-time gangster, old ass bastard!" We laughed, as Tara continued talking. "I think Jason and his boy had something to do with the missing drugs and gwop."

"Shit, I wouldn't put nothin' pass that grimy ass mutha-fucka."

"Your so-called man fucked up a whole U-Haul truck of drugs."

"What! He never mentioned anything like that to me."

"The DEA rolled upon his shit, and he hauled ass, along with Jamaican King."

"He ain't say nothin' about that to me. He must have felt embarrassed."

"Of course, he was. Andre and Jimmy were furious because they lost a lot of money. But the funny thing is that Robert and Jamaican King kept blaming each other for the mishap."

"Please stop, Tara! This shit is too funny. Robert says he's coming by tonight. I won't say a word to him about it."

"When are you gonna let him know that you're engaged and it's not to him? You should tell him to bounce."

"You're right, I'm getting there. Everything has its time and he's about to get his walking papers. But I can't do that now and still show my black ass around here."

"I hear you. I just wanted to know where your head is at and I see you're still on point."

We spoke for some time while sipping on Alize. If it weren't for Marques, who kept calling her to bring her ass home, she would have spent the night.

***

Robert never showed up like he promised, which was great. When he finally did it was three days after our conversation. He seemed edgy and he began telling me that he feared the people at his job were on to what he was doing.

"How is that possible?" I asked.

"I did invite Michael and Gary to several of Jimmy's pool parties."

"But even if you did what did they see? Did you show them anything? Did they see anything they weren't supposed to see?"

"Not that I'm aware of. The most they saw was some recreational drugs, which they also do. Anything else, I can't remember. But Jason, I don't know. He's the type that's always trying to impress. He always wanted to give them a tour of the fucking house and knowing that nigga with his big ass mouth and ego, I wouldn't put anything past him. All I know is that the police have been snooping around at the job and have spoken to several of my co-workers, including Michael and Gary. We barely speak now and the atmosphere at the office is very tense."

"The only thing I can suggest is to keep being yourself. The minute you start acting differently or showing some kind of emotion they've never seen before they're gonna be all over your ass. You've got to be cool, Robert. Come on now, didn't we meet in a chat room? You know what time it is. Don't let them play you. If anything, you play them."

I didn't give a damn about him and his problems. I had my own to deal with. However, I noticed he was nodding and agreeing with the things I said. He gave me a look as if to say, thanks. But the words never came out of his mouth. I was waiting to see if he would say anything about the so-called mishaps that took place and to my surprise, he did. He claimed that he wasn't at fault and that he felt that somebody had tipped off the police.

"What happened?" I asked.

"Jamaican King and I were about to hop into the U-Haul when out of nowhere we saw a bunch of DEA agents bum-rushing the truck. They must have thought we were inside the shit. That bust wasn't coincidental at all. That shit was a setup."

He went on to say that he believed Jason and Platinum had something to do with the robbery at Andre's place. He even mentioned Pretty Boy saying that he didn't trust him.

"Are you talking about the brotha who drove me and Tara back from our last run?" I asked, acting as if I didn't know who he was referring to.

"Yeah, I don't trust his ass."

"Isn't he your dawg?"

"Hell, no! Jimmy is the one who supposedly hired him."

During all this, Robert kept hinting that I should leave town with him.

"What are you talking about?"

"I want you to leave with me. I have enough money for both of us. Let's go to Mexico or the Caribbean. I have a funny feeling that this thing is gonna blow up. So why wait around for all that bullshit?" he snapped.

"You're right," I said, snickering to myself.

"Look, we can get married at City Hall, right here in Manhattan. We can do it tomorrow, or as soon as possible. No one has to know a damn thing. We just do our thing and leave."

"Damn, you're off the chain. You're moving too fast baby, slow down."

"Where is the ring?" he asked, looking at my finger.

"It's on the dresser."

"How come I never see you wearing it?"

"Because you're never around, duh! You know what? Let me go put it on, 'cause I ain't got no time for this nonsense."

"Nah baby, it's not like that, I was just asking that's all."

"Whatever."

This negro is something else, I thought to myself. His antics were scaring me. He was acting paranoid. He kept checking the windows to see if he was followed by the police. I didn't understand why he would come to my apartment if he felt he was being followed.

The one positive in all of this was that his mind wasn't on sex. It had been a while since we last slept together and I damn sure wasn't in any rush to sleep with him. I don't know what I would have done that night. Thank God it never came to that. He took a shower, hit the bed, slept like a baby, and left early the next morning.

***

Later that day . . .

After my conversation with Charles, I seriously began thinking about the occurrences that Jenny had mentioned to me, the strange cars, and the unusual behavior of several men on her block. But most important of all was the black Lexus with the tinted windows, parked directly across from her apartment building.

'*Do you know any of the men or the driver of the Lexus?*' I remember asking her.

'*No,*' she had replied.

I told her not to worry about it even though Jason and the things he said came to mind. I was still with the Playaz Club so there was no need for him to do something like that. Although I was convinced that everything was fine, I still had some reservations, so I decided to call her.

"Hey, how are you?" I asked when she answered the phone.

"Hi, I'm doing great."

"How's business?"

"It's good. The economy must be doing great. I've got a lot of buyers." She giggled.

"Girl, the economy isn't that good. People who have money don't worry about the economy. If they want a house, they just go out and buy the shit."

"You're so right."

She wanted to know how I was holding up and if I had begun spending from my trust fund.

"I'm doing fine and no; I haven't touched it."

"Good," she said. "Make sure you use that money wisely."

"I will trust me. Have you noticed anything unusual of late on your block?"

"No, you were right. The people in the car were friends of some brotha who lives in the building across from me."

"See, I told you not to sweat that shit. You've got too much going on in your life to be worrying about stuff like that."

"I know."

"I'm gonna go now. Say hi to Greg and Ebony for me."

"They're sitting right here. You know they can't leave this good pussy." I could hear them laughing in the background.

"You're nasty. Just make sure you're home later tonight. I might stop by depending on how I feel," I said, laughing.

"No problem, I'll be here. Talk to you later, bye."

I felt relieved knowing that everything was fine with her. It felt like a load had been lifted off my shoulders.

Episode 24

$\mathcal{T}$ ara was with me as our ride pulled up on the block. Sitting behind the wheel was Pretty Boy, and as we hit the New Jersey Turnpike my gut reaction was one of suspicion and it had me thinking. He was way too quiet as far as I was concerned. I doubt if he said ten words if that much during the ride. It was, "Hi, do you wanna listen to the radio?" and "Thank you." He had his eyes on Tara and I kept telling her to say something other than hi, but she wouldn't.

While Pretty Boy waited outside, Tara and I entered the safe house. Inside were Robert, Marques, Stacy, and four intimidating-looking men. Talk about being surprised. Lying on a huge marble table in the kitchen were drugs and money. But that wasn't all, across from where we stood several men and women dressed in overalls were staring at us. They were moving at a rather fast pace, loading several duffel bags and briefcases with drugs and money. Tara looked disappointed and frustrated.

"Is that our pickup?" I said under my breath to her, pointing at the marble table.

"Maybe, but I'm not sure." She stared at Marques, but his only concern seemed to be the task at hand. It was obvious that he never discussed his going to the safe house with her, and that pissed her off.

While the men continued packing, Robert told Tara to take the remaining drugs from under the table and put them in the duffel bags. I was so caught up with the frantic pace and everything else that was going on, that I never noticed a large number of drugs under the table. Robert, who was now staring at me, gestured for me to give Tara a hand.

"This place is busy," Tara said.

"Tell me about it," I replied. "Have you been here before?"

"No, but I'm glad I'm here now."

"What do you mean?"

"Can't you see what type of a setup this is?"

"Yeah, it looks like a wholesale distribution drug market."

"Okay then, look where those brothas are taking the duffel bags, and look how they are dressed."

"Damn girl, this shit is like New Jack City," I said, as I noticed Stacy walking toward us.

After signaling to Robert that we were finished, Stacy led us down a hallway, which led to an underground basement. *Damn, everywhere we go there's a fucking underground basement,* I said to myself. I couldn't believe what I was seeing.

In front of us stood several Amazon-looking women, along with several thuggish-looking men in overalls. They were all carrying high-powered weapons as they stood guard watching the workers who were busy stacking and counting several kilos of cocaine and cash.

As we continued walking, we were met by Hally Robinson who handed us three sets of overalls. Tara, who didn't like the idea of wearing the outfit balked at putting it on. Marques was quickly called to keep her in line. He took her aside and whispered something in her ear. Although I couldn't hear what they were saying, whatever he said must have angered her, because she made several attempts to leave. But after a bit of persuasion from Robert and Hally, she decided against it. I was so nervous and uneasy, that I couldn't hold my pee. Fortunately, there was a bathroom close by. To make matters worse, Tara said she had to take a number two.

"What the fuck you mean a number two?" an agitated Marques asked.

All eyes were on Tara as she stood her ground. I didn't know what to say as I looked on.

"I can't believe this shit, can you?" Marques said to no one in particular.

"Go ahead, make it quick," Robert said to her.

Tara spent the same amount of time inside the bathroom as I did.

"That was quick!" Marques said sarcastically.

"Hey, it's got a mind of its own, it wouldn't come out. What do you want me to do?" she said, with a scowl on her face. Stacy was laughing the whole time.

We were led into a makeshift changing room. I was somewhat suspicious of Tara and her bathroom antics, but then again, maybe she did have to take a number two. I counted so much money that day that it was ridiculous, and the guards watched our every move.

"I thought this was supposed to be a pick-up?" I asked Tara.

"That's what Robert and Jimmy told me."

"I'm in a fucking drug factory stacking and counting drugs and surrounded by a bunch of gun-wielding mutha-fuckas who would shoot me in a heartbeat. My dad is dying, and my best friend's life is in danger. I can't take this shit anymore," I said, crying.

"Chill girl, you can't let these people see you crying. Which friend of yours is in danger? Is it Jenny? Who threatened her?"

"Nobody, I'm just saying." I realized I had let my emotions get the best of me. And although she didn't push the issue, I knew she didn't believe me.

Once we were done, Tara, Stacy, and I got dressed. We were then led through the same underground tunnel where we first entered. Only this time we were heading in the opposite direction. When we finally exited the tunnel, we were at least two or three blocks away from our original starting point. As I approached our waiting car, I noticed that Pretty Boy wasn't behind the wheel and neither was our money.

"That place was off the hook, wasn't it?" Tara said.

"Yeah, it's off the chain!" Stacy gushed, sounding as if we just got back from vacationing in the damn Caribbean. "You guys have never been here before?"

"Nah," we both replied.

"As many times as Robert and Marques have been here, they have never taken y'all here? Wow! So, I guess you guys haven't been up to Bathgate either, huh?"

"No," Tara responded with an astonished look on her face. "I guess you've been all over, huh?"

"Yeah, I've been to Bathgate and the other stash house in Long Island. They usually move the works from Uncle Andre's crib to either Long Island or Bathgate and then to Jersey."

Uncle Andre, I thought to myself. But then I remembered her mother was sleeping with him.

"How do you know all this shit?" Tara asked.

"My mom, Tara, duh!"

I wanted to slap the taste out of her mouth so bad it wasn't funny. I wasn't saying a whole lot to her and she wasn't saying much either. We weren't friends but we tolerated each other because of the business we were in. I guess the ass-whipping I gave her had calmed her ass down.

Stacy kept yapping away as we drove back to the city. She was informative, explaining to us that the house in New Jersey's sole purpose was to cut, package and distribute the drugs. Anyone caught undermining the process was dealt with swiftly.

"What do you mean by dealt with swiftly?" I asked curiously.

"They get the gat," Stacy replied.

"Is that so?" Tara asked, taking a drag from her cigarette.

"That's what I heard."

"But have you ever seen anybody getting the gat with your own eyes?"

"No, but I've seen niggas and bitches get beat down," she answered, laughing.

Usually, when we completed our runs, it was the norm for our driver to have our money. Yet in this instance that wasn't the case. Stacy informed us that we had to wait until Robert got back to the city before we could get our money.

After dropping off Stacy at Sixty-Eight and Lexington Avenue, Tara and I headed to Sylvia's Restaurant in Harlem. The food at Sylvia's was top-notch exquisite southern cooking. Despite all the negative innuendos some people have said about the surrounding community, the people and the culture in Harlem were what defined it. So, to find excellent southern cuisine at restaurants such as Sylvia's and Amy Ruth's was not only a bonus it was also worth the trip.

The conversations inside Sylvia's were continuous and respectful. You could tell the people were enjoying themselves and having a good time. Tara and I ordered baked chicken, candied yams, and collard greens, and for dessert, lemon pecan pie. For drinks, Tara had a Pepsi Cola. I had a glass of country lemonade, a real down-home drink.

Tara and I spoke at length about our relationship with the men in our lives, school, family, and of course sex. We agreed that we wouldn't discuss the Playaz Club and we kept our word. It was great hanging out with her. Yet I sensed there were some things she wanted to discuss but held back. Whatever it was, I was confident that she would share them with me one day. *I wonder if she feels the same way about me,* I thought. I knew I had slipped up on several occasions by saying certain things I shouldn't have said. However, she never pressured me or meddled, and I respected her for that.

Like everything else, the evening came to an end. We hopped into a taxi and headed downtown. Our first stop was at her apartment, where we said bye to each other. I then called Charles as I continued in the taxi. I assured him that I would stop by his apartment later that night. I thought about calling Robert regarding my money but decided against it.

When Robert finally did call, he told me that he gave my share of the money, along with Tara's, to Marques. When I asked for an explanation as to why he didn't bring the money himself, his response was, "I was busy." He then asked. "Are you home?" After telling him that I wasn't, he wanted to know what time I would be back at my apartment.

"I'm not quite sure," I replied. "I'm thinking about spending the night at Tanisha's apartment." This was a lie because I was home.

"If you change your mind hit me on my cell."

"Okay, talk to you later."

I then called Tara and told her I was coming by. I could have waited until the next day to get my money, but I chose not to. I always felt that when it comes down to my money, it should be in my hands, instead of someone else's. Not that I didn't trust Tara or believed that she would do anything to cheat me out of my money. Because she wasn't like that, it's just how I felt.

I was surprised to see Marques when I got there. I could sense the tension between them. I had always avoided visiting Tara whenever he was there. I knew he was her man, but how he stared at me always made me uncomfortable because it was sexual. All this I figured stemmed from his friendship with both Robert and Jason, who must have told him that I had some good coochie.

Tara handed me the envelope with my money. Not wanting to disrespect Marques, I said hi. He barely said hello. He acted as if he didn't want to be bothered, so I left his ass alone. Tara and I were talking when his cell phone rang. He saw us watching him, and as he walked into the bedroom, he slammed the door behind him.

After getting off the phone, he got dressed and told Tara he had some unfinished business to take care of. She didn't doubt him at all. This was the nature of his job with the Playaz Club, so she didn't question it. Nevertheless, she was somewhat skeptical after hearing that he met up with Stacy at Sixty-Eight and Lexington Avenue, after we dropped her off. She never told me how she found out about it, but if she said it, I believed it.

No sooner than he was out the door, Tara informed me she wasn't sure what was going on between him and Stacy. But whatever it was she was going to get to the bottom of it. It certainly didn't strike me as if she were jealous, or that she gave a damn whether he was sleeping around or not. It seemed she was more interested in connecting the dots to the daily operation of the Playaz Club. I got the impression that she wanted to rip off the organization because all she talked about was getting paid.

While we continued talking, I excused myself and called Charles. It looked as if I wasn't going to be able to make it over to his place as I had promised. But I explained to him that I was running some errands and would be a few minutes late. He said it wasn't a problem. But suddenly it dawned on me that it was my time to start connecting the dots. I asked Tara if she would accompany me over to his apartment. Although I didn't ask his permission, I knew it wouldn't be a problem. She was aware of my engagement, but she had never met Charles, nor did she know much about him other than he was a professor.

As we drove, I began telling her how we met. At first, she was somewhat at a loss for words. She cursed me for having a man like Charles in my life and wanted to know why I still hadn't given Robert his walking papers. Moreover, she warned me to never break off our relationship via email, or because of Robert.

"No more email breakups for me." I laughed. "It's been difficult for me. It's as if I'm trapped. Sometimes it feels as if I'm living two different lives. I'm afraid that my actions might harm Charles. I don't want to bring him into our world, no way."

"So, what do you think you're doing right now? Girl, I'm telling you, if you don't put a stop to Robert and the Playaz Club, eventually you're either gonna pull him into your world or lose him. Are Robert and the Club worth it? Be honest, is it?"

"No, neither one of them is worth it."

"What you need to do is get your ass out of this bullshit and go on with your man. Why are you still a part of the Playaz Club? I know they have those bullshit rules about being a member for life, but don't sweat that shit. This is the good ole USA. This isn't some fucked up small-ass country where you can't relocate."

"It's not that easy, believe me, it's not."

"Then what is it? Does it have anything to do with the remark you made in Jersey about your girl being threatened?"

"Uh, no, it's nothing like that."

I could tell her mind was working overtime as she tried to figure out the reasons for me not leaving the Playaz Club. Although we were great friends, I thought she should be worrying about why she was still in the organization and loving the money as much as I and everybody else.

"I'll let you know soon."

"I hope it's not too late by then."

I immediately introduced her to Charles once we got there. From her reaction, I could tell that she thought he was handsome. She pinched me more than once on my backside and gave me the thumbs-up sign. Charles offered her a drink which she politely declined. Her cell phone rang. Whoever it was on the other end of the line was screaming at her.

"Okay," she said, as she explained that she had to go. Charles looked on with a puzzled look on his face.

"Who was that?" I asked her.

"It was Jimmy," she responded under her breath. "And he sounds pissed."

I knew something was wrong and I wanted to go with her. But she would have none of it.

"I'll keep you updated," she shot back at me.

"Okay, just let me know."

"No problem, bye. Charles, it was nice meeting you."

"It was nice meeting you also," he replied, as she headed for the elevator.

Episode 25

*T*ara got back to me the next day with some disturbing news. It seemed someone had ripped off one of Jimmy's drug houses and made off with nearly a million in money and drugs. The culprits they believed were two males and a female. The lone eyewitness supposedly was Jackie, who claimed she was on an errand for Andre, when he called and told her to keep an eye out for any unusual activity at several of his drug locations. The thing that bothered me was that she made several unfair allegations about me to Jimmy. She claimed that the female in the group had a walk like mine and that it could have been me. I was visibly upset, shaken, and feared for my life.

"She said that?" I said to Tara. I was pissed.

"Yes, she did. But I told Jimmy you were with me and that Marques could verify this also."

"So that was the reason for all that yelling on the phone yesterday. What did I do to that bitch for her to make up some shit like that?"

"Yeah, and my impression of Jimmy was that he didn't believe a damn word she said. First of all, she told Jimmy they were getting inside a tinted black Four Runner with their backs turned. Then when he asked, 'did you follow them, or try to get a better look at them', she claimed the traffic light caught her. The bitch is lying."

"Did Jimmy believe you when you told him I was with you?"

"He did."

"How do you know that?"

"He told me. Those were his words."

"Pheeeeew! I'm glad that shit is beyond me. But why would she say that about me? That's a fucked-up bitch!"

"She's done it before. She made that same claim four years ago and almost got the person killed. She's gonna get hers don't worry about that. She's a liar and a thief and I'm gonna beat her ass one of these days."

"You ain't the only one."

Tara and I concluded that whoever was robbing the organization believed that taking small amounts of drugs and money, would cast doubt on those closest to both Jimmy and Andre and the likely culprit may very well be Jason and his friend Platinum.

After the update, Tara said she would get back to me because she needed to know what the hell happened between Marques and Stacy. It was obvious she didn't get anywhere with Marques because she made the same comment several days earlier.

"You go, girl," I said to her. "You always tell me to check my man; well it's time to check yours.

"That's exactly what I'm gonna do. I'll give you a call later."

"Sure," I said, closing the door behind her.

***

I was watching television when my cell phone rang. It was Robert. He wanted me to meet him at the Garage. It was a private hangout for members of the Playaz Club. It was located at West Twenty-Third Street and Eleventh Avenue on the west side of Manhattan, by the Westside Highway. I had been there on many occasions, so it wasn't an issue. I threw on a pair of sweats and got into my ride. Normally, finding parking in this part of town was a pain in the ass. I was relieved upon finding a spot less than a block away. As I approached the building, the usual cameras that were normally at the front entrance were missing. *Damn, they make all this money and they can't install new cameras*, I thought to myself. There was a light on inside, however; there wasn't a soul in sight. I began calling Robert's name. I was getting worried and frustrated when I suddenly heard footsteps approaching.

"What's up, bitch? I see you got the message, huh?" Startled by the voice of Jason, I panicked and fell. I tried to make my way toward the door. "What's the rush? Quit being so antisocial, and by the way, the door is locked."

"Where is Robert? He said for me to meet him here." I began yelling out Robert's name.

"You still don't get it? Damn, you are a dumb bitch, Dana. Robert never called; it was me. I can't believe you went for it. I didn't think it would work, but damn, I'm good!" he smiled.

He had a haggard look on his unshaven face. His lips were chapped, and his bloodshot eyes betrayed his drawn face, which looked like he hadn't slept in days. There was a funky odor emanating from his dishevel-looking clothes. He briskly walked by me and sat on one of the leather couches directly in the corner of the room.

"Get your ass over here!" he demanded.

"Jason, I'm begging you. Don't do this to me," I pleaded.

His lack of concern for my well-being angered me, as he unzipped his pants and demanded that I suck his dick. I closed my eyes and began screaming within myself as the stench became unbearable the closer, I got to him.

The sound of a door slamming echoed loudly. I turned and looked in the direction of where the sound was coming from, only to see Jamaican King with a big ass gun in his hand, pointing it directly at Jason, who sat frozen on the couch. He had a startled look on his face as Jamaican King swiftly swooped down on him.

"Dana, get out of here!" he said, in his deep Jamaican accent.

"What the fuck is this? What the fuck is going on?" Jason screamed.

"The big man wanna chat to you. Don't worry every ting cool," Jamaican King stated, as he looked at me with a sly smile on his face.

"This shit is not right, no it's not," Jason mumbled.

"Shut up boy! You like teef? And now you graduate to raping and beating woman, huh?" I was about to walk out the door, when Jamaican King said, "Dana, you don't see nothing, you hear."

Visibly shaken, I nodded my head in agreement and walked outside. Not only was I stunned by what I saw next, but I was also hoping it was all a dream and I would wake up; because standing by his car next to Troy was Jimmy, puffing on his cigar.

"Hi Dana," Jimmy said, in that deep baritone of his. "Did Jason hurt you?"

"No Jimmy," I managed to say.

He hugged me, smiled at me, and whispered in my ears, "I never believed Jackie, and remember you didn't see or hear a thing."

"Okay, I didn't see or hear a thing," I repeated.

"Good girl, now go on home."

As I walked toward my ride, Jimmy and Troy entered the building. Time seemed to slow down as my car slowly rolled down the block. My body quivered uncontrollably, and my intuition told me that I had just seen Jason for the last time.

I drove around the city confused and dazed for at least an hour, unsure of what to do or where to go. Two things troubled me deeply, one was the look on Jason's face as he kept repeating, "This is not right." The second was the eerie baritone of Jimmy whispering in my ear, "You didn't see or hear a thing." It was unbelievably disturbing, as I tried to compose myself.

I was still undecided about where to go when I realized I was a few blocks from Jenny's apartment. But just my luck, she wasn't home. I called her at least three different times and she never answered. Almost out of options, I drove to Charles's apartment.

"You look a bit distraught," he said, as he greeted me.

"I'm just a little tired."

"You look as if you've seen a ghost."

"I'm just exhausted."

I kicked off my sneakers and sat on the bed next to him. My life was spiraling out of control or so it seemed. However, I decided not to say anything about Jason and the Playaz Club.

Tara was right, I said to myself, *if I were to lose Charles then so be it. But I damn sure wasn't going to get him involved in the Playaz Club affairs.*

Charles sensed that something was bothering me, but not wanting to get on my bad side he left it alone. Neither Jenny nor Tara returned my call that night.

***

There was a steady rain pouring when I awoke on Sunday morning. I hadn't slept well the night before and I was tired, and my body ached. As I looked in the mirror at myself, my face looked worn and drawn. I looked like a crackhead wondering where my next high was coming from. The last few days had taken their toll on not only my mind but my body as well.

I could hear Charles snoring as I brush my teeth. Seeing him lying there only reinforced my thinking that I had done the right thing by not mentioning the Playaz Club. After all, he was a college professor, who had worked too hard for what he had achieved, and I wasn't going to cause any disarray that could lead to him losing his job and perhaps getting hurt.

I made breakfast and turned on the television to New York 1, to get the latest news and updates. There was no mention of anyone getting shot or killed. Charles was still asleep when my cell phone rang.

"Dana, it's me. Where are you? Can you talk?"

"I'm at Charles'. Tara, what's wrong?"

"Listen up, we need to talk. What time is good for you?"

"Say about noon, is that good?"

"Yeah, it's cool and the black outfit looks nice. I'll pick it up later, bye."

I knew it had to be Marques who was snooping around for her to end the conversation as she had. Then again, she could have been around Jimmy and other members of the Playaz Club, because she hollered at me from an unfamiliar number. *But damn, it was early in the morning, why would she be at Jimmy's crib that early,* I thought to myself. I kissed Charles, who was still asleep, and left him a note. I was anxious to hear what she had to say, and as I pulled up on the block, she was sitting in her car as the rain continued to pour. I honked my car horn several times before she realized it was me. While we rode the elevator up to my apartment, I was very eager to hear what she had to say. I also wanted to tell her what had occurred between me and Jason. However, she abruptly cut me off before I ever got started and told me to wait until we were inside my apartment. Instead of saying anything, I kept my mouth shut and waited for her to start the conversation.

"Jason is dead!" she blurted out, once we were inside my apartment.

"Oh fuck, shit! Damn, are you sure?"

"Yeah, I'm sure. They found his bullet-riddled body in Staten Island."

"Staten Island?" I shot back at her, as she looked at me with raised eyebrows.

"This is what Marques told me. He said Jason and Troy were negotiating a drug deal with some brothas from the Staple houses, who decided to rob Jason. There was a gun battle and when the smoke cleared Jason was dead. Troy was able to get away unscathed."

"That's a lie," I said, in a soft voice.

"What do you mean it's a lie?" she asked with a startled look on her face.

"I was with Jason."

The expression on her face immediately changed from one of bewilderment to one of total confusion before asking, "What are you talking about? You were in Staten Island?"

"No!" I said as I began explaining everything to her.

Though I felt bad telling her about all the things that Jason did to me, I felt the timing was right for such a conversation. She asked several questions, which I answered. As I continued talking, her stare was very intense, and she seemed to collect and store every word I said like a damn computer. Nevertheless, I mentioned to her that Jimmy and Jamaican King told me to keep my mouth shut.

"Did they say they would hurt you if you opened your mouth? Did you feel threatened?"

"No, they were cool about everything."

"I bet they were," she remarked sarcastically.

"I'm not happy that he's dead. Despite the grimy shit he did to me, I never thought it would end this way. Do you believe Jimmy and them killed him?" I asked, knowing it was a dumb question.

"From what you've said, it looks and sounds like it. Yeah, I think they did."

"This is it for me; I'm through with this shit."

"You have to be smart about this whole shit like I always tell you. After what they said to you, do you think they would allow you to just get up and run off like that now? Do you think they wouldn't come after you? What you need to do is continue to act normal as if nothing happened or is bothering you. Trust me, if you do as I tell you, you'll be alright. I'm gonna break out with you. It's just that I have a lot of unfinished business with Marques and some of these mutha-fuckas. Once that shit is over, then we can both haul ass. I need to get paid before I bounce though. There's a lot of gwop going around. Everybody is getting paid, so why not me?"

"Dayum, I didn't know you were on it like that."

"Might as well. But like I said, just keep a low profile and relax. They all knew that Jason was dead. This ain't nothing new to them. You heard what that bitch Stacy said to us the other day about people getting dealt with gats when they stepped out of line. This is real. They get down like that, grimy. Have you ever wondered what happened to Gwen, Tiffany, Babs, and some of the other girls when they get locked down?"

"They don't bail them out?"

"Not bailing them out is only a part of it. The real deal is that they forget about them, no visits, none of that. These people won't even look out for their families."

"So, what about all that shit about taking care of your own?"

"That's exactly what it is, all talk. The only time they take care of you is when you're out on the streets working."

"You're right, Tara. I was sleeping."

"We are fucking with some ruthless mutha-fuckas. Why don't you come and stay at my sister's crib? She's on vacation and won't be back for a while. You can go to school and visit Charles from there. Have you told him about...?"

I cut her off before she could say another word. "No, he doesn't know a thing about any of this."

"Don't say a word to him about it," she suggested.

"I won't."

"I have to go and work on Marques."

"For what?"

"I wanna hear it from his mouth whether Jimmy and Jamaican King killed Jason. From what you've said he's a bullshitter. Don't worry, I got this. Here's my extra key and the address to my sister's place. I'll see you later."

"Okay, I love you."

"I love you too," she replied, as we hugged.

I then packed a small bag with some of my clothes, along with my books for school, and headed to Charles's apartment. I left my belongings in the trunk of my car and headed upstairs.

"You're back quick," he said, letting me in.

"I know. I was supposed to meet up with Jenny, but she canceled until later."

"Okay, well make yourself at home."

Although I had lied to him about Jenny, I was worried about her. I called her but there was no response. I hadn't spoken to her in a while and it was unsettling.

It wasn't long before Charles was all over me. He wanted me to spend the night, but I just couldn't. I figured if I gave him some coochie maybe he would stop being so damn demanding about me sleeping over. He couldn't help himself once he entered me. He kept yelling out my name. I was fucking him good. Despite this, he started getting on my nerves by answering the phone every time it rang. I made sure there weren't going to be any more interruptions by unplugging his home phone and turning off his cell.

I stayed with him for a while, and after taking a shower and changing into one of his sweatsuits, I kissed him and said bye. I drove to the Gramercy Park address that Tara gave me. Gramercy Park was one of New York City's most prestigious neighborhoods. It was the stomping ground for some of the city's rich and famous.

The apartment was well-kept and nicely furnished. Whoever did the decorating did a wonderful job. It felt strange being in the apartment alone. Yet, I never felt like I couldn't trust Tara. I knew she was straightforward and sincere as far as our friendship was concerned, but I was praying that she would hurry back.

When she finally arrived and was alone, I asked, "Where's Marques?"

"Who knows?"

"Oh well, I thought he would be with you. I guess I assumed wrong. What happened? What did you find out about him and Stacy? And what about Jason's death, did they do it?"

"I don't know right now 'cause Marques hasn't said another word about it. But I'll get it out of him sooner than later, trust me. As for him and Stacy, that's not important," she remarked, but her body language said otherwise.

"I thought you said this is your sister's apartment?"

"It is." She laughed. "Why do you ask?"

"As Stacy likes to say, duh, look at the pictures. Tara is hugging an old lady, who is she?"

"If you must know it's my grandmother."

"There's Tara dancing, stuffing her face, and kissing on a brotha who looks nothin' like Marques. And oh yeah, there she is as a little girl. And I still haven't seen a picture of her sister yet. I wonder why?"

"You're funny. I took over the apartment so now it's mine."

"You're not paying any rent over at Marques?" I asked, surprised.

"Hell no, he's paying that shit all by his lonesome."

"And you always had this place?"

"Yeah, let me tell you something, I only stay over at Marques' crib when I feel like it."

"Word, I didn't know that. All this time I thought you lived there with him."

"Uh uh, it's not like that sweetie."

"Does he know about this place?"

"No, he doesn't. I don't tell him all my business."

"Aren't you guys tight?"

"We're cool, but I have a job to do. It's like I said on so many occasions, I'm only in this to stack my papers. Marques is only a dick, plain and simple."

"You lost me right there, what do you mean?"

"A fuck, that's it. I only wanted him to get me close to the big dawgs so I could get paid."

"Damn, you a snap. So, what happened with your sister?"

"The bitch couldn't afford the rent anymore."

"You ain't right," I said, laughing.

"No, I'm serious. She still thinks she can come up here whenever she feels like it. But it's not like that and she needs to get that through her thick ass head. Here look, "she stated, opening the bedroom closet to make her point, "see, she still has some of her clothes and shoes in my closet."

"How come I've never seen you rocking any of these gears?" I busted out laughing.

"Girl please, that's not my style or taste," she said, as she too began to laugh.

She reached into the closet and pulled out several pictures of her sister.

"She's pretty. What's her name?" I asked, looking at the pictures.

"Chante."

"You mean like Chante Moore?"

"Yeah, and if you must know she's older than me."

"Yeah, you told me this before."

***

Our conversation finally ended, and we both fell asleep. I was still asleep when she woke me up saying she had to go and take care of some important issues. Before leaving she reminded me not to answer the door.

Although I was still sleepy, I figured I would get myself together and see what Charles was up to. I was about to call him when my cell phone rang.

"Hello."

"What's up?"

"Jenny is that you?"

"Yeah, it's me."

"Where have you been? I've been worried about you. Why didn't you return my calls?"

"I'm having too much fun. I'm in Aruba, girl."

"Aruba? You're in the Caribbean?"

"Yeah, it's nice. It was an invite I couldn't turn down."

"Who invited you?"

"Greg and Ebony, we're having a ball."

"You've got to be kidding?"

"I'm not kidding, look at the number I'm calling from."

"You go, girl. But why didn't you let a sista know you were going out of town?"

"I know I should have, or at least contacted you earlier. I'm so sorry baby girl. Anyway, I'm fine, and so are Greg and Ebony. I'll be back this weekend. So, what's up with you?"

"I've been staying at Charles's apartment more frequently now. Did I tell you I quit my job?"

"No, I can't recall."

"I did but hopefully I'll find something else."

"Why don't you come and work for me? You've always said you wanted to. But you have to change your wardrobe though."

Laughing, I said, "No hoochie mama, hot girl wears allowed?"

"Only when my male clients show up," she said, laughing.

Getting serious once again, Jenny suggested that I should get a job and use my trust fund wisely.

"I will."

"How is the situation with your dad?"

"It's still the same. The last time Tanya and I spoke she said he asked how I was doing. It's tough, but I'm holding on."

"I'm praying with you baby girl."

"Thanks, Jenny. Oh, I have some serious shit to tell you when you get back in town."

"Okay, I'll see you this weekend. Bye."

"Bye."

***

Jenny was still on my mind as I headed to the sociology department to see Charles. He wasn't in his office. However, I was told by the department secretary that he was on campus. I headed to the student union, where the teachers' lounge was located and there he was. He was talking with two of his colleagues. He excused himself and walked over to me.

"Hi, what are you doing here so early?" he asked with a smile.

I noticed several students and faculty members were staring at us, as we sat at a table in the student union cafeteria. We both wanted to kiss each other on the cheek, or at least a hug. Seeing the continuous stares, we decided against it.

"I'm okay," I said. "I just thought I would come in early and hang out with you."

"What did I do to deserve you coming here at least two hours before the start of your first class?" he asked, staring at me with those gorgeous eyes of his.

"Because you're special and I've been thinking about you all day."

"You're beginning to make me feel uneasy, but in a good way," he replied, his roaming eyes focusing on my breasts.

"Who said I wanted you to feel uneasy in a good way? I'm thinking more along the line of you being bad, as bad as you wanna be." I giggled. I felt my nipples getting hard as I tried to control my breathing.

"How bad do you want me to be?"

"Very bad," I replied, in my sexy cat woman voice.

"My next class starts an hour from now. Meet me in my office in twenty minutes."

"Okay."

He was sitting at his desk waiting impatiently when I entered his office. I closed the door behind me and deliberately bent over with my legs spread apart as I laid my bag on the floor. I could feel his eyes staring at my ass. As I turned to face him, I took off my jacket. His manhood was rock hard, and he pulled me close and began kissing me. This was one of Charles' better days and he certainly didn't disappoint me. We had a clear view of Washington Square Park, as he worked his magic stick. We had to be quiet because we feared getting caught.

When it was over, he grabbed a can of Neutra Air Freshener from inside his desk drawer and began to spray his office. I retrieved his books and other miscellaneous items from off the floor and placed them back on his desk.

"I'll talk to you later," I said, as I kissed him and headed to the ladies room-shaking what my mama gave me.

Episode 26

$\mathcal{T}$aking nothing away from the danger and predicament that I was in, nothing unusual was taking place other than a few minor runs that Tara, and I did. Jenny had returned from her vacation. I told her about Jason's death, but I kept quiet about the other details. She didn't say much about the news of his death.

"I have something else I wanna tell you," I said.

"What is it?"

"I'm ready to do the nasty with y'all," I giggled.

"Are you serious?"

"Yup!"

"It will only be me and Ebony?"

"What happened to Greg?"

"He had to attend some conference."

"Okay, then it's us three," I laughed.

The next day I visited. Ebony was sitting in the living room. It was obvious that she was unaware of why I was there. Jenny and I were in the bedroom chatting and having a few drinks when she made her move. It seemed she had waited for this moment. She was grinding, rubbing, and feeling on me. She kissed me and began playing with my breast. It felt wonderful. I was turned on. I opened my legs and she lifted my skirt and softly shoved me backward on the bed. Within seconds her lips and tongue were licking, sucking, and biting my clit. I was cumming like Niagara Falls as she drove me wild. I can't recall when we removed each other's clothes, what I do remember as we were in the sixty-nine position is opening my eyes and seeing Ebony standing by the doorway masturbating.

"Come here," I said to her.

"Is it okay?" she said to Jenny.

"Yeah."

I was beside myself as I watched her masturbate as Jenny and I continued making out. I was in sexual overdrive.

"You wanna fuck her?" Jenny asked me.

"Yeah, I wanna fuck her," I said, staring at her. "You wanna fuck me, Ebony?"

"Yeah," she moaned, taking off her clothes.

It was an afternoon of sexual bliss as we explored each other. Too bad Greg wasn't there because he surely missed out. This was more or less the last time that I was going to do something with another man other than Charles. So yeah, he blew it.

***

Four weeks had passed before I finally heard from Robert. I didn't know how to react when he called. He did mention Jason's death. He was very pissed and wanted to know if I knew anything about it.

"No," I said.

I told him I hadn't seen him for at least two months before his unfortunate death. It was clear to me that Robert wasn't aware that the upper-echelon members sanctioned Jason's hit. It wasn't just Jimmy who wanted him dead; it was Andre who gave the final word for the hit to be carried out.

"So where have you been?" I asked him.

"I was out of town."

"You're always out of town."

"What? You don't believe me?"

"I never said that it's just that…"

"Just what?" he asked, cutting me off.

"Nothing Robert, forget it." His attitude was condescending, disrespectful, and uncalled for and I had no time for either him or his nonsense.

"Have you seen that nigga Platinum; Jason used to run with?"

"Platinum? Who the fuck is that? Why are you asking me all this shit?"

He never answered me, instead he asked, "Where are you?"

"I'm getting my hair done."

"I'll stop by your place later. Be there!" he demanded.

"Yeah Robert, I'll be there. See you later," I said, knowing that his ass wasn't going to see me anymore. I had enough of the bullshit.

Staying at Tara's apartment was a great idea. No one knew I was staying there not even Jenny. The only person I told was Charles. He didn't like the idea. He kept insisting that I should stay with him. But after telling him that Tara and I shared the rent, he calmed down.

Tara kept me updated on the actions of the Playaz Club's inner circle. Even so, she still hadn't received a confirmation from Marques concerning Jason's death.

***

I was supposed to meet Charles in the student union, but unfortunately, he couldn't make it. He did call and apologize but I was still pissed at him. He wanted me to meet him in two hours at his place. He said he would make it up to me.

I was walking to my car when I noticed a black Lexus SUV with tinted windows double-parked next to my ride. I quickly became suspicious as the headlights came on. Walking at a slow and deliberate pace, I decided to approach my truck from the passenger's side. My suspicions were aroused as the SUV's reverse lights came on. I quickened my pace, only to see Robert getting out of the car, scaring the hell out of me.

"What's up, Dana?" he asked, with that crooked smile of his.

"What the fuck is up with you? You scared the shit outta me! What the fuck do you want?" I screamed at him.

"Why have you been avoiding me?"

"I haven't been avoiding you. I've just been busy," I answered, trying to calm down.

"Busy, huh? I tell you what, get the fuck in the car!" he demanded.

Overcome by fear, I hesitated for a brief second. He quickly overpowered me and shoved me into his Lexus.

"Why are you doing this?" I pleaded.

"You don't know?"

"No," I said in disgust.

"You'll find out in a few minutes," he rambled on with a scowl on his face.

I was now consumed by fear. *Did he know that I was one of the last people to see Jason before he was killed? What if Jimmy and Jamaican King told him I was involved?* I thought to myself. I was in a difficult situation and I tried to talk him into letting me go as he drove down Broadway. His stares were cold and scary. I was waiting for him to say something, but he never did. The car rolled down Broadway and he turned left onto John Street. The street was deserted. There wasn't a soul in sight.

He stopped in front of a John Street address. We entered the building, which was dimly lit. As we waited for the elevator, I was praying that someone would get off because I had made up my mind to make a run for it. My hopes were quickly dashed when the elevator doors opened, and nobody got off. While we rode the elevator to the third floor, I tried talking to him once again, but he wouldn't budge. Once inside the apartment, I demanded to know why he had brought me there.

"If I were you, I would be very cautious about asking certain questions," he barked. "Let me update you on several issues, Ms. Estick. Where's the ring? That's not the ring I gave you, is it? Who gave you that ring? Let me see, ah, Charles Anderson. It's him, isn't it, Mrs. Anderson? Isn't that correct?"

"So, what!" I yelled at him.

"You're not denying it, I like that. At least you're being honest and since honesty seems to be the theme here, I'll be honest also. I've known for a while that you were cheating on me."

"Cheating on you? Negro, please! You had a wife and you were fucking everything with a pussy at those pool parties. So, don't talk about cheating. I was keeping it real with you. I was fucking you and you alone until you started all the bullshit. You were never there for me."

"But I should've known that once a whore always a whore," he shot back at me.

"Fuck you!"

"You've got a lot of nerve. Remember that night when I called and told you I had some unfinished business to take care of? I was downstairs. I saw your skank ass get in your ride and drive over to that nigga's apartment. You drove the ride I bought you to another mutha-fuckas place. You guys were living it up, holding hands in the park, and going to the movies. And oh yeah, I've seen you guys on campus also. Isn't it against college protocol for an instructor to fraternize with the students? But no, you guys are bold. You are engaged to be married," he said in an enraged tone.

"Please Robert, whatever!"

"Knowing you, you probably fucked him on campus as well."

"What if I did, what is it to you? You ain't nothin' but a pussy!"

"Bitch, you better slow the fuck down and watch your mouth. I'm not the one to be fucking with! You don't even stay at your apartment anymore, do you? I guess you're cheating on the professor too, huh? Where have you been staying for the last few days? You were playing me the whole time."

"What's up with all the questions? The last time I checked you were a stockbroker and not a…" I began, as I was stunned by the slap, he gave me across my face.

"I told you to watch your fucking language, didn't I?"

"You watch."

"Watch what? Jason always said you were nothing but a whore. But I never believed him until I saw you with the professor. It was then that I decided to teach you a lesson. I was the one who hired those guys to beat your ass. You and everyone else were blaming Jason, dumb fucks! But it was me; I set your ass up."

I didn't know what to say. I could only smile within myself. Turning to him, I said, "You did that to me?"

"You damn right I did. I was the one who brought you into this. You weren't making this type of money before you met me, were you? Hell no! I treated you like a queen and how did you repay me? You repaid me by fucking your teacher. Shit was great in the beginning and then all of a sudden you began to change."

"You're a bitter man, Robert. You and I both know we were only going through the motions."

"Motion, potion, what the fuck are you talking about? Regardless of my wife and the other women, you meant everything to me. It wasn't just about the pussy."

"Robert everybody knew what was going on even Tara."

"Tara? Fuck her! I know that bitch had something to do with you ending our relationship. I never liked that bitch in the first place."

"She had nothin' to do with me and you. It was my decision and my choice. And I chose to see someone else."

"Why couldn't you have just said it was over, huh? That's what I get for fucking with a chicken head."

"You weren't saying that shit when you were sucking this chicken head's pussy and those nights you were fucking this chicken head. I never recalled you complaining. The only thing I remember you saying was 'Dana don't leave me. I love you.' You know what Robert? You're a sorry excuse for a man. You're starting to sound like Jason. I guess the apple doesn't fall far from the tree, huh?"

Raising his hands, he said, "What, you fucking little…"

"What the fuck is your problem? Hearing the truth makes you wanna hit me?" I mumbled, "You fucking pussy."

"What did you say?"

"I said I wanna go."

"You'll leave when I say so."

I felt helpless as I thought about the assault and to know that Robert was behind it hurt. How could he just stand there and say all those things to me? He said he loved me, but if this was his way of loving me, I damn sure didn't want to be around him when the hating starts.

"Jason is dead, and nobody knows a damn thing. What about you? What do you know?"

"Nothing, Robert." I began to cry.

"You and your fucking crocodile tears, when will it ever stop?"

"I wanna go. Please can I go now?"

He got up from his seat and sat next to me. Placing his arm on my leg he said, "I wanna make love to you one more time."

"Not now Robert, I'm begging you."

"If not now then, when?" he asked, staring into my eyes with that crooked smile of his.

"I don't know." I began to sob.

"I'll solve it quickly for you. Come here!" he commanded. He pulled me closer and placed his hands between my legs.

"I'm not in the mood."

"Relax; I'll get you in the mood."

Against my will, he unbuttoned my blouse, loosened my belt, and removed my clothes. I kept begging him not to do this. But he was only concerned with fucking me one last time. Within minutes, he was kissing me all over my body. Although I was pissed, I was getting aroused. He began eating me out just like I figured. I felt myself cumming as he sucked on my clitoris. He continued eating me out for another ten minutes.

"Move your hips," he kept repeating, as I made several attempts to keep my legs closed. He then worked his way up my body and tried to kiss me. Realizing that I wasn't going to let him do it, he went down on me once again. I tried to resist as his tongue entered me. I shrieked as his dick penetrated me.

"Didn't you miss this? It feels good, doesn't it? Look at you, your pussy is so wet and you're telling me my shit isn't any good?"

His dick was good. He was giving it to me like he always did. Tried as I did to lay still, but it didn't work. I began returning the favor as he lifted me on his dick. It was like old times, but there weren't any emotions behind it other than the physical act. I was only doing it hoping that he would let me leave.

Grabbing my ass, he pushed me up against the living room wall and screamed, "I'm cumming!"

Angry, pissed, and frustrated, I told him I never want to see him again. I reminded him that he had abducted me, forced me to his apartment, and fucked me without my permission.

"Get the fuck out bitch! And if you're thinking about going to the cops to tell them that I assaulted you, I would think twice about doing it. You must remember that you transported a lot of drugs across state lines. And if you push me too far, I'll make sure that you spend the rest of your life in Bedford Hill Correctional Facility for Women. Act like you know, bitch. Now get the fuck out and make sure you have my ring the next time I see you!" he angrily said.

That abrasive bastard had made me unleash a flood of emotions. He had disrespected me, and I couldn't do a damn thing about it. I was ashamed and embarrassed. I felt like a fool. I went straight to Tara's apartment and took a shower. I then called Charles.

***

"Baby, I'm sorry. But I was so tired when I got in. I took a shower and fell asleep. If you want me to, I'll come over," I said.

"It's okay. Why don't you go ahead and take care of your homework? You sound exhausted. I'll see you tomorrow. I love you."

"I love you too, bye."

Two days had passed without me seeing or hearing from Tara. Since the incident with Robert, I was spending the majority of my time indoors. I was worried and concerned about Tara's safety. The drug runs that she and I would normally make were more or less over. The whole operation was slowing down, especially for those of us at the bottom of the Playaz Club drug chain. Furthermore, I wasn't interested in making any more runs after everything that I had gone through. It was now going on three days and I still hadn't heard a word from Tara, when I heard keys tampering with the front door.

"Where have you been?" I said to her like an overprotective mother, before catching myself.

"I was on the job working hard."

"Jimmy had you worked two days in a row?"

"There's more to it than that. But what's up with you?"

"I'm cool."

"You say you're cool, but your face says otherwise. What's bothering you?"

"I saw Robert several days ago."

"You did?"

"Yeah, he came by my school and took me against my will to an apartment on John Street."

"Are you serious? Did he hurt you?"

Overcome with emotions I said, "Yeah."

After giving her a full account of what transpired, she took a deep breath and said, "I have something important to tell you. You have to promise me that you won't say a word to anyone. Can I trust you?"

"Of course, you and Jenny are the only two friends I have."

"I hope you won't let me down."

"I would never do such a thing."

After briefly studying my face she said, "I'm a drug enforcement agent."

"Oh, fuck! You're a fucking cop? Oh, shit! You're joking, right?"

"No, I'm not. The only reason why I'm telling you this is because of the friendship that you and I have. I've been on this case for the past five years. When I met Marques, I was already on the case only he never knew. We're now in the final stages of taking down the Playaz Club."

"We? There's more?"

"You do recall Pretty Boy, as you like to call him, right?

"Yeah."

"He's my partner."

"Get the fuck outta here." I was flabbergasted and dumbfounded all at the same time. No wonder he would stare at her like that. "What about growing up in Chi-town and going through all that drama?"

"All those things I told you did occur. But it was when I came to New York that I decided to get involved in law enforcement. And before you ask, I'm thirty years old."

"Damn girl, you've got the slang, the dress, and all that shit down."

"I told you I'm from Chi-town. We know what time it is."

"So those days you were away you were on official business?"

"Pretty much, we're on the verge of apprehending Andre, Jimmy, Marques, Troy, and Robert. We don't know the exact whereabouts of Jamaican King and Platinum as of yet. However, my people are working on it. We're gonna nail them, don't you worry about it. I'm gonna need a favor from you."

"What is it?"

"I'm gonna need you to testify in court against Jimmy, Robert, Troy, and Jamaican King. We can't afford to let scumbags like these guys get away with this shit. Think about Lil Jamel and all the other innocent kids who have lost their lives because of them. Don't forget all the drama and shit they put you through. I know you probably can't give me an answer right now but think about it. If you need to talk to your fiancé, fine." She sounded like Charles when he spoke to me after Lil Jamel's death.

***

I visited Charles the next day at his office. I told him to meet me after my classes on the corner of Eighth Street and Broadway. As we rode the subway to his place, he wanted to know what was so important that it couldn't wait. I began telling him about my childhood and all the awful things I had been subjected to. Moreover, I told him of my involvement with Kenny, Robert, and the Playaz Club.

I could see in his eyes that he was deeply hurt. He was noticeably quiet and subdued as we got off the subway and headed to his place. His demeanor hadn't changed, and I wasn't going to say another word, but he insisted that I continue. I was crying the whole time as I tried to explain myself. I felt like crap as I sat across from him in his living room. He sat there stunned the whole time listening. I told him that Tara was a drug enforcement agent and she would be able to tell him a lot more.

"Tara is DEA?" he asked, with a look of disbelief on his face.

"Yes, she is."

"This is serious, huh?"

"Yeah."

"She looks so young. How old is she?"

"Thirty."

"This is unbelievable. Why didn't you tell me about the Playaz Club and all those pathetic characters? Didn't we discuss something similar to this a few weeks ago?"

"Uh, uh."

"In our last conversation, you spoke about being truthful. It seemed the only thing you were truthful about was your father's health. Damn, I deliberately asked you if there was anything else that I needed to know, and you said no."

"It was too dangerous. They knew who you were and where you lived."

"They did?" he asked, his eyes widening.

"They threatened me and told me if I didn't comply, they would hurt you. What was I supposed to do? I couldn't let them hurt you. I would have rather died than let them do that to you. That is the truth. There were times when I would curse you for treating me so well. Whenever I was away from you, I was a nervous wreck, hoping and praying that you were safe. I have nothing else to hide. If you want to leave then you can. I don't know what else to do or say. Here," I said, taking off the engagement ring, and handing it to him.

"No, I don't want the ring. I've told you on numerous occasions that I love you and I still do. All I want is for you to understand that we have to communicate with each other. We're in this together now. So, we have to be honest with each other more so now than ever, or else the relationship won't work."

"I know," I said in a shaken voice.

"Come here. I'll go with you to see Tara. And yes, I think you're doing the right thing."

The next day Charles and I accompanied Tara and Pretty Boy downtown to see her supervisors and the prosecutors who were going to handle the case. I was promised immunity in return for my statements and for testifying against the Playaz Club. I felt confident and safe with both Charles and Tara.

With the help of Tara, I told them everything I knew about the Playaz Club. They told us they would recommend that we go into the witness protection program. Privately, I told Tara that I wasn't sure if I wanted to be placed in such a program.

What about Charles' teaching career? I can't allow this to happen to his career due to the choices I made, I said to myself.

Charles and I discussed it and agreed that I would testify. But we would leave the state at the end of the trial and start our lives anew elsewhere. We then explained this to Tara and the parties involved. Although they had their reservations, they accepted our terms.

Epilogue

My life had changed tremendously. I felt it was a fresh start and the beginning of something special. Still, I had to withdraw from school and give up my apartment. I was angry because I was so close to graduating. I finally sat down with Jenny and told her everything. She was pissed that I never confided in her. But I explained to her that it would have jeopardized her life, and it was a risk I wasn't willing to take. There's but so far that I'm willing to go and I sure wasn't going there. She understood. She was glad that I was all right despite all my troubles. We did lunch a few times, along with her two lovers and Charles. She thought Charles was nice and handsome. We also saw the beautiful and talented Chi-B and Masta. G, in concert at the Beacon Theater in Manhattan. It was a sold-out affair as the duo did several

R&B-Rap-infused numbers in English and Japanese from their latest CD.

I was home watching television a few days later when the regular program was interrupted. There on the screen were Robert and several of his stockbroker buddies. They were being led away in handcuffs. The whole thing was embarrassing because they were arrested at their workplace. Several of their faces were familiar to me. I knew they were all members of the Playaz Club. The look on Robert's face was one of disdain and bravado. He had a frown on his face, as he stared directly into the television camera. Noticing his antics, the officers grabbed him by his big ass head and shoved him into an unmarked police car. I didn't want to laugh, but the shit was hilarious.

"Yeah, nigga, what now?" I screamed at the television.

I knew Tara was a part of the operation. I tried calling her cell, but instead, I got her voicemail. I then called Jenny. I wanted to know if she saw the broadcast or heard anything about it. I got her voicemail also.

Later that evening with Charles by my side, Tara walked in with an expressionless look on her face, as if she'd seen a ghost.

"What's the matter?" I asked. She didn't say a word. "I saw Robert and several of the Playaz Club members being arrested on television this afternoon."

"Yeah, I know," she said.

She didn't sound exuberant or pleased with Robert's arrest, or so it seemed to me. Leading up to his arrest all she talked about was taking him and the others down. I was baffled. I guess Charles must have sensed something that I didn't.

He slowly put his arms around me, as Tara barely whispered, "Jenny."

"Jenny? Did you say, Jenny?"

"Yeah. I don't know how to tell you this but she's dead."

"No!" I screamed. That was the last thing I remembered. I fainted. I thought I was dreaming.

"Dana, Jenny is dead," she repeated.

"She can't be dead," I pleaded. "She said she would never leave me. She said she would always be there for me. Go look for her. Come on Charles let's go and find her. She ain't dead. She wouldn't do this to me, would she?"

"She's dead baby," Charles said in a comforting voice.

In a painful voice, Tara began telling me what happened. "They were executed at her realty business."

"They?" I asked, crying.

"There was a young lady by the name of Ebony Brown, who was killed with her. Do you know her?"

"Yeah, that was her partner."

"What do you mean her partner, her business partner?"

"No, they were lovers."

"Okay." She bit her bottom lip and avoided my eyes, and said in a quivering voice with trembling lips, "They were shot twice in the head."

"Oh, God!" I began wailing. "Jenny, tell them it's not true."

"Let her get some rest, Charles. Maybe she'll feel a bit better tomorrow. Maybe I can explain everything to her then. I'll talk to you later," she said to Charles.

***

It was noon the next day when Greg called crying. He said he was out of town and made several attempts to reach both Jenny and Ebony. Greg and I were still talking when Tara and three diesel-looking men with their guns drawn told me and Charles to get dressed. They weren't taking any chances or anything for granted as they led us out of the apartment.

We were then escorted to the morgue to identify Jenny's body. There she was. I couldn't believe it. I held onto Charles crying. I was hurting inside seeing her like that. She couldn't say hi to me. I was torn to pieces. I held her hand and kissed her on the cheek.

After composing myself, I called her parents. This was one of the most difficult things I've ever had to do. I was in a daze, but I somehow managed to tell them that their daughter was dead. The Thorntons spoke to Tara and several officers and arrangements were made for her parents to officially identify the body and for her remains to be transported to South Carolina after an official autopsy, which her parents wanted.

After leaving the morgue, we were taken to the Manhattan precinct, where they were holding the person responsible for Jenny and Ebony's death.

"Who did it?" I asked Tara.

"Platinum."

"Platinum?" I yelled, as several officers turned and stared at me. "Why would Platinum do that to Jenny? Not unless he did it for Jason or Robert. I still don't get it."

"Believe me, he wasn't a friend of Robert's. And it's not only Jenny and Ebony he killed. He also shot and killed Jamaican King. King's death was payback for what happened to Jason. But didn't you use to say that Jenny's life was in danger?"

"Yeah. Maybe Jason told him to do it before he got killed himself. I don't know, I don't know."

"Hmm. We know this much and that he killed her. But we want to know if he acted alone, but he's not saying," Tara said, with a disgusted look on her face.

I had never seen Tara like this before. She wasn't acting like her usual self. I began noticing the changes right after she told me she was a drug enforcement agent. Her mood quickly changed from her customary playful and joking ways to a sterner and more focused person. I guess she was letting me know that she cared and that her job was important to her.

"Where is he?" I asked.

"He should be coming out any second now. There he is, the guy in the charcoal suit," she said, pointing out the window at a group of prisoners being led to an awaiting van.

"Oh, God! Please, no! Help me! This can't be happening, no!"

"What is it? Do you know him?" she asked.

"That's Kenny," I cried.

"What?" she asked amazed.

"That's him. Oh God, it's him. He said he would get her one day. Oh, God! No."

"Oh shit!" she said, as she ran outside to catch up with Kenny and the other prisoners.

After telling the officers to hold the prisoners, Pretty Boy gestured for me and Charles to come outside. As I slowly walked towards them, Kenny who had his head down, turned and made eye contact with me. His eyes widened immediately when he realized it was me.

He glared at me with that familiar look of his, which was pure evil, and said, "I told you I would get that lesbian bitch, didn't I? You a lucky bitch 'cause when I found out that you were with the Playaz Club, they were hiding your punk ass. Did that bitch ever tell you I was clocking her for weeks? You a lucky bitch!"

"Fuck you, Kenny! I hope you rot in hell!" I screamed at him.

"Get his ass outta here," Tara said.

We were then taken in an unmarked police car, along with Tara to the Federal Courthouse, where we were whisked upstairs to the prosecutor's office. After our conversation, I was taken another two flights up, where I was placed in a room where I came face to face with several high-ranking members of the Playaz Club, including Andre, Jimmy, and Robert. Although they couldn't see me, I was scared as hell as I stood there with Tara looking at them.

"It's a one-way mirror. They can't see you. Remember the millions that were stolen?" Tara asked.

"Yeah."

"It was Jason and Platinum who committed the first robbery. The second robbery was pulled off by Stacy, Jackie, and Marques. I don't know if they were working together. But I do know there's a lot of finger-pointing going on. And it was King, Troy, and Jimmy who killed Jason."

"Those mutha-fuckas!" I said as Tara shook her head. "This is a big case isn't it?"

"Yes, it is."

"There are two things I have to ask."

"Go ahead."

"The drug bust that went down in Queens when we first met, were you the one who got me off? And your name, is it really, Tara?"

"Yeah, I was the one. Everything we did involve the police; I took care of it. No, my name is Tisha Jackson."

"Thanks, girl, and that's a pretty name," I said hugging her. "Is this it?"

"No, we're going after their international connection."

"Okay, are you gonna need me?"

"We won't need you for that."

***

The final arrangements were made for Jenny's body to be flown to South Carolina. Charles and I made reservations to fly down. Tara said she would meet us there.

The funeral was very painful for me. I felt sad for the Thorntons, Kim, and her relatives, as the mourners gave their condolences and paid their respect to the family. The church was crowded with family, friends, and even Tanya, though only meeting Jenny once showed up. Greg was there with several of Jenny's workers, who were accompanied by two of Ebony's siblings. Tara and Pretty Boy, whose real name I found out was Kevin Mitchell were also there.

She looked peaceful in her white dress. They did a wonderful job on her. It was her. I couldn't help myself as the tears rolled down my cheeks. The funeral procession headed to the Groveland Cemetery. I couldn't believe the number of cars and people — sending her off. As they lifted her body out of the hearse and carried it to her final resting place, I heard the melody from our favorite song coming from several speakers, which encircled us.

Then the words hit me, and I became lightheaded. "Ooh child things are gonna get easier. Ooh child things'll get brighter. Someday we'll walk in the rays of a beautiful sun. Someday when the world is much brighter…"

With tears streaming down her face, Mrs. Thornton looked over at me and said, "That was her song."

"Yes," I said, nodding and crying like a baby.

It was painful as they began lowering her body into the earth. I was delirious. I was hurting so much that I lost it. But as the song continued, I began singing along, "Someday we'll get it together and we'll get it all done. Someday when the world is much brighter…"

I hadn't said a word to anyone not even Charles, but as the last patch of dirt was about to cover her coffin, I said through the tears, "Jenny, I'm pregnant and it's a girl. You know she's got your name, right? And I'm gonna tell her all about her Auntie Jenny. I love you girl and I'm gonna miss you, bye."

As we drove away, I began to reminisce on the years we had together and all the things we did. I made a vow to myself that day that no matter where I go or how far I travel, I would visit her every birthday for as long as I live.

Tara reminded me that we still had some unfinished business to take care of back in New York City. I told her that I was more than ready to close this chapter of my life.

"I'll see you in New York," she said, as she hugged me and began singing. "See, we've got something in common." We both laughed as Charles and Pretty Boy looked on.

"Yes, we do. I love you," I said, biting my bottom lip.

"I love you too."

"We'll always have something in common, friendship and each other," I said, fighting back the tears.

I visited my father and although his condition had deteriorated, I introduced him to Charles. I told him once again that I had forgiven him and that he was going to be a grandfather. We were about to leave when his nurse and Tanya told me they doubted he would last another month. This was hard to take, especially after Jenny. But I had a strong man beside me and as Charles and I left together holding hands, I told him about our baby and the new life which awaited us as husband and wife.

The End